Lament
OF THE
Unclaimed

Lament
OF THE
Unclaimed

TONI MOBLEY

ISBN: 979-8-88785-025-2 (Paperback)
ISBN: 979-8-88785-026-9 (Hardcover)

Library of Congress Control Number: 2023948834

Any references to historical events, real people, or real places are used fictitiously. Names, characters, and places are products of the author's imagination.

Book design by Allison Chernutan.
Edited by Alex Vicarel and Carol Kudeviz.

Printed in the United States of America.

First printing edition 2023.

emily@fracturedmirrorpublishing.com
Fractured Mirror Publishing
Knoxville, Tennessee

www.fracturedmirrorpublishing.com

'Death is not the greatest loss in life.
The greatest loss is what dies within us
while we live.'

Norman Cousins

CHAPTER
One

My hands, blistered and bloody, ached but if I allowed myself even a moment of respite, I knew I would crumble. The dirt gave way easily beneath my shovel, but that had more to do with the near constant blanket of rain over the last few days than any effort on my part. Not that it mattered. My body was numb, but not from the weather or from the hours of slicing into the earth.

Having lived nearly a year bathed in blood, destruction, and chaos, you'd think death would be an easy subject to handle, and by now it was. Unless it came to those close to me. My calloused hands were shaking now, the cold air biting at flesh I could barely feel. It was enough to remind me I was alive, but that did nothing to make me feel better, because I was the only one left. My family, my friends, my neighbors were all gone; in this small town nestled amongst the mountains of smothering pines, I was alone.

Goosebumps prickled my skin as tears rolled blazing trails of warmth across my exposed cheeks. Even though my body was busy, my mind was not. It gave me too much time to remember why I was digging, and for whom.

Under any other circumstance, I could be proud of the fact it had only taken me three hours to dig this hole, but then I reminded myself it was because over the last few months I had plenty of practice. My eyes wavered on the mounds beside me; they were ringed by rocks I had carried from the nearby river and sprinkled with fresh flowers from a few days ago. The wooden spikes I had rammed into the dirt bore the names of those within.

Our world was over as soon as it had begun, and yet I did not weep for my fellow man. Right now, I didn't care about anyone, except the person who lay lifeless under the tarp beside me. The gentle pattering of scattered rain on the plastic only reminded me he was right there, or rather, that what was left of him was beside me. I was luckier than most; I had spent twenty-one years with him, and when *They* came, we were safe knowing that if we died, we'd die together.

"Except that wasn't true, was it?" I said through clenched teeth.

He wouldn't answer. After all, the dead can't talk. If they could, would he be proud that I sat with his corpse in my arms wailing for hours after he had died? I didn't think so, what dad would be proud to make their child cry?

Standing back from the lip of the grave I had dug for him, I distracted myself with the trails of water that spilled over the sides. Even though it was a light rain, a misting, tiny pools had gathered within the grave. If I didn't want to give my father a watery grave, it had to be now or never.

Gently prying the tarp from his face, I stared down at what used to be my father. His skin was cold, a sickish hue settling within the golden tan he had amassed from years of garden work. I couldn't bring myself to look, having shut his eyes after he died, but I wondered, would they still bear that gorgeous shade of caramel-laced green? Or would they have paled too, even more than the moment I had watched the light fade from them.

Securing the holes in the tarp with one of those bungee cords my dad used to secure lumber from the hardware store, I bent with my knees, dragging him to the hole in the ground. It felt so impersonal, like I was hauling a garbage bag to the curb. A weight had settled in my stomach and bile rose in my throat as, in one swift movement, I unceremoniously shoved his plastic-wrapped corpse into the hole. Something inside me broke, as shaking enveloped my entire body. It was all too much.

"Y-you asked me one thing, a few months ago," I said, voice cracking.

Swallowing the bile at the back of my throat, I continued. "You made me promise that no matter what happened, I'd reunite you with mom, and when the time came, we'd all be together again."

I glanced at the mound beside the grave I had dug. From here one could just see the edge of the dirt-stained quilt covered in faded flowers at the edge of his grave.

I couldn't bring myself to disturb her grave, but I was determined to honor his wishes. Mother would have wanted it that way. We had planned this long ago, before the world as we knew it vanished overnight. We had a family plot in a cemetery north of here, where my grandparents and great-grandparents lay. It was always Mom's wish that our family would be interred together, forever. But times change, and this was the best I could do.

"Goodbye, Dad, keep Mom company until I can join you."

With a heavy sigh, I yanked the shovel from the dirt and began filling the grave, letting the tears flow freely. My sobs were drowned out by the sound of thunder in the distance. It took me far less time to fill the grave than it did to dig it, and in the end, as I teetered above the mound that now housed what was left of my family, I screamed into the gathering darkness.

I was a ghost of whom I had once been, an empty shell formed out of a necessity for survival. My head was constantly filled with the sorrowful dancing images of those long gone—their names haphazardly carved into the great rock wall that towered above me. Its presence was suffocating, yet oddly soothing.

It was a cutthroat world out beyond the comfort of this den whose smooth walls bore the name of every person whom I had cherished. Their last breaths all taken beside me sometime in the last year, except my older sister, my only sibling. Part of me still hoped she was out there, wandering the wilderness—free. I remember the day I had said goodbye to her as she drove three hundred miles away to start her new life. I also remember the day, exactly a month later, when the world would change.

But days meant nothing anymore, the passage of time was more a hindrance than anything else. Lightning struck nearby, illuminating the six names like scars etched in marble. The vessels that once held their memories and mannerisms lay in a hastily dug cemetery below the cliff face.

Thunder rumbled outside and I turned to watch the dark, menacing storm clouds roll closer and closer. A blanket of despair enveloped the land, smothering it in a shroud of heavy silence and thick fog. Rain fell, beating against the rocks and dirt in a well-timed chorus that threatened to lull me to sleep.

Funnily enough, I was safer now, with the rain and the cold. We weren't entirely sure why they preferred the sun-soaked lands around the equator; perhaps for the same reasons we did. The temperate zones yielded the highest crops and highest concentration of humans. Two birds, one stone. But I knew I couldn't have picked a better place to hide, to call home. Others might not have used that word, but I was beyond caring what others thought at this stage.

There was a time when I couldn't even be seen in public without my hair perfectly curled about my shoulders and a full face of makeup, complementing my manicured nails and designer clothing. What a strange world I had once lived in. It seemed as if those memories were simply dreams—figments of an imagination running wild.

Now I lived in a constant state of ruin, subsisting on a diet of anxiety and scavenged leftovers. I would have to move soon, I had relied on this cave for as long as I could remember—back when there was more than just me. That was my motivation for leaving; I didn't know how much longer I could sit here and wallow in the memories.

I thought about going further north to where there was only cold, and only wet. But no one had ever returned from beyond this forest I called home, shrouded in an almost perpetual fog as of late. Whether they found new life or lost it beyond my den—I did not know. I had only met those going towards it, never coming back.

But what I did know was that *They* were not there.

At one point that was all we ever cared about, we who survived the initial onslaught. They kept to the southern half of the United States as we migrated northward to freeze or starve. It was hard to grow vegetables and fruit without the sun constantly being by your side. I'd taken it for granted, we all had. I was raised in a time of plenty, leading a life that was by no means rich, but compared

Lament OF THE Unclaimed

to now was a luxury. What I would do to share a fresh, home cooked meal with my family and friends by my side one more time.

I glared at the wooden pots of tightly packed spinach and lettuce that sat at the entrance to the den, water dripping slowly into them from a hole in the rock wall. It would have been inconceivable once upon a time to think you wouldn't be able to drive down to the grocery store for anything you needed.

At least the game was easy to come by: deer, pheasant, fish. One of the few things I could appreciate in this new world was that, with humanity now dwindling, nature had been able to flourish. How quickly they adapted to a world without our presence. It was hard to admit that the creatures responsible for our extinction had a beneficial impact on our world, to think that it was better off in their hands than in ours.

It had taken me months to master using my bow on a moving target, and weeks to learn how to whittle my own arrows and carve their salvaged metal tips to an acceptable efficiency. Trial and error were the bane of my existence. I wasn't known for my patience, if something didn't work well the first few tries, I would simply give up: sewing, clarinet, dancing. To think my childhood dream was to become a seamstress; I gave that up quickly.

At least I knew how to cook.

I suppose I could thank my mother for that. She was a lot like me: hair as golden as fresh straw, eyes that shined the glittering turquoise of a warm tropical ocean. But I suppose that's where the similarities ended because she was dead now—and I was not.

Some days, I wished I were.

When the world ends you either adapt or die; I learned that very quickly. I pulled my knees up against my chest, hugging them tightly. I didn't know what to do, now that I was alone. Part of me thought it would be better to give up, to surrender. I mean, why shouldn't I? The world was clearly better off without us; I hadn't seen a hint of smog on the horizon since the fires died down. The air was fresh, it was clean. No trucks cut through the sounds of nature, churning out thick, black smoke as they hogged the roads. The only litter that was left was scattered in places not yet assimilated by our new overlords.

Something deep within me fought against the voice that bid me to surrender. Some primal instinct, I suppose, that dragged me from bed every day at the crack of dawn to check my traps, to venture deep into the abandoned recesses of towns and villages to look for supplies, scavenging long-dead technology once hailed as groundbreaking to use as scrap for the tips of my arrows.

Oh, how far we had fallen.

The world was cold and grey. Wind howled through the treetops, bowing and breaking their branches, sending them tumbling to the underbrush. Crawling from bed, I peeked out the den entrance and watched as a thick fog fell from the mountains above and dripped into the yawning valley below, blanketing the world in silence.

It was eerie before the end of society, after the evacuations, after the order to stay inside. The silence was like the morning after a blizzard. The world was quiet and still; only the birds and squirrels had the audacity to break the serenity.

I was okay now, with the emptiness of it all—I had accepted my fate. As I looked off into the shrouded treetops in the distance, I reminded myself that I might be okay with how my story would end, the inevitability of it all, but I certainly would not surrender without a fight. Although I might one day end up being the last human on Earth, I would not let them forget who we were, whose world they had so callously assimilated.

Today, I surrendered myself to staying within the smothering confines of the cave I called home. Tomorrow though, I would scavenge, I would scout—I wouldn't sit here and wait for the end. I would bring it right to my doorstep.

Rain continued to beat the earth, its furor loud and unrelenting as lightning arched across the sky. Thunder rumbled low in the distance; the sky became dark. There was nothing more I could do for today, except sleep, in preparation for tomorrow.

Tomorrow I will do something—anything. I repeated that to myself over and over until sleep reluctantly gripped me.

CHAPTER

Two

The morning was as rambunctious as the middle of the night had been, except now the fog bank lifted to reveal a soaked landscape heralded by howling winds and misty rain. Under any other circumstances I would have considered it far too dangerous to risk going out, but I needed more supplies. I had made it a habit to know the movements of everything around me, if a single rock looked out of place, I'd camp the high ground and wait it out to find out why.

Most of the time it was the result of some animal moving through the area or the result of soil erosion. After all, earthquakes were as common here in Oregon as they were in California. A few times though, it had been Them—and even fewer times, it'd been one of us. But I didn't have to worry about that this far out, the smartest of us had either moved as far north as we could—or out across the seas and oceans. I heard Hawaii was popular at the end of the world. Too bad I had no way of knowing if it were as much of a haven as the few migrants had claimed.

Pulling on the thickest pair of jeans I had, some waterproof boots, my winter jacket, and a nearly empty backpack with a full water bottle, I suited up my belt with a sheathed hunter's knife and slid my quiver and bow over my backpack. I made it a habit of traveling as light as I possibly could, because, as of late, my scavenging had always resulted in a bountiful harvest. This just made it that much harder to admit that humanity really wasn't the right master of this planet. We may have been "top of the food chain," but we certainly didn't deserve it. The world thrived in our absence.

I paused by the rock wall, the names of the fallen called out to me. Possessed by guilt, and for no reason I could comprehend, I pulled my knife from my pocket and added a name to the list. Below my mother's and father's names, I wrote my own: Wren.

With one last glance around the cave, I took a deep breath and departed. I hid the entrance with a reed mat before picking my way down the cliff edge towards the river below. The rain was light like the mist that rose from the spray of a waterfall, but it was quick to soak through my clothes, chilling me to the bone. The winds had died down considerably as I made my way through the forest, yet the sun still struggled to break through the dense cloud cover.

My destination lay east, huddled amongst the redwoods and pines straddling the river. I found an area where a tree had fallen across a thinner section, letting me use it as a natural bridge. On this side of the river, the forest was crisscrossed with both asphalt and natural hiking trails leading to a campground. I generally avoided it as most humans that came through the forest said they stopped by it on their way north, and I certainly wasn't looking to make friends. It was just easier that way, the less people I knew, the less people whose deaths I had to carry with me.

It was a small town, Cave Junction. Before the end of humanity as we knew it, this town was a popular destination for tourists to rest on their way south to the more impressive Redwood National Forest. But it contained a decent number of homes and motels that offered me an almost exclusive reserve of supplies. Most people who made their way through Cave Junction skirted the town itself in favor of the campgrounds, opting to hide in the shadows of the trees.

Fortunate for me.

The last time I had been here I had made sure to hide everything in even stockpiles throughout the town. That way, if anything were to happen and I'd lost access to one or more locations, I wouldn't be caught completely without resources. Today I was opting for a simple trip to the Visitor Center. It was a rather understated grey and white colored building right off the side of the road. It'd been left to nature long enough that tall weeds and bushes hid most of it from view now.

Skirting the outside, I did a full circle of the building and the surrounding forest, my ears straining for any noise that didn't quite belong. In our absence, the forest was teeming with life; bugs, birds, rodents, all sorts of creatures whose voices were once drowned out by the monotony of humankind now filled the void we left

behind. It was inherently beautiful, but also deadly—
for me. Our unwelcome guests were exceptionally quiet,
their footsteps almost unheard until they were right
next to you. I had to rely on every sense I had to keep
one step ahead.

Today was like every other day, seemingly void of
any human activity except my own. I propped open the
door and walked inside. Although the building looked
decently sized from the outside, it was quite small inside.
Like every visitor center, it held displays filled with
pamphlets and maps, and rails with clothing. Souvenirs
littered the ground from where they had fallen from
kiosks. What I was after was hidden in a small alcove I
had dug out of a rock display behind the desk.

Cans of vegetables and fruits, blankets, medical
kits, towels, and a myriad of other useful trinkets I had
acquired sat in a neat orderly pile inside the alcove. I
knelt, shoving a few cans of vegetables into my backpack
along with a box of band-aids and sanitary napkins, a
bottle of hydrogen peroxide, and a spool of fishing wire.

I replaced the rock over the alcove and swung my
pack over my shoulder, leaving the Visitor Center to
follow the road north into the town. A few roads jutted
out from the main one, leading to an expansive mobile
home resort. I had hidden stashes in two of the homes on
the northern edge, but they were substantial collections,
and I was saving them for the eleventh hour.

Eventually the trees opened to a clear view of the
small town nestled amongst the surrounding hills. A

light mist had gathered, swirling around the buildings. In the distance, the snowcapped mountains rose up to meet the darkened sky. I picked up my pace until I was hidden in the shadows cast by the small, red-walled cafe which used to be bustling with visitors. There were so many memories of this place, and yet it was the most mundane ones that choked me up. I was nearly overwhelmed with the memory of sitting at one of the outside tables with a cup of coffee and plate of eggs, listening to my mother gossip with her loquacious friends.

I lived in Cave Junction when I was a child, but I was born in nearby Grants Pass to a carpenter and teacher who dreamed of a simpler life in the countryside. When I was seven, they did just that, and Cave Junction became our new home. Now I was the only one left, and I stood there looking through the window at the abandoned shop left in disarray, covered by the webs of the spiders who now called it home.

My heart ached so badly my head began to spin, but I took a deep steadying breath, reminding myself that the reason I was the only one left was because I had to go on, even if it were purely out of spite. If I died, no one would be left with their memories, and I wouldn't let that happen until I managed to find a way to avenge them. Sometimes I wondered if that really was a good enough reason to keep going. Maybe that was just the human part of me, a byproduct of two hundred thousand years of evolution.

But when I saw them in my mind, those faces as they laughed and loved, as they went to work every day and came home to their families, it made it hard to give up. They had hobbies, my father liked to play tennis with his friends on Saturdays and my mother loved to paint. My sister—I nearly choked thinking about her—she was fond of dancing and singing, even if the latter was only behind the closed door of her bedroom.

And me? It was almost incomprehensible to imagine I liked dabbling in cosmetics and watching fashion shows, but I'd had no direction in life, nothing to strive for. Before the end of the world, I had already accepted my fate; resigned to underpaid customer service roles where the only thing I would be good at was taking abusive, snarky comments from middle-aged nobodies who took out their aggression on random service staff because they were unhappy in their own lives.

None of that mattered now, everything was different. I had no hobbies, no likes, no dislikes—only the need to eat, sleep, repeat. Survival was the only thing I had to look forward to, and I stood there wallowing in guilt and pity, feeling sorry for myself and everyone else— until I noticed a movement out of the corner of my eye.

Our eyes met at the same time, he stood like a deer in headlights across the road, unsure whether to run. I did what everyone else did now, I nodded at him, watching as his shoulders slightly lowered and his eyes darted left and right. He was clearly checking if I was alone. I slid my hand nonchalantly over the knife under my jacket, ready to use it if I needed to. Once he seemed sure there was no one else, he quickly crossed the road, skirting the cars in the parking lot to stand a few feet in front of me. A simple bin separated us. I was unnerved by how close he was, but his demeanor shouted anything but danger.

Up close I could see he had it rough—his face was pockmarked in recent scars, his beard scraggly, and his hair oily. A torn backpack that was clearly empty sat limp across his back. His eyes downcast, he cleared his throat, "D-do you have any food?"

I loathed the fact that I had to interact with him, but I knew the safest course of action for me was to simply give him something, and I knew the best way to do it. "Check the bin."

He frowned, looking down at the bin between us. Hesitating for just a moment, his eyes met mine and whatever he saw must have placated the fear in him as he pulled the lid off the bin.

"Where did you get all this?" His voice nearly cracked.

I was relieved that he believed that was a lot. It saved me from having to sacrifice too much. After all, it wasn't much of a loss, it was one of my smaller stockpiles I had made out in the open specifically in case of an encounter with another person. I was surprised it had lasted this long.

"Take it," I said simply, my eyes drifting to the storm coming in on the horizon.

"Thank you," his eyes filled with tears as he began unloading the cans, bottles, and boxes I had hidden in the bin. After he had shoved as much as he could into his bag, he held one can of spaghetti out, pulling back the lid. He fished around in his backpack for a fork and dug in, watching me carefully.

I hated small talk, but I knew he was as apprehensive of me as I was of him, so I tried, "Has it been a while?"

He nodded, "A few days."

"That should tide you over for about two weeks if you're careful. Where did you come from?" I took a seat at one of the tables. He sat down in the chair opposite me.

After chewing a mouthful of food his eyes sank to the ground, watching a leaf blow in the increasing breeze that had rolled in ahead of the storm. "Originally? Portland."

That caught me off guard, "Wait, you're traveling south?"

He nodded.

"Why?" Had things changed? Was the north no longer safe? I could feel my anxiety bubbling to the surface, but I kept it in check as I searched his eyes waiting for a reply.

He finished another bite before clearing his throat, "Everyone I've ever known is now dead. There was no point staying. It's cold, its wet, winter is coming—if it's my time I'm certainly not letting nature take me. I'd rather die at Their hands—fighting."

I was momentarily silenced; he had the same wish I did. I watched him finish the can, before he plopped it onto the table. My gaze drifted to the bin beside us. I couldn't believe, of all the things to be annoyed about, it was the fact that he wasn't going to put the can in the bin—that bothered me.

"My wife's family had a place out near Lake Selmac. I owed it to her to see if they were still alive."

"You've gone a bit too far for Lake Selmac, it's off the 199." He'd obviously been traveling for a while, and with no food, he was fatigued—bound to make a mistake.

He took a shuddering breath, a shadow settled upon his face. "Lake Selmac is *Theirs* now."

I frowned; Lake Selmac was at the most only nine miles to the north of here. I hadn't seen or heard anything that would have hinted that a large force had settled in the area. In fact, I hadn't seen any of them for a long while, not since— "What do you mean?"

His eyes were downcast as he whispered, "They've turned the shoreline into some sort of…I don't know, camp? It used to be all marsh and redwoods down there off Lakeshore Drive and Reeves Creek Road, now it's strewn with these weird buildings—I don't even know how to describe them. But they're everywhere."

"You saw them yourself?" My skin crawled imagining them taking over that beautiful shoreline with their grotesque monstrosities, turning what was once ours into their own. I'd never actually seen them do it, but I'd heard enough stories to piece the image together.

"Yeah, I hightailed it out of there as soon as I figured out that's what was happening."

"Why come east, though? Must have been a pain coming through the state park." We both glanced towards the towering redwoods as they swayed in the breeze.

"I figured there would be less of them this way. They seemed to have…a fondness, for our buildings."

I frowned, "What do you mean?"

The wind picked up again, icy against my exposed face and I pulled my hood over my head. He glanced up at the dark, brooding clouds before standing up, "Listen, you seem like a smart person. I really appreciate the food; I wish I could do something in return, but the only thing I can give you is a warning that might save your life. It doesn't seem like they've come out here yet, it was clear in the woods and on the main road coming in. But if you need to leave, don't go into the towns or cities."

I hated having to ask, but I needed to know, "Why?"

"Because they belong to *Them* now." With that he turned and continued along the Redwood Highway south. I sat there watching until he disappeared around the bend.

A thunderous boom sounded in the distance and a flash lit up the darkened sky, the storm would soon be upon me. It was too risky to try making it back to the Den, I'd have to wait it out in one of the nearby homes. I knew this town like the back of my hand, every nook, every cranny—and since the end of the world I now knew what the inside of every house looked like, too.

I jogged down the road behind the cafe to the riverside, barely making it to the front door of a two-story colonial house before the downpour began. The sound was deafening, echoing through the open door of the empty tiled house. I shut the door firmly, triple checking that it was locked before doing the rounds of all the windows and doors. Nothing was disturbed, nothing was out of place, not even a hint of an inhabiting spider.

Just as I had left it.

The last time I was here I wasn't alone. Back then I was surrounded by those I loved. It seemed like such a long time ago as I stared absently at the sofa in the lounge. My mother, with her long sun-soaked hair tied into its signature bun, would sit on the beige leather couch telling us everything would be okay. My dad always stood by the back door, cup of coffee in hand, the water in the river below set alight by the noon time sun, glittering like a thousand crystal shards.

Thunder rumbled above and I was broken out of my reverie, my heart aching from the memories. I flung my backpack on the sofa and sat down to eat a can of peaches, unable to resist the syrup that I had once detested. Maybe I just missed sugar? After all, it was once in practically every packaged food on the shelves.

Now I savored it, eagerly holding the can above my head until I was sure I had every drop that too-small can had to offer. I glanced outside, my heart sinking as I watched the rain pour off the roof in what seemed like an impenetrable sheet of water. It wasn't even midday. An entire day I could have used to hunt, or fish, or scavenge, and instead I was stuck in this house—with my memories.

Groaning, I tore myself from the comfy couch and perused the bookshelves for the one book I knew I would find. It was right where it was the last time I was here, when I had watched my sister sneakily grab it from the shelf to read in the bedroom upstairs. I traced my fingers along the spine, lost in thought as I followed the small indentations in gilded lettering before pulling it from the shelf.

I'd read this book once before, in high school, when I was forced to. Reading wasn't exactly a hobby of mine, at least—not before. Now the Den was littered with books and manuals on topics of survival and combat, on how to adapt. Without those guides, I might not have made it this far. Funny how fast priorities shift when your life is on the line.

Now, it was probably the only thing I had left to remind me of my sister. She loved the classics. So many beautiful editions had graced the floating shelves in her bedroom, lovingly displayed in alphabetical order with lights that no longer worked to highlight their presence. My heart ached at the memory; my eyes began watering.

Somewhere out there, she could still be alive, safe and sound—at least, that is what I told myself. A year before the invasion she accepted a scholarship to a prestigious university in San Francisco. It was one of the first cities that was completely assimilated. My only solace was that she wasn't in one of the cities that was obliterated to a smoking crater, like Los Angeles. I shook the images from my head. In the beginning the news stations and tabloids were careful of showing too much. By the end they didn't censor *anything*.

"To Kill a Mockingbird," I said aloud, flitting through the pages, more for a distraction than any real care for reading it.

Another clap of thunder sounded above, pulling me from the darkness that always gathered at the edge of my mind, threatening to swallow me whole. I sighed, putting the book back on the shelf. The rain was relentless as it poured from the roof. I stood by the back door watching it.

Until movement in the trees across the river caught my eye.

I immediately stilled, my eyes unblinking as I stared at the trees. Was it just a breeze? An animal? Maybe I had imagined it? Although there were still people out there, and movement in the trees wouldn't be unusual—I hadn't survived this long because of a lack of precautions. A few moments passed, the thunder continued to boom, flashes of light suddenly lit the forest, and I relaxed—some animal, possibly a raccoon, scurried itself up one of the trees.

Sighing, I lounged across the couch, letting the beat of the rain and roll of the thunder lull me into a gentle slumber.

I didn't know how long I had been asleep when I came to. The rain outside had lessened, but not by much. A weird noise had been scratching at my ears, pulling me from my sleep—and I froze. There it was again, by the front door.

I was on my feet in the blink of an eye, my backpack slung against my back, and my knife drawn. Slowly, I followed the noise as it traveled from the front door along the side of the house. Whatever it was, it was outside— and then I heard it, the distinct sound of boots walking along the wet pavement. I didn't bother waiting to find out if it was a human or one of Them, as whoever was outside continued to move along the side of the house. I had to decide, and soon. I wasn't safe inside the house; at one point they might try to come inside.

I ran for the back door, my hand on the handle, and waited with bated breath. I didn't take my eyes off the kitchen windows where the person had been. My heart beat fast as I took a step closer to the door, ready to race out into the storm.

In a single breath, a shadow loomed over me, and shards of glass flew by my face before I could even contemplate what had happened. They scattered around the room, tinkling like little pins on the tiled floor. I screamed, running into the lounge and diving for the other side of the couch. I landed on my stomach, the air knocked from my lungs. Without a backwards glance, I gathered myself to my feet and ran up the stairs to the bedroom and locked the door behind me.

Angry, heavy steps ascended the stairs, the sound of them thudding against the wood rang through the house. With my heart beating in my ears, I pried the window open and glanced down at the lawn below. Rain still fell from the sky, coating the landscape in shades of grey. The road leading to the café was covered in a gathering mist.

The door shook behind me, like a battering ram assaulted it, but I knew it was fists that pounded against it, trying to force it open. Darting across the room, I unceremoniously tossed the books off the bookshelf and dragged it across the door. Just like downstairs, the room erupted into chaos. In the blink of an eye, the wood splintered like the shards of glass, flying across the room, thudding against the walls and floor, revealing my assailant.

My entire world froze as I stared into the cold, golden eyes of one of *Them*. His strong jaw, high cheekbones, short auburn hair, and toned physique—any other time I might have considered swooning. He wore a leather vest and pants, a bandolier of knives was strung across his chest, and twin swords sat at his hip. Even from here I recognized the glint of well sharpened blade.

His eyes narrowed, a smile playing on his lips. They pulled back to reveal his long canines. I didn't give myself a chance to second guess as I turned—and jumped out the window, landing in the soft, wet grass below. With the wind knocked from my lungs, I struggled to my feet, slipping and sliding until I managed to meet the gravel of the road. I ran as fast as I could towards the other houses. I knew I could not outrun him—*it*—but fighting was out of the question. I'd seen what their kind were capable of, and I wasn't interested in ending up like the people I'd seen on the television. No. My only hope was to outwit the monster that now stalked me.

A cry rang out and several sets of boots followed closely behind me as I rounded the corner of one of the nearby houses. A long alleyway connected the yards of the houses, and I ran its length, glancing left and right for an opportunity to hide. I noticed the fences were too tall or would take too much time to climb. It was when I neared the end of the alley that I could hear them gaining on me. I willed my legs to carry me as far and as fast as they could. My lungs burned and my thighs ached, but I pushed until I found myself in a narrow glen surrounded by towering trees.

It was then that I realized my mistake. One of them walked out from behind the nearest redwood, obstructing my path. I stopped dead in my tracks, glancing between him and the mob of three approaching from behind. They all stopped within ten feet of me, watching—waiting. I stared them down defiantly, my heart pounding in my ears and somehow deafening the sound of the rain hitting the treetops above.

The one from the house, with the short auburn hair, took a step forward, procuring a blade from his bandolier and brandished it towards me. I slid my hand under my jacket, pulling my knife free—I had no choice. I had to fight. I was no match for even one of Them, but that wouldn't stop me from trying. I cursed myself, I knew this day would eventually come, I had just hoped I had more time. But I wasn't going to make it easy, if they wanted a fight, I would give them one.

His smirk only grew when he took a step towards me. In the blink of an eye his knife had missed my throat by an inch. I instinctively jumped backwards, right into the creature that had blocked my way. He promptly pushed me forward, causing my knees to buckle as I slipped in the mud. One of the others snickered and the auburn-haired one took another step forward, beckoning me with his hand to get up.

I pushed myself out of the mud and ran towards him. He caught my hand and flung me across the glen—back into the mud. With my knife firmly in my grasp, I again pushed myself to my feet, wavering under a newfound pain in my side and flung myself at him. My knife connected with his arm, leaving a thin, red line of blood. He paused, his eyes glancing at the pathetic excuse for a cut on his arm, before narrowing them at me.

He growled, low and guttural.

I stood there transfixed, unable to react in time before he knocked the knife from my hand in one swift motion before his hand circled my throat. His sharp claws dug deep, crushing my windpipe and drawing blood. He waited several agonizing moments as I hung there desperately gasping for air, then threw me across the glen. This time my back collided with a tree and I collapsed into the dirt, winded. I clutched at my side as I drew terrible, deep breaths into my screaming lungs that were wracked with pain. I knew I had probably broken a rib, maybe even two, but there was nothing to be done about it. As long as I staggered my breaths it was slightly tolerable.

Pulling myself to my feet, I stared him down. His eyebrows raised and he regarded me like one would a small child. He nodded; I picked my knife up out of the mud. The monster waited patiently while I staggered forward towards him, my knife aimed for his throat. He simply side stepped my advance. A foot swinging beneath mine sent me cascading into the mud again. This time he did not wait for me to get up, he straddled me holding down my arms. Sharp nails pierced the delicate skin of my upper arms, and I cried out, struggling in vain in his vice-like grip.

He growled, his lips pulling back to reveal sharp, blinding-white canines that once earned the title of vampire when They first appeared. He slowly lowered his face to mine. I did the only thing I could think of— I headbutted him. He reeled backwards and I kicked him off me, swinging my knife towards him. He recovered far faster than I anticipated. As I would have sliced his arm again, he brought his fist up to connect with my jaw and sent me flying into the mud. Once again I found myself on my back, fighting for air.

Shivering and covered in rain and mud, I stared at him. I huddled under the pouring sky, the pain from my jaw and ribs made it hard to concentrate on simply breathing. He said something to his companions, and they all chuckled, looking at one another with knowing smirks. They knew they had won. I couldn't fight much longer, and I was no match for them. Like a sheep that had wandered into a wolf's den, this was my end.

They approached, encircling me until they almost managed to block out the rain. I sat there, waiting for the blow, waiting for it to all to end. The one with russet hair kicked my blade from my hand. I was too numb to feel it, but I watched it thud to the ground out of my reach, the hilt sticking out of the mud.

I accepted this was it, and took a deep, painful breath. My gaze was locked onto Them. I wouldn't close my eyes; I wouldn't give them the satisfaction. But just as I anticipated the final blow to come—another one of Them emerged from the alleyway, calling to the pack that surrounded me.

They immediately separated, letting their new companion come to stand before me. My gaze drifted from the jet-black boots secured by gilded, charcoal greaves up past his equally dark pants and vest to his face. Even heavily cloaked, it was easy to discern how he was very different from his companions.

Whereas his companions were like models, he was what the Romans would have considered a god. His presence commanded the attention of everyone near him, and they were quick to back away, their eyes downcast. He pulled back his hood, revealing cold, golden eyes, long white hair, and the stony face of someone who had seen countless wars. He looked me over, and although his gaze drifted to his companions, my eyes never left him.

The auburn-haired one murmured something in their ancient silken tongue, which sounded as smooth as laced honey to the ears. The leader held up his hand, dismissing whatever he was saying and spoke again. The others exchanged a brief glance at one another before taking a step back. They shied away from the auburn-haired one, like he was plagued. The leader stared him down, and for a moment he looked as if he would resist whatever he was being told to do, but eventually he nodded his head in defeat. Holding his right hand to his left breast, he led the others away into the forest. The leader watched them depart, his gaze cold and dismissive.

Several moments passed before the leader's gaze met mine. I hardened my resolve, prepared to struggle even though I knew it was no use. My ribs ached with every breath, and my jaw felt like I had been kicked by a horse. Although I was still dizzy from the blow earlier, I wouldn't let that stop me from delivering one final push before my demise.

One final act of vengeance.

He raised his hands to his neck and fiddled with the clasps of his cloak, sliding it from around his broad shoulders.

Frowning, I leaned back as he towered over me.

He bent to drape the cloak across my shoulders, and I winced when he pulled the hood up over my head.

I froze, confused. Surely, he would deliver the blow now, he just didn't want to see my face as he did it. That made sense. I felt the same way when I hunted. I could never stare my prey in the eyes when I completed my hunt. Whether they were deer, rabbits, or fish. But I never understood their kind to not enjoy the thrill of ending their hunt.

Several agonizing minutes passed; my eyes were glued to his boots while I waited. Each painful breath was a struggle not to shiver, though from the wet or the fear, I was not sure. I hugged the cloak tighter; droplets of rain fell from the hood to join the puddles on the ground. Then before I could even react, I watched as my bow hit the mud in front of me, and the boots retreated. I hadn't even realized I dropped it in my haste to get away from Them. I looked up in time to see him disappearing into the forest, without so much as a backwards glance.

Just like that I found myself alone again, the wind howling amongst the trees was my only company. I don't know how long had passed before I decided to pull myself out of the puddle that I had been soaking in, grasping my bow in my shivering hands. I gingerly bent down to retrieve my knife, gazing into the distance while the clouds above darkened.

I slowly made my way back to the Den, back towards the only home I knew now, the only place I could call safe.

CHAPTER
Three

I made it back to the cave, but I didn't remember the journey. I had tossed all my clothes aside to fall naked into my bed. Every inch of me ached and throbbed, soaked to the very bone. The night was long, and I jolted awake at every little noise, while every bruise set my body alight with shocks of pain. And the shivering; my very soul felt cold.

Eventually the shadows gave way to the light, and a cold breeze filtered through the reeds, rousing me from the fitful sleep I had managed to obtain the last few hours of the night. Birds chirped cheerfully outside, a welcome chorus as I peered out into the day. Water dripped from the trees, and a light mist had gathered around their trunks, but all was quiet—all was well.

Until I glanced down at my naked body. Awful purple and black bruises covered my legs, ribs, and my wrist. Plenty of jagged cuts and dried, crusted blood clung to my too-pale skin. The angry red welts were a jarring sight, but it reminded me of how close I came to death.

The faces of my assailants were a muddied jumble of nothing. But that leader of theirs, his face was clear as day, those hardened golden eyes felt as though they had pierced my soul. A bit of me shuddered in fear. Though

I knew they were gone and that I was safe here, worry gnawed at me.

But I still had work to do. I'd lost my backpack of goods, along with a decent portion of whatever dignity I had left. I'd have to return to town to scavenge whatever I could, and right now I was desperate for some alcohol to disinfect these wounds. The last thing one needed in post-apocalyptic America was an infection.

What a great time to be alive, I thought bitterly.

I glanced at the pile of soaked clothing I'd left in a heap by the foot of my bed. The cloak that creature had given me lay atop it. Frowning, I leaned down to straighten out all my clothes to dry on a rack I had fashioned from some metal pipes. They stank horribly but there was nothing to be done about it. I picked up the cloak last, holding it outwards to let my eyes roam over it. I hadn't noticed the fine craftmanship, the thick material embroidered with strange symbols in bright colors upon the hems. Embroidery of exotic and fantastical creatures pranced amongst leaves and flowers and was unlike anything I had ever seen. But the most impressive thing was possibly the symbol etched onto the left breast.

Sitting regally in a swirl of gold and white thread that weaved in and out was a leaping creature that looked very similar to a deer. Its head sat tall and proud on a strong neck and thick body, but resembled a horse more, with two sets of thick horns, one curling towards its face from behind the ears and the other set stood atop its head, branching out into the most majestic set of antlers I had ever seen. Then I noticed the long wings that extended from the creature's back and I took a moment to try and visualize something so powerful and inspiring as it meandered its way calmly through a meadow. Did such a thing truly exist? And if it did, did it now exist here, on Earth?

I shook my head, urging my racing mind to clear itself for the real task at hand—checking my traps in the woods and attempting to recoup what I had lost. I sheathed my knife in my pocket as I left the cloak to dry on the rack. Sitting discreetly by the reed mats at the entrance of the cave was the compound bow their leader had decided to leave for me and a quiver filled with brightly feathered metal-tipped arrows I had found a few months before in a cabin in the woods. I slung the quiver and bow across my back before pulling back the reed mats to emerge into the soaking world.

A ray of sunlight pierced the cloud cover to momentarily blind me. I threw my hand up, shielding my eyes, as I perused the horizon. The trees glittered like gems, their boughs and leaves still dripping from yesterday's downpour. New shoots sprouted from their branches, fresh green leaves drooping under the heavy weight of a single drop of rain.

It was a familiar scene, but every time I saw it a part of my heart was moved by the simplicity. Even amongst such chaos and devastation, life moved on. Someday, maybe even the idea that humans walked this planet would be almost as unbelievable as the dinosaurs that came before us.

The day was cold and cloudy, yet the world was alive with the twittering of small birds in the canopy. Squirrels chased one another in the underbrush, their constant chatter drowning out the birds and bugs. Hopefully that meant the traps yielded promising gains. There was only so long you could survive on nuts and berries before you went insane. Or at least I thought so, my sister would have me think otherwise—sometimes I thought she was part squirrel.

A tug at my heart, the smile disappearing as fast as it had appeared. I couldn't think of anyone now without feeling that pit of despair yawning beneath me, threatening to pull me in. A sinking feeling followed me everywhere, it gnawed on my very bones, exhausting me during even the most mundane of tasks.

I sighed. It did nothing to dwell on the past, one day I'd end up like everyone else—but no one was here to plant me into an unmarked grave. Nobody to mourn my passing. My body would lay open to the elements, the next meal of somebody's feral poodle.

Something wet slapped against my hair, dripping down across my face. A ray of sunshine flitted through the trees, as a rainbow was cast in the distance, striking up from the forest to disappear into the clouds.

I made my way cautiously through the forest to the first trap behind an aging oak tree, its heavy twisted boughs were a favorite of the forest denizens. Unfortunately, today wasn't my day, the trap was empty—the bait untouched. Running my hand through my hair, I kicked several leaves at the base of the cage to help disguise it better before trudging off down the cliff side towards the river.

That burbling, grumbling, roiling river rushed past with such ferocity you could hear it from miles around. I had a trap at the top of the waterfall and one below it where the river bottlenecked. For quite some time salmon was plenty, I caught so many I had to teach myself how to pickle and salt the fish to make it last. But the spawning season came and went, and before I had time to debate eating the questionable crustaceans that began to populate the rivers, the woods surrounding me exploded with new animals.

Elk, deer, bear, fox, wolf, raccoon, opossum. In the absence of humans, nature took control. I had my pick really, not that I particularly wanted to eat any of that, but when you're starving you don't have much of a choice. I could only justify that I was helping the fragile ecosystem somehow with my systematic culling of the old and withered animals that were too slow or injured to escape the tip of an arrow to the heart.

Ahead, the trees fell back revealing the dark surface of the raging river as it headed over a rock ledge to tumble several feet into a quiet, rippling river. Here, I gingerly knelt beside the river, sucking in a breath at the ache in my ribs and jaw, and thrust my arm into the cold waters to pull the crab trap up. It was a flimsy thing

I had found in the back of an abandoned truck, but it had served me well.

"Not today it seems," I muttered discouragingly to myself. Shoving the trap back into the water, I crawled over the rocks as I made my way down the embankment towards the next trap.

But that one was also empty.

Which meant there was only one left.

I tried to stop myself as my eyes followed the river downstream towards the town. But I couldn't think of the ifs, I had to go, it was my last chance at an easy meal before I had to waste my entire day hunting down an animal that could easily maim or kill me. In my weakened state, I was easy prey. For wildlife, for fellow man, and for *Them*.

I couldn't stop the shiver that overcame me because I knew now what the town meant. They might still be in the vicinity—which didn't make much sense to me. They hated the inefficiency and lack of culture we have—*had*, and yet they'd occupied most of our former cities, warping them into some perverted version of where they came from.

We were also stupid. Because that's where we hid from Them. The cities, the towns, the villages. We just sat in our homes and waited for them to take us. We listened to our leaders, our government, our military— by the time evacuation was even a consideration, it was too late. We stood there, in plain sight, and we suffered dearly for it.

Lament of the Unclaimed

My memories of those last few days, over a year ago, came rushing back. I jolted to a stop; my feet felt like concrete boots had been slapped onto them. I violently shook my head, trying to dispel those thoughts—the images. Wrenching my feet from the spot, I forced myself, step after step, following the gently rippling current downstream. Down, down towards the grey colored wood of the Visitor Center where it sat desolate and wasted in a clearing off the main road.

A light breeze had picked up as I skirted around the nearby cabins, my eyes on every window and door. Almost all were boarded up—untouched since those early days. Here and there I came across the tracks of deer and small vermin, evidence of their voracious activities laid out on the trash piles scattered throughout the once densely populated areas.

I hated litter back then, and I hated it even more now. I almost felt hopeless coming across every piece that flitted by, knowing I'd never be able to clean it all. Fortunately, They abhorred garbage as much as I did, every town they occupied was so clean you would have no second thought licking the very pavement. I suppose if I had to attribute their dominion to anything good, it would be their ability to transform a trash heap into a garden.

The last trap was up ahead. I had it set in an alley between two houses where an unusual amount of animal traffic seemed to occur. It never failed, either. The main problem was hauling whatever I had caught back up the mountainside to the Den. Usually I was graced with opossums, raccoon, rabbits, or rodents. Skunks were the worse though—they weren't worth the effort to rid yourself and their skin of the smell.

Thankfully, I'd never been hungry enough to resort to eating a skunk.

Cautiously, I backed up against the side of the house, inching forward slowly to glance around the corner. Adjusting the bow over my shoulder, I slunk into the alley; a ray of sunlight brightened the narrow way. The trap stood behind a trashcan and pile of abandoned firewood at the far end of the alley. I'd thought of procuring the wood for myself on numerous occasions, but I figured most of the critters the trap caught used it and the trashcan as a home. It was far more useful where it was for the time being.

I pulled back the sheet covering the front of the trap and my heart immediately sank—it was empty. Even the bait was gone. I had caught nothing. Audibly sighing, I bent down to replace the cover on the trap and stared off into the woods. Now I had to spend the rest of what little sunshine there was trying to hunt something down.

That's when I saw a shadow saunter past the alley, and I turned to watch as a young buck began scavenging for acorns. If there ever was a time that I considered some celestial being was looking out for me, it was right in that moment.

I didn't think, I acted straight away, afraid to lose such a good opportunity. I slung the bow quietly off my shoulder and knocked an arrow, walking out from the safety of the alley. The young buck continued rooting through the leaves, his back to me. A breeze cleared the few wispy tendrils of hair that were tickling my face—I was downwind, he would have no idea I was there.

I couldn't have asked for a better set of events. But hauling that hundred-pound boy back up the mountain was a whole other challenge. I'd worry about that after, worst case scenario I'd just take what I could carry and store the rest in a house for later. Lifting the bow, I watched the buck move at the tip of my arrow. Waiting for that moment where his chest would line up perfectly and award him a quick, clean death. He slowly turned, every movement of his was agonizing to me as I slowed my breathing, my arm straining to hold the arrow. The effort it took to stay so still, the increasing pain in my ribs, caused my vision to waver slightly.

Then he did it, his chest aligned perfectly with the tip of my arrow.

I took a deep breath, steadying myself. Before I could release the arrow, a branch snapped from behind me and the buck raised his head to stare into my eyes, then bolted. I loosed the arrow and watched as it hit the spot he where he had been, disappearing into the leaf litter as he disappeared into the forest.

Whirling, I prepared for the mental anguish I'd feel when my eyes met a squirrel or perhaps a curious stray dog. I was not prepared for that familiar long white hair that gracefully framed a sharp, masculine face set with watchful golden eyes staring back at me. He seemed as startled as I was, unprepared for coming face to face with one another. But he certainly remembered me, and I him. My bow dropped from my hands with an audible thud against the ground.

Shit.

Now that I could see him more closely, my eyes not shadowed by rain or pain, I could let them roam freely over him. He was tall, like his kind usually were—and clothed in the most peculiar of clothing. He wore a deep purple tunic banded by a bright reddish leather brace hugging his chest, emphasizing every muscle, every curve. Leather gloves that matched the brace on his chest also matched the bracers on his wrists, and the boots on his feet. You couldn't deny the power—the handsomeness he exuded, but that didn't stop the feeling of dread as my heart sank and my stomach quivered. His golden eyes narrowed, no doubt fully aware of my observation. I felt like a deer in headlights, as we both looked each other over. His face was calm, belaying no emotion, no hint of what he thought or planned to do.

Then he did something I didn't expect.

He spoke.

"Run, little human," he said nonchalantly, his voice held a soft lilt, almost musical.

It wasn't surprising he spoke our language. I mean, we did teach it to them when they first came here. Or rather, when we first let them in. We tried a diplomatic approach because we knew we were hopelessly outmatched. And it worked...for a while.

I stood my ground, counting the steps between here and the tree line. I couldn't risk running back down the alley, who knew where the others were. I did know that if I ran in the direction the buck had that there was a small cottage two miles into the forest that couldn't be seen from the main road. It was my best shot.

That was when I heard another call out from the alley, his voice drifting closer. I couldn't afford to be trapped, I couldn't outrun one, let alone two.

"Run," he said, glancing behind him. "Now." His eyes narrowed and he called out softly in his language to his companion.

I didn't even let it process that he was essentially saving me—that he was letting me go, *again*. I turned and fled. Willing my legs to pump harder than they ever had, I dashed beyond the tree line and kept running. Jumping every log and root that fell across my path, enduring every tree branch that whipped against my bare skin. Stinging and far more sore than when I had awoken, my chest heaved, and my legs began to trip on every leaf. I finally rounded the driveway that led to the cabin two miles from the Visitor Center. I hadn't even glanced back to see if I was being followed. My breaths came in angry gulps, my ribs were on fire and every bruise seemed to be magnified.

Once I calmed down a little, I realized my most dire mistake. I had left my bow behind. That creature might have let me run for whatever sick, twisted reason he had, but my bow was evidence that I was there. The thought struck me, I would need to abandon the Den. It was too close, and it was a risk I couldn't take. Before, they inhabited the homes on the outskirts of Cave Junction, a coincidence that I could possibly overcome. But now, they were inside Cave Junction and the Visitor Center... the campgrounds were just a short walk from there. None of us were safe anymore. The other humans that had made their homes at the campgrounds weren't safe. They could have already met their fate and I would never have known. I felt a tear slide down my cheek as the realization kicked in of what I now had to do.

But I would first have to return to the Den. Gather what supplies I could and say goodbye to my family. I knew I couldn't stay there forever, but I thought I'd have more time. My father was the last to die, and he had only been cold for a few weeks.

Sitting in the dirt at the foot of the stairs I gave myself a few minutes to recuperate, for my heart to settle and my legs to recover. I knew I should be taking it easy, letting my ribs recover before I set off again, but I couldn't afford that luxury. As much as my body pained me, it was my mind that caused me the most discomfort.

Why did he let me go? Again. He could easily have overpowered me, and with an accomplice nearby I didn't stand a chance. This interaction was unlike anything I had ever experienced with Them, and now it had happened twice. But I couldn't let it change my resolve, he had to have an ulterior motive. Hunters enjoyed the hunt more than securing their quarry. They were monsters, he was a monster.

I wasn't going to stick around long enough to give him that opportunity.

It was a tiring trek back to the Den, not a single trap yielded anything (I may have double and triple checked on my way back) and I realized I was going to have to go hungry tonight. It wouldn't be the first time, but it had been a long time since I was unable to trap or hunt anything.

"How could you be so stupid, Wren?" I berated myself.

Shoving my spare clothes into my backpack, I ran circles around the Den, tossing things aside to make sure I had everything I'd need. I didn't have the luxury of a vehicle or pack animal (or even a second backpack). It was hard to stand there and decide whether I needed that tarp more than a second pair of boots, or to know that I would have to abandon the bed and memory foam pillows I had grown so fond of.

I leaned against the entrance, sighing as I watched the sun dip below the tree line. I just had one more thing to do before I left, and it would end up being the hardest thing of all. I gently traced the six names carved into the rock wall. No one would know their lives—or their deaths—once I left here. They would be lost. Random names carved onto a cave wall for who knows why.

Two graves sat at the base of the cliff below the Den, both were ringed by large river stones and marked by a wooden cross adorned with a wreath of decaying wood and flowers. A single rock sat at the base of the cross with the name of the person who lay slumbering beneath it. One whose dirt was still a tad soft; they were as close together as I could get them—considering they died months apart.

"Mother," I whispered, my fingers grazing the wreath. She was so full of life, so nurturing—so selfless.

It had been her undoing.

I turned to the last grave. The one I had slept beside the first few days, those horrible, terrifically unbearable three days after. My sister was like my mother in every way—but not me, oh no, I was easily a daddy's girl. I was like the son he never had; I was the go-to for three in the morning fishing expeditions down at the lake. The first choice for organizing Superbowl parties with the block. He taught me to ride a bike, pitch in Little League, he was even there when I tried and failed at crafting my very own chair (ten-year-old me didn't think chairs needed four legs).

"I'll miss you, too, Dad. Keep Mom company for me." A single tear dripped down my face.

With that final goodbye, I hefted the backpack more securely against my back, and the cloak that creature had given me was slung through the straps. As I set off, I endeavored to check the traps one last time before all traces of sunlight were gone. Raging against the pain,

I scoured the woods. It was as if Their presence had vacated the forest of all life. Although I still heard the birds and vermin scurrying about, none wanted to show themselves. They especially didn't want to become my next meal.

I was stuck, my stomach growling angrily as I made my way down the hill in the direction of the national forest. I decided on a whim I would attempt to get close to Lake Selmac, regardless of what that wanderer had said to me earlier. There was a greater chance of Them being in the towns along the way, but the chance to find food was even greater. The only real plan I had was to eventually get to the ocean, commandeer a boat, and make my way to one of the many islands up north, where the snow and rain was abundant, and They were nowhere to be seen.

Or so we always said. I wasn't so sure how true that was anymore.

The sun was truly gone now, luckily there was just enough moonlight filtering through the treetops for me not to trip across every root and rock in my way. But that didn't mean my hike wasn't wrought with peril. It also didn't stop me from walking into several cobwebs or taking a face full of pine needles more than once.

After what seemed to be hours, the forest thinned, exposing a long winding road. I paused briefly at the shoulder, debating whether going west towards the coast was truly the right choice, or if traveling as far north as I could was the better call. The soft blue light of the moon slowly winked out. The wind picked up, and with it, a soft rain began to fall. No doubt soon I would be soaked to the bone; my thin jacket and jeans would do little to deter the rain once it became more than a modest sprinkle. I then remembered the cloak hanging from the straps of my backpack and worked quickly to throw it over myself.

"Just what I need," I muttered, debating whether it was worth it to risk bringing my flashlight out. At this rate, I would exhaust myself just straining to see ten feet in front of me.

I sat at the edge of the road, hidden by the trees, letting the rain gently pat against the hood of the cloak. I had to admit, it did a wondrous job of keeping me dry. But that was all I really had going for me now. The lack of food was beginning to gnaw at me, my movements were sluggish, and I could feel the dizziness settling into my bones. The tightness of the bruise against my jawline probably didn't help the strain. I would have to decide what to do. Soon.

But I didn't have to make a choice—because that's when I saw it, the lights bobbing along the road just beyond the trees. Only a few at first, and then many. Uniform, militarist, as if they conferred to a specific stance and never strayed. Pressing against the tree I was hidden behind, I peeked out to watch as they bobbed closer.

My heart nearly stopped, and I had to slap my hands across my mouth to prevent my gasp from being heard.

Figures emerged from the dark, rainy night. A series of eight tall figures shrouded in thick cloaks, their muscular bodies adorned by heavy leather tunics, swords hung at their waists. Bright lights of pure energy floated nearby, held in place by some invisible tether.

Them.

But it wasn't Them causing a fervor in my gut, and my eyes to burn—it was the six shorter figures walking slowly in the middle. They weren't shrouded or protected from the rain. They wore long, pale robes tied at the waist by twisted belts.

Humans. All women. They were anywhere between twenty and thirty years in age, different races and heights. But there was one human that caused my breath to hitch, every muscle in my body became taught with disbelief.

Bright skin and soft, blonde hair billowing gently in the breeze as she walked with her head held high, back straight—a lithe, athletic body. The high cheekbones, the full crimson-tinged lips, and eyes as bright as the tropical sea…

"Katie." I couldn't help the strangled gasp that escaped my body.

CHAPTER
Four

Katherine.

My sister.

Alive.

And enslaved by *Them.*

My eyes burned and every muscle strained as I beheld her.

She wasn't dead, she didn't have any evidence of injuries or malnutrition, she looked right as the rain that fell between us. She was alive, and she looked— healthy. Her skin was tanned and glowing, her hair was soft and bouncy. Everything about her would have had me second guessing the end of the world.

I don't know what possessed me, I was mesmerized as I took a step forward onto the edge of the bouncing lights. It was all that was needed. A guard looked in my direction and raised the alarm to his companions. The humans all looked up at me, and my eyes locked with my sister. Her bright turquoise eyes widened; she shook her head before she mouthed a single word.

Run.

Two guards made their way toward me as I stood debating my fate: be captured and stay with Katie—the only family member I had left—or run, abandoning her. I watched her a moment longer, deliberating, but I couldn't read her. Her face was a blank slate as she stared back at me, impassive, unyielding. Should I run? Should I stay? Everything in my being told me to run.

I'll find a way to save you, I'll find my way back to you. I promise.

I won't leave you at their mercy. I wish I could have verbalized it, but I tried my hardest to say it with my eyes before I turned my back on her—and ran as fast as I could. The moon was still shrouded by the rain clouds, and my flight was slow and agonizing. It felt as if hours could have passed when, in truth, it had been mere moments. I constantly tripped, leaves and rocks ripping at my exposed flesh, my jeans tore at the knee as I fell again. My ribs burned, and it felt as if every cut and bruise on my body suddenly was amplified.

I could hear my pursuers shouting behind me. They were gaining ground, and fast. I didn't know what they said or how far away they were, and as I turned around to stare at the lights bobbing not more than twenty feet behind me, their shadows silhouetted against the trees, the ground disappeared beneath me.

Tumbling into the darkness, I felt the forest lash out at me. My skin stung, and I was certain it wasn't just rain that dripped down my extremities. As soon as I hit solid ground I jumped up and ran again. There was no time to stop and examine every pained bit I could feel. I would have to risk injuring myself further before I could tend to my wounds.

As I rounded a small hill, the trees thinned, and the bushes disappeared to reveal a manicured lawn leading up to a small town. I paused only briefly, but it was long enough for one of the monsters to catch up with me. He stood at the top of the hill and as his golden eyes met mine, he called out to his partner somewhere behind him.

I took off across the lawn towards the first building, rounding the corner. I glanced left and right before dashing towards the door of a small shop. The sign had long since decayed beyond recognition, but I didn't care what it held, I needed to get inside. The door was locked, and so were the shops next to it. I could hear Them behind me somewhere, the lights clouded by a dense fog that had begun to creep into town. The rain was still light, fresh, but it had seeped into my clothing, even underneath the cloak—chilling me to the bone.

The next set of buildings were locked as well, but oddly enough none were boarded up. I didn't pause as I ran down an alley and up a side street to the next set of buildings. A cat sat on a barrel outside of a supermarket, licking its paw and regarding me. I ran towards the entrance, begging it to be open, but to no avail.

The bobbing lights crept ever closer, the voices of the guards pursuing me were muffled but carried through the gentle breeze. They would soon find me; adrenaline alone kept me going. There was one building that stood out to me, up a narrow road on a small hill. It seemed to overlook the small town, with a view that commanded the entirety of the redwoods.

Lament of the Unclaimed

It was tall and made completely of stone, and the windows were adorned by beautiful oak shutters with a trough of flowers beneath. It looked like a mill and barn converted into a house. Mustering what little strength I had left I ran towards the door, wrapped my hand around the knob, and turned it. The lock clicked and the door slid open silently. I ducked inside and shut the door behind me, locking it. The inside was dark, but surprisingly not musty at all. It held the faint scent of flowers—rose and gardenia, perhaps? Certainly not what you'd think an abandoned building would smell like.

Lowering my hood, I rubbed the water, dirt, and possible blood from my face, wincing at the pain in my jaw. I waited for my eyes to adjust to the darkness, faint light trickled in from outside; the moon had finally shown itself again. Then I heard the voices, glancing around the room for a place to hide I noticed the layout: six small tables, three on the left and three on the right covered in neat piles of books and papers—and at the very end of the room sat a longer dark wood desk that had an even larger pile of books and paper on it. I ran for it, ducking beneath the desk and pulling my backpack to sit in front of me.

The desk's back faced a window with delicate blue curtains, from which I could see the silhouette of one of the guards walking by, his body lit up by his faithful ethereal ball of light. I slowly slid the knife that once belonged to my father from my pocket. Its smooth wooden handle was oddly comforting as I sat there in

57

the dark. I saw the second guard's shadow meet by the window, and they talked in hushed tones, their words inaudible even though I would more than likely not have understood a word.

Water dripped from my hairline into my eyes, and I tried to blink it away furiously. The guards stood there for a while, listening, before they disappeared, the balls of light shooting off ahead. The darkness returned as the moon retreated and I quivered there, too afraid to move. Listening to the rain gently beat against the roof, I waited for my breathing to calm, and the realization of what I'd seen came flooding back.

Katie was alive, and she was with *Them*.

Questions ran through my mind as I leaned back against the desk. I wanted to explore whatever predicament I had now found myself in, but I was afraid to make any noise that might betray my position. If they found me here, I would be in trouble. There was only one way in or out as far as I could tell, and that was the door I had come in.

They could be right outside the door for all I knew, waiting for me. My only chance was to stay here until the morning. Until the light would reveal what lay out in the dark for me. As impossible as it was, I caught myself nodding off. I didn't have much choice—or control over it, my body was telling me it needed to rest. If the fatigue didn't lull me to sleep, the pain radiating through my body would have done the job.

I wasn't going to argue.

The morning greeted me with a ray of sunshine to the face, and I stretched—uncomfortable from the decision to sleep under the desk. Gingerly standing up, I used the chair to support me and shoved my backpack into the corner under the desk. With my knife still clutched in my hand, I peeked behind the curtain. The window provided a view of a rising set of hills and trees too tall and thick to really see beyond. But they led west, and if I followed them, it would probably lead me back towards Katie.

Even though my gaze swept left and right, past the buildings and into the forest, I knew there was something odd about this town. It wasn't like Cave Junction, at least not the Cave Junction as it was now. There was noise. Lots of it. Not just the noise of the wild waking from its slumber, birds chirping and bugs buzzing. Oh no, it was the noise of *civilization*. The noise of conversations and footfalls, of doors slamming and glasses clinking. This town was alive, and I had the horrible thought that maybe I had just signed their death warrant.

But I didn't have time to dwell on it. The wood creaked above my head, and my heart raced with the realization that I was hearing footsteps. In the far corner against the back wall, steps led upward into the darkness. Someone was there, and I didn't know if it was a human—or one of Them. Startled and panicking, I made the decision to crawl back under the desk, pulling the chair up to hide me, with my knife clutched in my hand.

How could I have been so stupid? Such an easy mistake, my dad must be rolling in his grave. With that much commotion outside it was highly unlikely the town was populated by humans. It certainly wouldn't go unnoticed, especially not after my intrusion last night. A part of me hoped it wasn't a human, because then it would be my fault if They came back.

I sat as still as I could, taking slow, shallow breaths as I listened to whoever was walking down the stairs and the rustling of whatever they were wearing and the tap, tap, tap of their shoes as they approached the desk and placed something on it. The front door opened, followed by the shuffling of many pairs of boots. There were easily four other people in here with me now, and I couldn't miss how the air shifted in their presence. At least, I hoped they were people. My breath hitched as I mentally begged someone to say something. There was a knock at the door and whoever was by the desk called out to them, calling a name I couldn't quite discern. A set of heavy boots thudded across the floor, heading towards the desk.

They spoke to one another, and my heart instantly sank at the recognition of those soft, lyrical words. It wasn't one of our languages. It was *Them*. Every set of boots I had heard must have belonged to them, and there I was—sat under the desk like a frightened puppy flinching at every noise. Papers rustled, books closed, and fingers drummed against desks in contemplation. Whatever this building was used for before, it was now some sort of gathering point for Them.

The voices next to me rose and fell, but the creature who had come down the stairs maintained a calm voice, while the newcomer seemed hasty, annoyed, even. His boots thudded against the floorboards and steadily grew louder as he approached the desk. As he approached *me*.

His feet were clad with rough, leather boots that pushed back the hems of the rich, chocolate brown leather pants that disappeared beneath a cream-colored robe. What struck me the most was the clothing he wore was intricate, regal, even. He must be very high ranked. You didn't see many of them swathed in robes—battle leathers and plates were their go-to wardrobe.

I held my breath as I willed him not to look under the desk, not to pull the chair back. But if I thought before that there ever was a guardian angel looking out for me, he must have turned his back, because the chair quivered slightly as the creature pulled it back and sat down.

His golden eyes locked onto mine, but he didn't so much as blink as he looked back up at his companion, listening to the other creature drone on and on. It was *him*, the creature from the Visitor Center. He was here—I never forgot a face, definitely not one of Theirs, and he was ignoring me as if he hadn't seen me. I knew he did, despite the lack of emotion across his face. Just like when I first saw him. The grip on my blade was so tight my knuckles were bone white, I was waiting—waiting for that moment when he'd reveal that I was here and six or more of them would come at me. I was prepared to die if I couldn't escape, no matter how ached and strained and tired I was. I wouldn't let them have me.

My eyes strayed over him; the impossibly shiny ivory hair that graced his shoulders was highlighted by an oddly curved golden circle set against his pointed ears. One hand cupped his chin as the other drummed on the armrest of his chair, occasionally answering his companion. Eventually he held up his hand and his companion muttered before the sounds of his boots traveled towards the door and it slammed shut.

He rolled his eyes before pushing up out of the chair and disappearing towards the door. He muttered something and I heard the gentle shuffles of several sets of feet leaving. I peeked my head out from behind the desk as the last of the creatures left through the front door, The snowy haired one had his back to me, and I didn't second guess it, I tip-toed towards him.

As he shut the door and clicked the lock, I held my knife against his throat, having to stand on my toes in order to be tall enough to reach him. He sighed—a ghost of a smile playing on his lips as he glanced back at me. His golden eyes swirled, and I felt a shiver run itself up my spine. His gaze was intense, and I felt almost pinned to the spot, frozen. But I strengthened my resolve, pressing the blade more firmly against his flesh.

"Interesting response," he mused, "certainly not how my kind thank their saviors."

I pressed my knife against his throat even harder, sure that at any moment it would cut him. Then I leaned in, "Thanks," I said acidly, debating the best way to escape, if slitting his throat would be necessary—but in the blink of an eye he took the choice away from me.

He had pried the knife from my hand and tossed it to the ground before grasping my wrists and pushing me against the wall. He held my wrists to either side of my head, his eyes twinkling as a smirk formed.

"Let me go, you filth!" I spat, kicking out in anger and trying my best to free myself from his firm grip.

"Vicious," he laughed.

A knock sounded at the door and as he glanced up, it sounded again, more urgently. He released my wrists to wrap an arm around my mouth, dragging me behind the door and against him as he cracked it open. He muttered something under his breath, too low for me to comprehend, but I felt a cool breeze wash over me. The tingling sensation traveled across my skin, and I had the mind to think I had imagined it, but the sensation was hard to consider natural.

My heart beat rapidly in my chest as I considered what would happen next. If he had wanted to, I would have been outed already, the past two encounters with him were enough to slightly calm the anxiety building up within me, but my fate was undecided, and my guardian angel lay quiet.

"What?" he asked, and the word resonated through me before I realized, he didn't say it in English—but in his language, and I could understand it.

"I'm sorry for bothering you, Aer Vaelythor, but I have been instructed by the guards to alert all residents to an incident that has occurred." I couldn't see the speaker, but he spoke with an authority that had me rigid in the creature's arms.

I felt his grip tighten on me, but not in a painful way. My hands fell limply to my side as I waited to hear the rest. Struggling was useless, for now. The easiest way to get out of my predicament was wait it out, until it was just me and him.

The creature holding me spoke, "Continue."

"An unclaimed human was spotted in the woods last night, female, twenties, she managed to escape custody. Last seen running through the town center."

"Interesting," he mused, "is she dangerous?"

"As far as we are aware, she is unarmed." The creature handed my captor a paper, "in case you see her."

"Thank you—Aerol, was it?"

"Yes, Aer Vaelythor." I could hear the smile in the creature named Aerol's voice. As if my captor remembering his name was an honor.

"That is all?" I didn't know what 'Aer Vaelythor' meant, but it didn't translate over, as if it was his name or a word that had no translation in my language.

Aerol must have nodded because my captor closed the door and released me. I took a few steps back, debating if I could make it to my knife before he killed me. He either didn't notice my intent or didn't care; he regarded the paper he was handed before showing it to me.

"It seems you're famous."

I took the paper from him, retreating several steps away before looking over the carefully drawn image of myself. They didn't miss a single detail, from my ratty, wet hair hastily thrown into a ponytail and the dirt smudged against my cheeks, to the bruise on my jaw. I hadn't thought they'd gotten such a good look at me, but then I remembered that moment when I stood there in the open—watching my sister walking in the rain.

"How could I understand you? When you were talking to him?" I whispered, my eyes glued to the drawing. I could see the knife glinting on the floor in my peripherals, as if beckoning me to try again. But I had to handle this situation cautiously, he had saved me—twice, if this didn't count as a third time.

"It was a simple spell," he answered casually, watching me.

My heart skipped a beat.

"You *spelled* me?" I growled, crumbling the paper in my hand. When had he done that? I didn't even notice...but I had, hadn't I? It was so casually done, like a whisper.

I stilled, if they had the power to do that without us even noticing—what else were they capable of? My skin prickled, no wonder They had conquered us like measly ants.

"Someone worked hard on that," he nodded at the paper.

When I didn't reply he turned his back on me to go through a pile of papers, "I did it for your benefit. There will be no repercussions from it, it simply allows you to understand us."

"Who said I wanted to understand you?" I glared at the back of his head. The mental anguish that roiled inside me easily overtook the physical pain that ravaged my body. I wanted to be outraged, I desperately did. But I couldn't muster that feeling, I didn't understand why I couldn't—and, honestly, that scared me the most.

Not his actions, but mine.

He must've done more than let me understand their language, there must have been something else he did. It made no sense that his kind would conquer humanity and then he'd behave the way he had. Having that group of thugs in Cave Junction leave me alone, warning me to run at the Visitor Center, hiding me from the rest of his kind here, and then spelling me so I could understand them. It made no sense, none of it did—something was wrong. This was some sort of sick joke. Maybe he was bored of straight out killing humans and now preferred to play with his meals first. I eyed the dagger, weighing my chances.

Somehow, even with his back turned, he must have guessed my intentions because he said, "You can try if you want, but I can guarantee you won't succeed."

"I almost did," I replied, my eyes narrowing.

"You weren't even close."

"Cocky from someone who let a human hold a knife against their throat," I spat.

"Ah, the keyword there—*let*." He turned around, his eyes just as cold and distant as they were that day in the clearing.

Part of me wanted to ask why, but I began to feel dizzy. The world had been blurry at the edges since I woke, but I had pushed to ignore it. Everything was beginning to close in as if I had been running on pure terror and adrenaline and now, finally, I was empty. I was in more danger now than I had ever been in before, neck deep in the den of my enemies—with intentions I could not comprehend, and my body was telling me it had had enough.

His eyes narrowed, "You're injured."

"No, I'm not." Probably the most obvious lie I had ever told, but I certainly wasn't going to admit to him how suddenly and acutely aware I was of every bruise, cut, scrape, and sore muscle in my body. In fact, I wasn't sure which part of my body *wasn't* in pain. My ribs screamed in agony with every breath, and as hard as I fought to ignore it, I suddenly found myself unable to.

He frowned, watching as I slowly let myself slide against the wall to sit on the floor. He was speaking to me, I saw his lips move, but I didn't hear anything that he said. I was so angry at myself, angry for letting this happen, angry for succumbing to such an easy death literally at the feet of this monster.

I drifted in and out as I felt myself lift from the floor where I was slumped. Strong arms held me close as the room spun. Darkness shadowed the edges of my mind, and I could do nothing but watch myself get carried towards the stairwell. Sleep took me before I could think of doing anything to save myself from what awaited when I awoke.

CHAPTER
Five

A bird chirped somewhere, rousing me from a dreamless slumber. I heard rustling nearby and froze, remembering where I was, and what had happened. I gently moved my wrists and ankles—no chains, no restraints. I even expected my back to be stiff and sore from sleeping in some cell, but a fistful of soft quilt and silken sheets told me otherwise. I could feel several pillows propping me up as well. Cautiously I opened my eyes, ready to see a horde of guards with their weapons drawn.

My captor sat across from me on a wooden chair set by a desk like the one downstairs, a tray of food and sour smelling concoctions in a bowl sat in his hands. He noticed my stirring, setting the tray on a table beside the bed. I wasn't sure where I was, the last recollection I had was of being carried towards the stairwell. *The loft.* If he wasn't going to sound the alarm, then he would have carried me to the loft to keep me hidden. Hidden, but why? What possible benefit did my life have to him? Maybe he kept me alive for his own benefit, to use me as some sort of experiment?

An experiment. He must have kept me to study me. There was no other logical explanation for his actions.

Once, twice, three times—you didn't go out of your way to spare something unless it was somehow valuable to you. But I wasn't sure what he could learn from me that his kind hadn't already gathered after they took over the entire planet. I remembered all those humans that were walking on the road with Katie, wherever they were headed this creature must have kept me for that purpose as well. I took solace in the fact that maybe I still had a chance to see my sister.

"Oh look, it still breathes." He smirked, mixing some of the sour concoction with a dash of what I presumed was water before handing it to me.

"I'm not drinking your poison," I said, trying to keep my eyes from wandering over the bread, cheese, and fruit that lined the tray with lust.

He rolled his eyes, still holding the mixture aloft, "It's medicine."

"Why should I believe you?" I sat up in the bed, my hands shooting to my face as the room began to spin.

He glowered at me, "If I wanted to kill or harm you, you've given me plenty of opportunity."

"I suppose it doesn't help if you mess with your field study," I said angrily, snatching the concoction from his hand. I didn't want to take anything he offered, anything at all—I didn't want to be here. But I couldn't help Katie if I was sick or injured or neck deep in a viper pit. Besides, if he truly wanted me for what the other humans were destined for then maybe I would get reunited with her after all. I would just need to play along.

"Field study?" He questioned, amused. But I wasn't having any of it, I threw back the covers and tried to stand, staggering so badly as bouts of pain radiated through what seemed every part of my body.

"I would advise against you standing up right now," he said casually, watching me.

I glowered at him, "I'll do what I want."

He regarded me for a moment in silence before returning to the desk and sifting through several papers. The once crumpled ball with the drawing of me was pinned to a cork board above the desk. Along with a map of the surrounding area stabbed with red, blue, and yellow dots. I squinted, noticing that Cave Junction was marked with a red dot, the national forest with yellow, and Grants Pass and Lake Selmac with blue.

It dawned on me then the significance of that board— it showed the enemy movements. It showed what areas were under *Their* control, what were neutral, and what still belonged to man. I tried not to gawk as I went from one corner of the map to the other, counting the reds, blues, and yellows, remembering the names of the areas which were marked blue and making a mental note to avoid them. The only problem was, I wasn't entirely sure where we were, this town wasn't marked on the map at all, but the buildings seemed old enough to be ours. I saw the Redwood Highway and the small road where it split north of Cave Junction, and I was certain I had followed it west. But in all that commotion, running for my life, had I really gone west?

Mustering whatever strength I had left, I slowly walked towards the window, peeking behind the curtain to stare out into the foggy wilderness beyond.

"Where are we?" I asked, watching the dark clouds passing overhead, threatening to unleash upon this small unknown town.

"I would advise you not to go outside right now, if that is what you plan." He was watching me now, a handful of papers in his hand.

"I don't care for your advice; I want to know where I am," I said in annoyance.

I turned from the window to stare him down and he shrugged, "It's north of where we had met last."

North? How did I end up north? Somehow in the confusion of being hunted and seeing my sister alive I had must have completely missed the Redwood Highway to end up… I closed my eyes and rubbed my temples, trying to recall what towns were between here and Grants Pass.

When I opened my eyes again, I noticed my right hand was covered in a patch and my left wrist was in a bandage. A moment of clarity overcame me as I realized more of me was also wrapped, but that didn't come close to my main concern—I was clean, and dressed in a soft, pink gown. My hair was soft and smelt faintly of roses, cascading gently across my shoulders. I berated myself, how could I have not noticed that before? I froze, my brain slowly catching up—that meant he had undressed me.

"You..." I couldn't muster the words to describe how I felt just then, so exasperated, I simply indicated my clothing.

"You had multiple injuries that were on the cusp of infection, including a fractured rib and foot," he said, nodding at the bowl by the bed. "That will help with the pain."

A fractured foot? I dumbly looked down, noticing how swollen my left foot was compared to my right one, a barely visible bruise had begun to form. I hadn't even noticed...I mean, I did stick that landing hard down that ravine or gully I tumbled into. But certainly not enough to fracture my foot? As for pain, I wasn't really in too much pain, was I? My skin stung as if I had a hundred invisible paper cuts across it, but it wasn't unbearable. I always had a high tolerance for pain, I felt the normal aches and pulls that I thought should be there—and a dull throbbing in my foot. I'd never broken a bone before, let alone fractured one; maybe that was normal? Then I remembered my rib, I had done something to it when I was attacked back in Cave Junction, he said it had been fractured as well. At least it wasn't fully broken, a broken bone would delay my journey back to my sister's side.

I turned to him. "I still can't believe you had the audacity—" he raised a hand before I could finish.

"I did nothing, my familiar did the work that is causing you such outrage. I only treated your wounds. I am not unaware of the fondness humans have for their modesty," he replied, his eyes skimming papers until he found a thick parchment with deep blue ink written across it, a seal of gold and ivory forming a crest at the bottom.

I ignored the mention of a familiar, it meant nothing to me. Maybe it was what They called an assistant? Or a slave. It didn't matter, though, my main concern since I woke up had to be addressed, the events of me passing out were buried in a haze of fog.

"Did you knock me out, too?"

"No, you did such a good job yourself I didn't think it was necessary," he replied sarcastically, not bothering to look up.

I tried not to audibly sigh with relief as I glanced at the mixture on the tray debating whether it truly would ease my pain; I wasn't yet so desperate that I would resort to consuming one of Their concoctions. But the food called to me—sung to me, my stomach growling in response. The soft, golden bread drizzled with what smelled like honey had me salivating, it'd been the better part of a year since I'd had the joy of experiencing bread. The fruit and cheese were delicately arrayed in a careful circle around the bread on the center of an ivory porcelain plate. Strawberries, blueberries, orange slices, even a pair of figs.

"I figured I should feed you at least, for going through the trouble of surviving the night." He nodded at the tray. He seemed to have accepted that I wasn't going to consume his weird medicine.

I stared at him, trying to read him, trying to find a

motive. It was hard for me to admit that somehow, he seemed...*genuine*. His actions from the moment I met him, well, they were confusing. He had saved my life, spared me. Time and time again. Even now, although I hated to admit it, he was saving me. He wasn't like the others. I couldn't be sure it wasn't an elaborate ruse, but I couldn't shake the feeling, the stigma, the proof, of what his kind was capable of. He wasn't doing this for me, he had a gain in saving me—somehow. I wouldn't let my guard down. I'd get what I could from him, find out where Katie was headed, and I would save her.

A knock sounded at the door, and I froze. My captor slid the parchment into the fold of his sleeve and made his way to the stairwell.

Just at the cusp he turned to me and said, "Try not to make any noise," before disappearing down the stairwell.

The door opened a moment later and a familiar voice echoed up from below, it was the same voice that had spoken to him when I was hidden under the desk, only now I understood what he was saying. I slid from the bed and inched my way towards the stairwell to listen. Luckily the visitor came inside, and they walked to the desk at the back of the room—directly underneath me.

"You called for me, Aer Vaelythor?" the voice said, yawning.

I heard the rustling of paper before my captor replied, "I need the contents of the shipment from the City of Angels altered."

"Altered?" The question was followed by more crinkling of paper before the chair slid back across the wooden floor.

"I need it to read 'live cargo'," he replied, there was a sound like the scratching of pen on paper.

"Yes, Aer Vaelythor," I heard his heavy boots walk away before they stopped. "Can I ask, what we are moving?"

"Nothing, it's already here." His melodic voice crooned.

"This sounds like one of your crazy ideas again," the visitor replied in exasperation.

"Have any of my plans ever served you wrong, Yaern?"

I heard him—Yaern, snort, "Promise me you won't get into too much trouble?"

"I certainly can't promise that," I heard his chair slide back, "but, Yaern, I need you to act in haste—and with discretion."

The hesitation was palpable, but he must have accepted my captor's word because he merely replied, "Yes, Aer Vaelythor," before the door opened and he left.

I leaned back against the wall next to the stairwell, my back and thighs aching, my foot finally began to hurt—a sharp pain every time I flexed it. I inwardly sighed, my eyes lingering on the bowl set on the tray by the bed. Between my hunger and pain, I didn't think I could get very far. I certainly couldn't help Katie in my current state.

Using the wall to pry myself off the floor I half hopped towards the window to peek behind the curtains, careful not to let anyone who might be outside see me. This window sat above the bed I rested on, offering me an unobstructed view above the treetops to the town and the endless sea of towering redwoods and pines beyond.

The sky was dark, roiling clouds bringing thunder and rain rolled across the horizon. A bolt of lightning arced across the sky, illuminating the town. My heart sank low in my chest as I mentally tallied every one of Them that scurried for safety from the downpour, there were not just a few here and there, oh no, this was an outpost, a heavily occupied one. The entire town seemed to be filled with the creatures—all male that I could see, clad in armor and armed with weapons. A convoy was stationed outside the supermarket I had tried to open earlier; they loaded and unloaded random bags and crates.

I had unknowingly found myself within a military outpost. I cringed at the thought of what that meant. That now, I would be stuck here, at the mercy of the creature whose kind slaughtered and enslaved my people. Who ended the reign of humanity just as it was beginning to get better, just as we were at the forefront of technology, saving ourselves and our embattled planet.

Who knew where they were taking Katie, they could be in the next state over by now. I had no way of knowing, no way to find her—and now I was trapped. She looked healthy, but she also looked scared, and she told me to run. The only word she tried to say to me, she hadn't seen me in almost a year, and her only word was to save myself. *Run.*

That's exactly what I did, too. I ran. I saved myself and left her at Their mercy. Like a coward. I couldn't save Mom or Dad, and now I couldn't save my older sister— the last person I had left in this miserable world. The one person who always stood up for me, who was there to coach me through the hardest times of my life, and I left her to handle the hardest time of her life—alone.

I knew the tears were coming but I didn't bother trying to hide or hold them back, letting them silently fall down my cheeks like the rain drops that slid across the window. I watched as the cat I had seen last night ran from the porch of a shop to a house across the street, pausing to shake the water from his fur.

A heavy, yet comforting weight settled on my shoulders, and I turned to see the ivory-haired creature standing there, a solemn look on his face as he adjusted the blanket he had placed on me.

"I-I said don't...touch me..." I stuttered, choking back a sob. I dropped my head to rest against the sill, pulling the blanket closer around me.

He stood there a moment, before turning to stare outside the window next to me. "What is your name?"

It took a moment for me to register what he had said, for me to figure out how to reply. He wanted to know my name; the one thing that let me know I was real. That I was a living, breathing human with a story as varied and rich as those that had come before me. The one thing I had, that was truly me, and this monster wanted to know.

"What does *Aer Vaelythor* mean?" It was the only thing I could think to say, if he wanted answers then I wanted some, too. If I could use it against him, to save Katie, I wouldn't bat an eye.

He raised his eyebrows, his eyes sliding to mine, "Curious little one, aren't you?"

"I could say the same about you," I turned back to stare aimlessly out the window, "why doesn't it translate like all the other words?"

"It's a title." He said it simply, almost evasively. There was an edge—a pause, at the way he replied. It was important somehow, and I needed to figure out how. It was obvious he wasn't a grunt like the others, whoever he was he carried authority, and that would come in handy later.

"That sounded convincing," I scoffed.

He let out a small laugh, "Do I get to know your name?"

I watched the rain drip down the window, watched as it pooled in the streets outside and disappeared into the drains. The world was quiet, and all I could hear was the *pat, pat, pat* of the rain on the roof that was nearly twenty feet above my head.

"Am I your prisoner?" I suppose it was the one thing I really wanted to know. Could I leave when I chose to? If I did, would I be hunted down?

"No," he answered calmly.

"Then I'm leaving," I replied, gingerly pushing myself up off the bed and walking past him towards the stairwell. The room was fuzzy at the edges, and I felt weak, but if I could escape now then I would.

"You're not my prisoner, and I would never treat you as such," I looked back at him over my shoulder, a darkness seemed to shroud him as his face hardened, "but it seems I cannot guarantee your safety if you are not by my side."

"What do you mean?" I whispered, damning myself for letting my voice sound weak and afraid.

The concern was almost palpable as he said, "The others are not so kind."

"So, why do you care?" I asked, trying to inflict as much conviction as I could. I didn't know why, but I felt myself flinch as I said it with that tone, as if even I knew it was harsh. I berated myself, who cared? He was one of Them. He deserved far harsher than that, and he was lucky I was in no mood to do worse. That was the end of the story.

A flicker of emotion crossed his face, disappearing as fast as it had appeared. "You wouldn't understand."

"No, I don't. You're right," I replied hobbling down the stairs towards the door. I heard him moving fast behind me.

Pain shot through my foot as I cleared the last step, and the room spun even faster as I found myself approaching the wooden floor. I closed my eyes just as I thought I would hit it, instead I felt strong arms close around me, pulling me into a tight embrace.

"Why are you humans so stupid?" He muttered by

my shoulder.

I shivered, as the racking sobs took control of my body. I felt so pathetic, so useless sitting here in the lap of my enemy while I cried like an insolent child. I was pathetic, so weak and cold from hunger I couldn't fight myself free of his grasp. I couldn't fight for my freedom, and I couldn't fight for Katie's. I couldn't do anything, I stood by and watched as everyone that had meant anything to me died, everyone. I had this opportunity now to take revenge, and instead I allowed the devil to coddle me like a pet.

I tried to push him away, tried to muster any strength or conviction, but then I surprised myself when my body slowly leaned forward and I buried my face in his shoulder, letting the tears soak through his robe. I couldn't admit it, not aloud at least, that at this very moment, the thing I craved the most was—contact. I hadn't felt someone's arms around me since my father passed. Weeks of loneliness, several long, agonizing weeks of having no one there to talk to, to be consoled by. I needed this. I hated myself for it, every fiber of my being was disgusted at the fact that this *thing* was even in the same room as me, let alone touching me. I was disgusted that I needed to rely on him, disgusted that, in order to save my sister, I would have to let this creature play master. But most of all, I was disgusted by the fact that all he had shown me was compassion and kindness.

How could you hate something that wouldn't let you?

Without a word he lifted me in his arms and carried me back up the stairs, setting me on the bed and pulling the blankets around me. He picked around the food tray, beginning to remove pieces when I grabbed his hand, stopping him.

"Leave it," I said, not meeting his questioning gaze.

He nodded, replacing the food before leaving for the stairwell, turning around at the last moment to watch me. A strange emotion played about his face, disappearing before I could identify it. He muttered that he would be downstairs if I needed anything as he descended into the darkness.

The rain still beat against the roof, the world outside was cold and miserable. As soon as I was sure he was distracted I no longer held myself back and tore apart the bread, greedily devouring it. Without even giving myself a break, I shoveled the figs into my mouth and swallowed them down with a cup of what tasted somewhat like sweetened tea. The plate was empty within minutes, and I sat there disgusted with myself as I stared at the bowl of medicine.

I sighed, my stomach still grumbling, begging for more. Although my mind kept telling me no, my throbbing foot and aching rib begged for me to drink the concoction. Gingerly, I picked it up and brought it to my nose, sniffing carefully. It smelled sour—bitter, maybe akin to a rotting lemon.

Taking a deep breath, I swallowed it in one go, wincing at its bitterness. I hoped desperately that I did the right thing, consuming something I knew nothing about. Trusting in a monster. The taste was almost unbearable, I tried to wash it down with the little tea left over, gagging at the aftertaste in my mouth.

I didn't know how long it would take to affect me, or even what effects it would have, but he made it seem like it would relieve me of my pain, then again—I supposed that's what death did. I was sure he wouldn't have fed me poison though, after saving me and clothing and bandaging me, I doubted he'd seek my end through something as mundane as poison. He had wasted resources on me, and you don't do that for an enemy if they weren't still serving the purpose you sought them for.

There was a knock at the door, and I heard his chair slide back as his boots clicked across the wood. He seemed a sought-after individual, handling a lot of paperwork and questions. Half an hour went by and finally his guest left after a lengthy, tedious discussion regarding textiles and paint.

He made his way up the stairwell, a roll of parchment in his hands which he placed on the desk opposite me before taking a seat. He glanced at the empty tray and bowl; his eyebrows raised.

"Feeling better, then?"

I paused, I hadn't even noticed—the throbbing in my foot, the aching in my joints—had been replaced by a feeling of dullness. It was infinitely better than what I had been feeling before. I felt good enough to walk, to run, to fight. I almost laughed at myself, maybe not enough to make a run for it, but certainly enough to move about, to observe.

He must have guessed at the emotions playing across my face that I did very little to hide, because he said, "It didn't fix your injuries, it only dulls your senses. You still have a fractured foot and rib, not to mention your myriad other minor bruises and cuts."

I nodded slowly, my gaze drifting to the window. Lights from candles and sconces were being lit, letting an eerie orange glow befall the town. In some ways though, it was soothing—peaceful. This town looked more homely now than it probably did back in our time, with our halogen bulbs and smog. That was one of the things I didn't miss—the pollution and our blatant disregard for nature.

It still rained outside, but the cloud cover wasn't as dark. That allowed me to see a small convoy making its way from the east. It was an assortment of creatures riding on their unusual choice of mount—if ever there was an inspiration for a unicorn this was it. They were like horses with long luscious manes and tails flowing around them, but they also had two horns that shot up from their skull like a gazelle. Often their manes were braided and adorned with bells or brightly colored lengths of twine. At least in the beginning they were. Now they were outfitted with leather barding and pointed face masks that turned an ethereal beauty into a haunting malice. They were mounts fitted for war.

My eyes were glued to them as they paraded through the town, hauling an open wagon set with barrels and crates. There was another wagon behind that one, and as soon as my eyes registered what sat in the back clad in pale, pastel gowns, I jumped up. Pushing myself as close to the window as I could, I counted, three, five, eight—*eight* humans, huddled in the wagon. Their eyes downcast, as they were hauled to whatever destination was in store for them.

"Where are they taking them?" I breathed, almost forgetting whose presence I was in.

He appeared at the side of the bed, following my gaze. He replied nonchalantly, "To be claimed."

I frowned; it wasn't the first time I heard that phrase. I had an idea of what it meant, but I hoped I was wrong. The humans didn't look dirty or mistreated, but their fear was palpable. Like my sister's.

"What does that mean?" The wagon disappeared behind a building, the rear guards covering up the end. There was no escape for them.

"They will be put to work as needed," he said simply.

I stared up at him, noticing the twitch in his jaw. It almost seemed like he didn't agree with the practice any more than I did.

"Work doing what?"

"Physical labor, menial tasks, whatever they are deemed most suitable for."

"What about those who can't contribute like that, what do they do with them?" I felt like a lead weight had settled deep in my gut. What use would they have for someone like that?

He glanced at me from the corner of his eye, "Everyone has a use, one way or another."

It took me a moment to consider the implications of what he was trying not to say, of what that meant. He watched me carefully as I began to piece it together. The fact that Katie looked healthy, was groomed, and clothed in pristine condition, I doubted she engaged in hard labor, toiling away at a mine somewhere.

I jumped up off the bed, wincing as I felt my ankle roll. But I didn't have time to even think about it. Katie was in trouble, big trouble—and I'd be damned if I was going to sit here all comfy and safe while she served as a toy to Them.

"Where are my clothes?" I needed my boots and my jacket, and my backpack. Where were my things? I hadn't even thought about it.

"I had to dispose of them." He indicated a pile of garments stacked neatly on a trunk by the wall. "You can use these."

I whirled on him, "I don't want your kind's clothing, I want mine!"

He stood still, watching me. I tried to hold back the anger, how could he stand there and think it was fine for me to wear *Their* clothes, next he'd have me eating and talking like one of Them, too. Maybe I was his to claim now, and he thought he could do what he wanted. The rage built up in me like steam in a kettle. Oh no, I wasn't going to let that happen. I was seething, I needed to find Katie. I needed out. I needed it—now.

The sun had disappeared, the night was pitch black save for a light mist that was gathering around the streets and building, illuminated by the eerie glow of their sconces and candlelight. I could see most of the creatures had left by now, either holed up in the houses or gone somewhere outside the town. We always said that night was the safest time for us to be out, it seems we weren't too wrong about that.

I rushed to the pile of clothes and pulled a long tunic over my gown, securing it with a belt at the waist. There were no pants, only a pair of socks and slippers left, so I hurriedly pulled them on. That's when I noticed the cloak he had given me was cleaned and neatly folded on the pile, I threw it over myself without a second thought—the crest that was on it might come in handy.

He stood by the window, watching me. I didn't know what he would do, if he'd attempt to stop me or let me go. He said I wasn't a prisoner, well—now was the time to prove it. I carefully made my way down the stairwell and towards the door. I heard him before he gently grabbed my arm as my hand touched the doorknob.

"It's not safe out there," was all he said to me.

I glared up at him, "If you're going to stop me, you'll have to kill me."

Wrenching away my arm, I pulled the door open and walked out into a world of shadows. Mist whirled around my feet as the light rain clung to my clothes. I wasn't sure what I was doing or where I was going, but my best bet was to go in the direction the other humans were.

My sister could have been part of an earlier convoy and they might all be going in the same direction. The guy in Cave Junction mentioned an encampment near Lake Selmac, it was the best lead I had. Lake Selmac was north, now all I had to figure out was which direction would lead me there.

I quickly hobbled across the wet grass and down the hill towards the back lots of a row of shops. They all lined the main street that led out of town. As I turned the corner, in the distance across the bridge I noticed a row of sconces illuminating the sign for a hotel—and it was occupied. The wagons from earlier were parked out front, the weird unicorns nowhere to be seen. There was probably a farm somewhere further down the road where They stabled them. But that also meant that if the prisoners were here, so were the guards.

I went to pull my knife from my pocket when I realized I had no pockets, and no knife. He hadn't even told me where it was, as if he had disposed of it as well—or hidden it from me. I remembered then, having my knife sitting in the middle of the house when I had collapsed, it wasn't there now. But I couldn't turn back, once I got the information I needed, I could think about returning to the mill to retrieve my things. For now, it was full steam ahead. In and out.

Scurrying around the hotel, I found an alley with two doors, both labeled as an exit. The first one I tried was locked, the second opened without so much as a squeak. I quietly snuck in, closing the door behind me. It was dark and almost impossible to find my way around or to even know what was a foot in front of me. The glow from a candle ahead lit up a small corridor lined with several doors. They were all hotel rooms, numbered from ten to twenty.

The larger, nicer rooms were probably at the front of the hotel, and that was where I'd most likely find the guards. Here in the back, the tinier, less desirable rooms were surely where the prisoners were kept. I tried all the doors to my left first, they were all locked, I frantically tried the other side with no luck.

Running my hand through my hair, I decided to turn down the next corridor when someone rounded it. Jet black hair tied back in an intricate bun, shoulders slumped, and eyes as dark as the night itself, the young girl stared at me—mouth agape.

"You're unclaimed," she said, looking me over. Her arms were burdened by a basket of towels and what looked to be dressing gowns.

"I don't have much time; I need to know where the others are," I whispered, glancing up and down the corridors.

She blinked at me, before glancing nervously behind her, "You shouldn't be here, you need to run."

I grabbed her arm, "I have to know, please."

She averted her gaze, "They're in the conference room."

"Thank you," I let her go before whispering, "Where are the guards?"

"The conference room," she muttered, so low I almost didn't hear her.

That posed a problem, but maybe I could avoid that altogether. "Where do they take the prisoners from here?"

She adjusted the basket against her hip, moving past me to glance down the corridor, "I don't know, okay? Please, you must leave. If they catch me talking to you… it'll be bad for us both. Just do yourself a favor and get far away from here."

Without waiting for a response, she hurried down the corridor, disappearing into the darkness at the end. I cringed imagining what her role here was, to imagine what Katie might have to do or if she was going through the exact same thing right now. I waited a moment longer before following her, my eyes scanning the walls for a map of the hotel. I had no idea where the conference room would be, I didn't even really know where I was.

The corridor she had taken ended in a small room with a stairwell, ice machine, and vending machine. Both were empty and unused, but surprisingly not unkempt from disuse. Pushing the door open slightly, I peeked inside; the stairwell went up to the second level. But what I was most interested in stood just inside, a map against the wall.

According to the map, the door I had tried earlier

that was locked outside opened into the foyer where the conference room came from, I was stuck in section B and the main half of the hotel was in section A. The stairwell led to the second floor which had a walkway that led to the next section. Good, I didn't want to risk going outside and being caught trying every door to get in.

Closing the door quietly, I made my way up the stairwell to the landing, gently opening it to stare into the corridor. All was quiet and calm. The girl was long gone, I had no way of knowing if she had gone to a nearby room or taken the walkway to the next section.

The walkway was open on both sides. Arches decorated with vines outlined it and were lit by sconces in the shape of conch shells flickering candles sat within. A misty breeze flew through, and I instinctively shivered. I hadn't planned this well, I didn't even know what I was going to do when I found the other humans. All I knew was that I needed to find out where Katie had been taken.

So far, so good. The glass doors at the other end of the walkway were unlocked and emptied into two corridors. One went left, the other went right and ended in a staircase. There was noise drifting up from below— the conference room. Pushing up against the wall I tiptoed down the hallway to glimpse down the stairwell. At the bottom, a door was left ajar, light twinkling from within. No one seemed to be outside guarding it as I shimmied down the stairs, pausing at the doorway to peek inside.

"I told you to run, what are you doing?" hissed a feminine voice from behind me.

I hadn't even noticed there was another corridor under the stairs. That could have ended so badly for me, my heart lurched thinking about what could have happened. But it wasn't one of Them, it was the girl from before. Her eyes were wide as she grabbed my arm and tugged me back from the doorway, dragging me toward the corridor she had come from.

"Are you stupid?" she asked, pulling me further down the corridor. There were only three doors down this corridor and the first was labeled 'Staff Only.' She stopped me right before the third door, straining to listen to whatever it was she was looking out for.

"We only have a few moments before the guard changes, please," she looked me over, from head to toe, fear in her eyes, "just run."

"I have to know where They're taking them, I have to." She showed no reaction, "Please, my sister…"

Her eyes widened, I had struck some chord, her lip trembled before she whispered, "They took my sister, too. Listen, I don't know where they take these prisoners or even if your sister was taken to the same place. But there's a place about two hours north just off the Redwood Highway. There's this ranch up by Lake Selmac. They took me there, too. From there all the humans are sorted for…what they're considered most suited for."

She didn't want to say it out loud, and she didn't have to. I now had more information than I could have ever hoped for. If they were all brought through the town as a checkpoint before reaching that ranch, then there was a good chance that Katie's group was on their way there. They were headed in that direction.

North.

"Thank you," I said, grasping her hands. I glanced down the corridor, the noises from the conference room were still but a drone in the background, not a soul had entered or left. If I were going to make my escape it had to be now.

"There's a side door around the corner that takes you to the parking lot, you should be able to get to the trees before anyone sees you." She mustered a solemn smile for me before I released her hands, and she swiftly made her way down the corridor towards the conference room.

This was good. Much better news than I could ever have hoped for. I tried to quell my excitement, knowing was the easy part—now I needed to figure out how to get there. Although, it couldn't be too hard to find a ranch off the 199 on Lake Selmac, could it? Especially one crawling with monsters. That was two humans now who confirmed there was definitely something suspicious going on at that lake.

Running my hand through my hair, I turned down the corridor and collided with something solid, sending me to the ground. I looked up sheepishly, ready to berate myself for being stupid enough to walk into a wall. Standing in the hallway, between me and the exit, was one of *Them*. He had long black hair that cascaded across his shoulders, giving him an air of authority set against a chiseled jaw and sharp emerald eyes. He was dressed in the riding leathers that their kind enjoyed, a band of knives and a sword sat around his waist. He regarded me a moment before it suddenly clicked, he knew I wasn't supposed to be here.

"You're—" I didn't give him time to finish, jumping up I rammed into him as hard as I could, sending us both to the ground. I didn't pause as I staggered to my feet and made a beeline for the door, yanking it open and bursting out into the night.

He was only a moment behind me, and I mentally screamed for my legs to go faster—carry me farther. But the tree line, just within my grasp, suddenly disappeared as he appeared in front of me. Grabbing hold of my wrist, he pulled me into restraint against him and, try as hard as I might, his grip was absolute. I was caught.

"Stop struggling," he growled, pulling his arm up against my throat.

I certainly didn't listen. If anything, it made me struggle harder. I lashed out with my legs, kicking his shin, but he didn't flinch as he used his free hand to pin my left arm behind my back.

I panicked against his grip, it was getting harder and harder to breath, when a voice called from the mists, "You're not damaging my merchandise are you, Raekhan?"

I felt the creature named Raekhan's grip lessen, before he growled, "Aer Vaelythor, you keep company of such filth, now?" He pushed me to the ground, my knees scraping on the asphalt. My ivory-haired savior emerged from the mists, golden eyes glowing, his turquoise gown brushing the asphalt gracefully as mist swirled around him. It pained me to admit how utterly godlike he looked.

"I sent her for supplies, seems she didn't make it that far." He didn't once glance my way as he casually closed the distance, standing before the one named Raekhan. In the fractured light of a nearby sconce they looked complete opposites of one another, a god of light—and a dark god of death. Opposites and yet, one and the same.

"Perhaps you should mark her then, Aer Vaelythor—it was an easy mistake to assume she was unclaimed and," his lips pulled back to reveal his sharp glinting canines, "*for the taking.*"

"Are you trying tell me what to do, Raekhan?" His golden eyes glowed with such a fire it looked as if the flames of a blistering sun burned within.

Raekhan glared at him, defiant, yet something in his stance told me what his words didn't. He was afraid of my captor—my savior. There was something to fear about him, and even this mighty warrior seemed to know better. I wasn't so sure now whether I wanted to truly know who, or what, he was.

The darkness feared the light.

"Of course not, Aer Vaelythor." His fury barely contained as he took a step back, adjusting the belt of knives.

"You may take your leave," the white-haired creature said.

Raekhan stood there a moment, before his eyes slid to me and he growled. I couldn't help the flinch, so instinctive—and satisfying to him. He smirked before tossing his hair over his shoulder and disappearing back into the building.

I sat on the ground, shivering in the dampness. Waiting. I didn't know what to do, should I run for it? If I did, would my captor send Raekhan after me?

"Of all the Aerendor to run into, why did you have to cross paths with the Master of the Hunt?" he asked, exasperated.

With my eyes glued to the asphalt I muttered, "What's an Aerendor?"

He paused before answering, no doubt waiting for me to look at him. But eventually he answered, "that's what my kind call us."

The name seemed so fitting. Exotic and yet dangerous. Maybe a part of me had heard the name before, on the news long, long ago when this all began, but I didn't remember. That was my problem, I relied so much on the internet for everything I hadn't bother trying to remember anything myself. I guess that's why I didn't do so well in college.

"Thank you," I whispered.

He deserved it. He had saved me yet again, and all I had done so far was curse him and make things difficult. For whatever reason he had, he'd shown only kindness to me. And it was all because he was one of Them—an *Aerendor*, that I judged him like I judged them all. But it did nothing to convince me that his kind weren't to be exterminated, my family—my friends, everyone was still dead. And it was still *Their* fault.

His footsteps echoed on the asphalt, his turquoise gown flowing into view where I stubbornly stared at my feet. He knelt before me, extending his hand. Somehow, I didn't find so much revulsion this time when I grasped it and let him pull me from the ground.

"Who is he?" I asked, wiping the dirt and asphalt from my knees. Light pink skin glistened in the sconce light, the night air's kiss stinging.

"He's the Master of the Hunt, Raekhan. He commands the hunters in this region for collecting."

"Humans, you mean," I finished for him. Raekhan hunted humans, to force them into servitude for the Aerendor.

He pulled the hood of the cloak over my head, dusting the dirt from it. He swept his hand outwards, towards the mill, ushering me to start walking. I begrudgingly put one foot in front of the other.

Guards stationed at the front of the hotel that weren't there before glanced at us, and immediately averted their gaze when they noticed my companion. An Aerendor with his face obscured by a cowl stepped off the path to let us through, his eyes downcast. Everyone we encountered seemed to give us a wide berth. Whoever my savior was, maybe I should take his kin's heed. I should be more cautious in getting on his bad side.

Just as we got to the mill door, he turned to me, looking me up and down, "Was it worth it?"

I was still wrapped up in my own little world, trying to decipher what their reactions could possibly mean and simply mumbled a, "Huh?"

"Did you find that which you seek?"

I deliberated telling him, telling him what I was looking for. But at the end of the day, he was still one of Them, an Aerendor. I couldn't let him use Katie against me, and I certainly couldn't risk putting her further in harm's way. His kind still held control over mine, and no matter what he had done for me I wouldn't let him get in the way of my rescuing Katie. No one would.

"I found a clue," was all I mumbled, moving past him into the mill and up to the loft.

He stayed downstairs, occasionally I'd hear a paper rustle or a book close—his chair sliding back and forth. A pale slip dress was folded neatly on the trunk, and I briskly changed, slipping into the bed. But he didn't come back upstairs, and I fell asleep devising my next plan for escape.

My next plan would get me closer to rescuing my sister.

CHAPTER
Six

The morning came and went, the sun sat bright and high above, threatened by a dark looming smear on the horizon. Rays of light twinkled through the window above me, warming my face. I was reluctant to pull myself from my reverie, resentfully content in the comfort of the bed.

Sighing and stretching, I sat up—staring out through the window. The town was alive below, Aerendor came and went about their busy lives, not a human to be seen. Convoys of wagons and carriages carrying supplies filtered slowly in and out, choking the roads. It would be hard to sneak through all that to make my way north; again I would have to rely on the cover of night to execute my escape.

The door clicked and swung open, heavy boots moved with purpose across the floorboards. They stopped by the desk, hoisting something heavy on top of it. I heard the sound of papers rustling and a mumbled word before the boots approached the stairwell.

A dangerous thought occurred to me—what if it wasn't the white-haired creature I was so familiar with on that stairwell right then, what if it was a different one of Them? I froze. He had warned me the others weren't so kind, and I wasn't prepared to figure out what that meant. I had more than enough experience from my debacle last night with the Master of the Hunt. I jumped up out of the bed, wincing as pain shot through my foot and my ribs, sending me to the ground with a thud.

"Aer Valythor?" Called the mystery voice from below. A pause before footsteps made their way up the stairs.

I cursed myself for my stupidity, there was nowhere to hide up here. The room was smaller than below, loosely decorated with a bed, desk, side table, and a trunk that was far too small to climb into. I was stuck. No weapons, no way out. It was obvious that "Aer Valythor" wasn't here, it was up to me, and I was lightly clad in a thin, white slip gown.

There was only one option, I hurried towards the stairwell, my back up against a wall that slightly jutted outwards. It'd be enough to hide me so long as whoever was here didn't step onto the landing. The boots stomped up the stairwell with a fervor, pausing on the last step.

Don't come up. Don't come up. *Don't come up.*

My mentally screaming at him did very little to influence his choices though as he cleared the landing and turned to look at me with those same bright, golden eyes. He was tall and muscular like the others, with short, thick russet brown hair…I immediately froze, and he realized it as soon as I did. We knew each other, because he was the same Aerendor that had attacked me in the clearing. He wore their standard riding leathers with a forest green tunic tied at the waist by a bandolier burdened by pouches and a short blade hidden in its sheath.

"You," he said simply, his eyes narrowing, "I knew you were still here. I guess Raekhan wasn't lying."

I stood there like a deer in headlights, unsure what to say or do. Unlike before, though, he didn't seem ready to fight me. I found room to breathe with the idea that since he mentioned the Master of the Hunt then he possibly knew what my captor would do if he hurt me. I stared him down, the russet hair and unyielding eyes, then I remembered his voice—his voice was familiar. So were the heavy boots. I was certain this was the guy who was here before, who was talking downstairs—Yaern. Now I had a name to go with his face, not sure what use it did me right now, but later it could prove useful. Their names could come in handy when I finally found my sister.

"Curious, why hasn't he claimed you?" he asked, cocking his head sideways. His eyes roved over me, like he was looking for something. It wasn't in any way menacing, but I had to admit it was quite unsettling to be examined like some animal at the zoo. I took a step to the side, trying to increase the distance between us. He smirked as he raised his hands, attempting to reassure me of his intentions—or lack thereof.

"You can relax, human. Unlike before, I am not here for you." He took a step back, lowering his hands. "I know you can understand me, I'm sure he's spelled you for that."

"What do you want?" It was easier now to have a bite in my voice, when fear and adrenaline wasn't clouding my senses.

"I'm simply here for Vaelythor." He looked around, as if he could have possibly missed him in that too small of a room.

So, his name was Vaelythor. He claimed it was a title, but why wouldn't he admit that it was his name? His name must carry a lot of weight; I couldn't underestimate his significance.

Yaern sighed, "Have you seen him?"

I paused; did I admit to him that I hadn't seen him? Or would that end badly for me? Vaelythor and this one—they seemed quite close. He had visited the mill several times since I'd been here. Which meant Vaelythor probably knew he'd come by, and he might be on his way right now.

"No," I said quickly, my eyes instinctively going to the blade at his belt.

Weapons always unnerved me—guns on police, tasers on guards, even a child wielding a slingshot sent me into a moment of panic. Even now, knowing how my survival depended on using a weapon—I abhorred it.

He noticed my gaze, "my name is Yaern, what is yours?"

I hadn't told anyone my name yet, not even the creature who repeatedly saved my life. But to be fair, he hadn't told me his either. Yaern seemed to be the only one going out of his way to give me information.

It could be useful for later if I played along now. I was hesitant to release something so valuable to me, the only valuable thing I had left, and I deliberated giving him a fake name.

But really, what did I stand to lose?

"Wren." My name sounded so foreign on my tongue, my lips struggling to pronounce it as if I hadn't heard it before. It had been a long time since I had voiced it; even longer since I heard it on anyone else's lips.

"Like the bird," he said smiling. "It's a pretty name."

Averting my gaze, I hugged my arms around my chest and mumbled a thanks. Yaern looked around the room again, for what—I didn't know. Did he honestly think his companion would be hiding from him? And yet, he still seemed disappointed.

"I don't suppose you were given any documentation?" He didn't give me time to respond as he continued, "ah, I suppose not. That wouldn't make much sense, he wouldn't risk an Unclaimed with such sensitive information."

Yaern walked towards the window, pulling back the curtains to stare out over the town. What was he doing? Was he going to wait here for his companion? Wait here, with me—alone. I cringed at the thought, I already loathed the idea of being stuck in the company of his kind.

I knew it would be best not to show any weakness in front of Them. Taking a silent breath, I walked towards him to stare out the window, just as the clouds that hung low on the horizon closed in—smothering the sun. He glanced down at me, his gaze following mine to a convoy that had just arrived, loaded heavily with an assortment of barrels and crates. It was always barrels and crates. I inched closer to stare out, my eyes searching the faces of everyone that milled about, I highly doubted Katie would be among them, but it didn't stop me from trying.

"You're looking for someone, aren't you?" I glanced up at him, his golden eyes seemed to see right through me. He was much more intuitive than I gave him credit for.

I'd have to be careful with this one.

I kept my mouth shut, my eyes on the convoy. I couldn't give anything away, if I did…it would make finding my sister even harder. What if they tried to stop me? What if they figured out who I was searching for and did something to her in response? No, I couldn't risk it.

"Well, little bird, perhaps you could entertain me with a story?"

I turned from the window, "a story?" I could feel the goosebumps rising on my arms, a chill down my spine—a warning. I would have to be careful what I revealed, it was obvious he was fishing for information. Two could play at that game.

"Indeed," he replied, his eyes sparkling.

"What story would you like to hear?" I asked sarcastically, he knew that I knew what information he was after.

"I'm particularly interested in how you two met." He was clearly still upset about that day in the clearing, being denied his kill. I stared him down, the silence between us was deafening. Once he figured out I wasn't going to answer he seemed to change tactics, instead of playing coy he straight out asked me what he wanted to know.

"Where did Vaelythor find you? You weren't on any of the convoys. I'd remember a face like that," the way he said that last bit left a chill in my very blood, but he quickly moved on, "and you certainly weren't part of any shipment he ordered." Yaern turned to me, his golden eyes boring into me, "which means, you were the feral one—weren't you? The one Raekhan has been searching for."

He reached forward to lightly grasp a lock of my hair, letting the strands fall like golden thread. He cupped my chin, tilting my face, "So pathetic a creature, and yet somehow you managed to escape Raekhan and fall into the favor of an Aer."

"It seems you are quite popular with my charges," Vaelythor said from the landing, his tone tight.

His hair was half up, braided around a simple golden circlet, letting a few strands fall about his face. His deep golden eyes seemed unamused where they lay upon us, his hands held together in the folds of his maroon robe, a rich ebony shawl of intricate golden embroidery set upon his shoulders. He looked every bit the noble. Unlike any of the others. It was as if he were royalty, and everyone else were commoners.

Yaern immediately took a step back, bowing his head with his arms slack at his side. His eyes on his boots, he spoke in a hushed and hurried tone, "I was waiting for your arrival, Aer Vaelythor. Wren and I were simply getting to know one another better, isn't that right?" A sideways glance, an innocent gesture—but I was all too aware of how threatening it was meant to be.

Vaelythor walked towards us, pausing to look me over. His gaze seemed concerned, as if he was worried Yaern had done something. I stared him down, frowning when he turned his gaze to Yaern.

"I see you acquired my shipment." he said simply, extending his hand.

Yaern pulled a small roll of parchment tucked into a pouch at his belt, handing it to Vaelythor. He unfurled it, glancing over the weird shifting symbols that lit the page. Whatever was on it seemed to appease him, and he smiled at his companion.

"It seems everything is in order. You have done well, Yaern," Vaelythor exclaimed, patting Yaern on the shoulder.

Yaern smiled, before turning his gaze on me, his eyes darkening, "Aer Vaelythor, permission to speak candidly?"

Vaelythor's eyes narrowed, as if he knew where this was headed, he replied curtly, "Speak."

"You have to claim her or Raekhan has the authority to—" Vaelythor held his hand up, instantly silencing whatever he was going to say.

"Raekhan's authority does not outmatch mine, no matter what his idiotic father seems to think. He should stick to what he does best."

I froze, hunting humans—that's what he did best. But that voice in the back of my mind whispered *and yet you managed to escape.* I almost audibly scoffed, he certainly couldn't be the greatest hunter, let alone the Master of it.

Vaelythor seemed to think the same. "A useless title for a spoiled brat," he scoffed.

Yaern smirked, holding back a smile before clearing his throat. "Shall I take my leave?" Vaelythor nodded his head, and Yaern left without a glance back. The door downstairs opened and closed, leaving us alone standing around the loft, staring one another down.

"You told him your name?" Vaelythor asked.

I watched as the golden specs in his eyes swirled, like a whirlpool sucking life into the darkened depths, "What concern is it of yours?" I nearly berated myself for sounding so harsh, one might consider this another instance of him saving me. But I was still apprehensive of my situation, of the Aerendor—of his motives. I was still waiting for the moment when I would be shackled and forced into their human network of slaves.

He regarded me coldly, "I suppose none."

"You'd suppose correctly then," I walked past him to stare out the window, watching as the town went about its business. Yaern was in the distance talking to a group of what looked to be guards, weapons were glinting from their backs, belts, and bandoliers.

I don't know where it came from, but a waft of freshly-cooked goods assaulted my senses, drawing my attention to the nightstand. Vaelythor had somehow arranged a small box filled with an assortment of sealed glass containers on the table when my back was turned. Completely forgetting my annoyance, I left the window to glance down at the marinated meats and steamed vegetables, and what looked like rice.

"Why?" I asked, barely loud enough for myself to hear, my hand pausing just above the box.

There were four different containers: one of pork, chicken, beef, and fish. Each one was accompanied by an assortment of vegetables: boiled baby potatoes, sautéed carrots, grilled mushrooms, and steamed broccoli. I hadn't had this fine and varied of a meal in…a very long time. I felt my eyes begin to water, the memories I had tried to quell for so long threatening to come to the surface. The last time I had anything like this, it was my mother's birthday just before the world went to hell. Just before they opened the rift.

We had gone out to her favorite Italian restaurant for pasta—she had her signature chicken marsala and I had lasagna. I felt a tear slide down my cheek as the image of her sitting at the table, her face alive and smiling, she wore the new rose embroidered dress Dad had bought for her that morning, her golden hair pinned back with a butterfly clip.

"Do you not like it?" I had almost forgotten he was there, so wrapped up in memories of a life long gone. Of people, long gone.

It was odd that his first concern was that I didn't like the food. He didn't consider anything else, like that I hadn't eaten a meal like this in a long time, or that memories of when I did would sit like a stone in my gut. But then again, why would he? He was the invader; all he knew was that he was the conqueror and we were the conquered.

I took a deep breath, "it's fine, it's just—" I shook my head, he wouldn't understand, and I loathed to be the person to explain it to him. I took a seat on the edge of the bed, my eyes roving over the food with such lust I knew he could read the expression on my face easily.

He sat down at the desk across from me, looking over the containers I'd opened, "Which do you prefer?"

I frowned, staring up into those golden orbs of his. Clearing my throat, I looked back down at the food, everything was undeniably perfect. But if I had to choose one thing I did not particularly hunger for, it was the fish. It wasn't that I didn't enjoy fish. It was more that crustaceans and river dwellers had been ninety percent of my diet for more than a year. I was kind of sick of fish and it was hard for me to acknowledge that I suddenly had the choice to be picky. What little livestock was still around was hoarded by people who were more likely to shoot than share. I set the fish aside from the other glass containers.

I shrugged when he gave me a look, "I'm bored of fish."

He stood up, taking the container of fish back to the desk. I watched as he placed it down, folding his robes around himself.

"Are you going to eat with me?" I was mentally punching myself for the suggestion. What was wrong with me, why would I even ask such a thing?

"Only if you will indulge me in conversation," he said, his eyes twinkling.

I tried to hold myself back, but as soon as that first strip of beef hit my tongue, I couldn't control myself. I greedily devoured it all before he had even eaten half of the fish. I forced myself to be slower with the chicken, eating the steamed broccoli first, one piece at a time. It was pure torture. As if this was somehow part of his devious plan, to win me over with food before forcing me to work. What helped alleviate my suspicions was the obvious confusion he had with eating the fish. I wouldn't quite say he enjoyed it, he almost seemed—confused. To what it was or how to eat it, I wasn't sure, but his torture did bring me joy.

His kind—the Aerendor, had only been here just over a year. I didn't know if he came with the initial assault or was part of the greeting team. Or if he'd only been here a week. Part of me was scared to ask, but I needed as much information as I could get.

"How long have you been here?" I forced the words to tumble out.

"Where?" He played with the piece of fish at the end of his fork.

"Earth."

He paused mid-bite, "Two months."

Two months. This town must have been assimilated and convoys established within that time. Indeed, it seemed like he was quite good at what he did, but he didn't seem very knowledgeable about humanity. Maybe the others weren't either. That might make my job so much easier.

"My turn?" he asked.

I nodded.

He sat there watching me, his head cocked sideways as he crooned, "What is your name?"

With my fork poised to attack a piece of chicken, I paused to look at him, confused. "You already know my name."

"I suppose so. But I want to hear you say it."

What game was he getting at? He wanted to hear me say my own name. What could he possibly gain from that? He did seem a bit touchy when Yaern mentioned it earlier, he even commented how I had given him my name. But whatever, I'd indulge him.

"My name is Wren."

I'd usually get sly looks and muffled smirks from people when I told them my name. My entire family had normal names: Katherine, Elizabeth, James—and then there was me: Wren. A little songbird. Robin was a common name, there were two in my middle school growing up. But there was never another Wren.

I expected a sly comment. "It's a beautiful name, *Wren*."

I felt oddly shy, my cheeks heating, I had to quickly change the conversation, "And yours?"

He raised his eyebrows, "Have you not guessed it by now?"

It was my turn to play the game, "Ah, but I want to hear you say it."

He chuckled, an actual laugh—the first genuine one I'd heard from him. "Vaelythor."

"Vaelythor," I said. Testing the name on my lips for the first time, I had to be sure I said it correctly. "Can I ask another question?"

He nodded. I almost felt hesitant to say anything that might dampen his mood. But I needed answers.

"What does it mean, to claim a human? Is it... painful?"

I had no idea what it entailed, but it obviously involved something that let the other Aerendor know the human belonged to one of them. Maybe it was like branding, a burn mark across your skin for all to see. But Katie, the other humans, that girl from the hotel—they had nothing I could see that marked them.

He placed the empty container on the tray, placing his fork beside it. I could see some emotion so fleeting across his face, but I knew it was there. It was as if he fought with the idea of what to tell me. He stood up from the chair and walked to the window, pulling the curtains away to let the little light trickle down from behind the clouds, filtering into the room.

"I suppose you would compare it to branding, what your kind do with livestock." He must have seen the look of horror on my face because he quickly clarified, "it's hardly traumatic. We place a sliver of energy upon your forehead, its shaped into the crest of the House you serve, announcing to everyone that the human is under that Aerendor's…protection." He seemed to choose that last word ever so carefully.

I hadn't noticed any such thing on the other humans, on the girl in the hotel—or my sister. Maybe it was only visible to the Aerendor, or those who had been claimed; the girl in the hotel seemed to notice my lack of branding quite quickly. Would I need to be branded to find out? My stomach churned at the thought of it. Was it worth the risk for knowledge to forever be marked as their property? My stomach churned, we truly were slaves, no better than cattle to them. I couldn't help the disgust that no doubt was splashed across my face plain as day.

"Will you claim me, then?" I rasped, my voice hoarse and filled with venom. I wouldn't let that happen, I *refused*. He could bribe me as much as he wanted, but there was nothing I wanted that was worth more than my freedom—than my sister's freedom.

He rolled his eyes, "I do not dabble in the ownership of inferior creatures."

I stood up from the bed, seeing red, "*Inferior* creatures!" I seethed.

"Is it not the truth?" he shrugged.

He showed no emotion as I stood up, trying to tower over him to show my rage, but my body ached, and pain shot through my foot as I nearly lost my footing. He tried to reach out to steady me, but I pushed him back.

"I told you not to touch me!" I couldn't believe I had been so stupid as to think that he was any different to the others. *Inferior creature*, I nearly scoffed. He didn't treat me like the other Aerendor did because he didn't find me useful like they did, I was simply another creature occupying the same space as him. What he hoped to gain from it I still didn't know. But I also didn't care.

I needed out. Now.

I disregarded his warnings as I threw his cloak over my slip, shoving my feet into a pair of slippers before descending the staircase. He was right on my heels, quietly following me. My hand on the knob before he finally spoke.

"It's not safe, Wren." He tried to warn me as I stood there in the withering candlelight.

I whirled on him, "You don't have my permission to use my name like you know me! Whatever game you're playing, whatever experiment you're doing—I won't be a part of it. I'm done entertaining you!"

He stood there, eyebrows raised, as I yanked the door open and marched out. Not used to inferior creatures, aye, well get used to this! I wouldn't bow like a dog, and I certainly wouldn't let him claim me. If he or his kind wanted me, they could have a corpse.

A few Aerendor glanced up as I stomped away from the mill. Vaelythor stood in the doorway watching me leave. Again, I hadn't planned a single thing, something I apparently excelled at. But there was no going back as I made my way towards the tree line, following a side road as it curved around the bend of a hill. I wasn't even sure if I was going the right direction, all I knew was that I wanted to get away—far away.

The world moved around me, business as usual in the forest, birds chirping and creatures scurrying about. I didn't know how long had passed before I realized I was ill prepared, the pain in my foot was rapidly climaxing as every heaving breath felt like a thousand tiny needles stabbing me in my ribs. I didn't have any food, water, or a weapon. I couldn't help second guessing my actions—I was unbelievably careless—*stupid*. A stupid, inferior creature. I collapsed to the ground, my knees sinking into the soft dirt, and screamed.

I vented my rage in the forest surrounding me, my voice deafening the snapping of the branches as I tore at everything within arm's reach. Every memory that had rippled from the dark recesses of my mind burst forth like water through a broken dam. My mother, my father, my sister, my best friend, my neighbors, my dog. Every single reason I had to keep breathing, to keep living. I let it out, all of it—not caring who heard or who saw.

When there was no more, when I had screamed for so long and so loud that my voice was rasping, I let the wracking sobs take over and I bent over in the dirt. The tears flowed so fast and hard, I could barely catch my breath.

I wasn't aware of the passage of time until the sun began its descent into darkness, as the shadows gathered at the edges of the trees. The world was quiet, the day beginning to still. I looked up to watch the sun cast its last rays over the treetops. North. I picked myself up from the forest floor and moved through the forest, the crimson-gold rays at my shoulder as I ventured north.

Towards Katie.

CHAPTER
Seven

The night was long and dark, but thankfully uneventful. I sought respite in a hollowed log sometime after the moon had reached its zenith in the night sky, before the clouds came in again. I was sore and muddy, only realizing after I had made considerable distance between myself and the Aerendor-occupied town that I truly had no real idea what I was doing. Or even where I was. I was more in danger now than I had been before, with the purple and orange hues just twinkling on the horizon, daybreak was around the corner—and with it the unknown.

Gingerly I crawled out from my hideaway, wind gently kissing my exposed flesh, I pulled my cloak tighter around me. My eyes went skyward, marveling as the sun's rays caressed the leaves, it left a hollow feeling that I couldn't quite place. Nature didn't care for our squabbles, it carried on, content to follow the path it had since the beginning of time. Was there one for me, too? Or was I destined for nothing, to wander the world aimlessly until I, too, died?

Like the rest of humanity.

A twig snapped nearby, and I quickly dropped to the floor, surveying my surroundings. Only now was I berating myself for being so careless, I didn't bother to make sure I was alone—or that I wasn't followed. Several agonizing minutes passed, but the birds continued to chirp, and the squirrels never ceased their endless squabbling. Whatever passed through the forest, it did not concern them.

I allowed myself to relax, the sun was only just above the trees now, light streaking through the forest allowed me to continue my journey northward. The terrain barely changed, moss covered redwoods reached towards the sky, their roots caressed by ferns. Here and there I crossed hiking paths—their trails barely visible where the earth had begun to retake them. A small panic began to build in me, my anxiety bubbling to the surface as I glanced nervously around me; what if I was lost? I assumed I was somewhere north of Cave Junction, but what if I was wrong? What if my journey north brought me out to the middle of nowhere—way beyond Lake Selmac? I knew these trails, I knew these woods, and yet everything looked the same. My heart began racing.

That was, until I heard the river moments later.

Words could not convey the sense of relief that washed over me when I heard the gentle gurgling of the Reeves Creek. Up ahead the trees thinned, revealing a grey pebbled shore gently caressed by barely moving waters, their depths so clear and pristine the reflection of the forest looked as if it were painted upon it.

At the cusp of the riverbank, I stood letting the water just barely touch my slippers, letting the sounds of nature soothe me. It was good that I hadn't crossed the river yet, that meant I knew exactly where I was. If I took the hiking trails and stayed within the forest it was just less than a three hour walk to Lake Selmac—if I were able to keep a steady pace. My foot ached horribly, and I was suspicious of how swollen it felt. My rib was tolerable, a pain easily ignored and overshadowed by the throbbing in my foot.

What else could I do though, but keep going? I trudged through the shallowest parts of the river and continued my somewhat tranquil walk through the forest. The world moved slowly around me as I found myself beginning to limp. My guardian angel must have felt pity for me because I found a trail early into my walk, mercifully allowing me to avoid trampling through the thick underbrush. It only made it slightly easier for me, but now I had too much time to think— without having to worry about where I placed my feet, I found my mind wandering.

Wandering to how I had gotten here, how time after time I kept finding my life in the hands of that *monster*. Every. Single. Time. My friends and family weren't spared their wrath, but for some reason this creature thought to spare me the sweet release of death. To what end? Was it really some sort of experiment? Or was it all a show so that his Master of the Hunt could hunt me down like some rabid dog? Or was there actually a chance that maybe, just *maybe,* he wasn't like the others.

The trail broke off ahead, a small glen on the side of the path revealed a picnic table and a small campfire ring. It hadn't been used in a very long time; knee-high weeds threatened to smother everything. At one time a family used to sit here with their basket after a relaxing hike, telling stories and eating sandwiches together. At one time, that was my family. Not necessarily this little alcove, but we used to hike together around the trails outside Cave Junction. But not just here, everywhere. Southern Oregon was my family's playground, and we knew these roads and trails better than we knew ourselves. We loved it here.

My sister was always distracted by the way the light danced among the ferns. My mother would stop every couple of minutes to take a photograph. My father, though, he and the dog were inseparable—they belonged in this forest, owned it. Every Saturday we would walk these trails, without fail, rain or shine.

All the way up until the military gave the order to stay in our homes, my sister was far away then—it was only my mother, father, me, and the family dog. We waited in our house, just like our neighbors, waiting for the evacuation. It never came. As the world went dark and silent, our entire network of satellites and devices ceased to be anything but chunks of processed metal in a matter of moments. The saddest thing? We knew it was going to happen.

They promised they were going to share their technology, make us stronger—better as a species, and I suppose they did. In a way. They weeded out the worst of humanity: no more conglomerates forcing a monopoly on precious resources, no more corrupt politicians loading their pockets from the suffering of those less fortunate. But we also lost the best of humanity, those advocates who fought tooth and nail for the freedoms of others who were unable to fight. The truly good who only sought the improvement of the world and the betterment of their fellow man.

I knew that was partly why I still fought to survive. For my loved ones who no longer had that choice, who sacrificed themselves so that I could survive. But guilt was a strong muse, I didn't play much of a part in protecting this world. I didn't bring my own bags to the grocery store, I used plastic straws, and half the time I passed by a homeless person without even acknowledging their existence. In the grand scheme of things, I could have done so much more, just one small difference can make an impact—that's why I partly hid stash piles around Cave Junction. It wasn't so much for me, I liked to pretend it was so that I always had 'options,' but I easily could have stocked the Den from floor to ceiling. I kept them in town, precisely so others would have something if they were desperate—like that man I had met. The one who had warned me about Lake Selmac.

That was when I heard it on the horizon, *pop, pop, pop.* Like the sounds of popcorn kernels in the microwave. To an innocent, privileged girl growing up in the safety of the suburbs those noises would be most peculiar, and up until a year ago I would have never been able to place it. But there was no doubting what that noise belonged to; it was the distinctive sound of gunfire.

Somewhere up ahead was a skirmish—I had no way of knowing if it was between humans and other humans, or humans and *Them*. I also knew I had no choice; I would have to try and skirt around them and hope I went unnoticed, They could have infiltrated the entire forest by now—I wasn't safe until I could get somewhere I could see all of my surroundings. Where every rock, tree, and bush that slightly moved in the breeze didn't have me scurrying for safety.

As I neared the edge of the forest the gunfire became louder, an explosion of pops in rapid succession followed by the unmistakable wailing of terrified human beings. I heard them crashing through the underbrush, tree limbs snapping and rocks flying as heavy, clumsy feet carried them through their panic further into the forest. In the distance I saw them, hooded and masked, clad in tattered plain clothing running for their lives, some with weapons, some without. None of them bothered to look in my direction.

I tried to quiet the unease settling in my stomach, the heavy weight that pulled down every step I took. The gunshots grew further apart, now every shot sounded as if it rang within my skull, rattling my very bones. I shivered, pulling the cloak closer over me, as if the flimsy cloth could protect me from an automatic rifle. But I couldn't allow myself to worry about that, I had to get through the forest, I had to get into the suburbs on the other side so I could see for myself what was really happening at Lake Selmac.

The forest thinned ever so slightly, the ground declining beneath my feet, I took a few more steps forwards—and I burst forth onto a bitumen road. Yawning before me was a walled compound filled with rectangular buildings. It was a trailer park. I froze, listening. The world was eerily quiet, the air still, as if it waited with bated breath for what was going to come next.

"What are you doing?" cried a voice next to me, and I turned to stare into the dull, blue eyes of a teenage girl. She was a little shorter than me, skinny—her black hair an oily mess that hung from her head like seaweed at the pier. She grabbed my arm, dragging me towards the trailer park, "Run!"

I didn't stop to consider that I had never seen this trailer park before, I had never seen this road either, or the flowers planted out front, the decrepit wooden sign welcoming you. I also didn't think as I followed her, weaving through the park, stopping and starting after she was sure of her next move. We paused behind a blue painted trailer home with barrels out the front, a *Do Not Disturb* sign hung limply from the porch. The girl glanced left, right, even up into the sky before resting those tearful eyes on me.

"What's going on?" I asked, my eyes drawn to a crow in the tree above me, his stare was haunting as he watched us expectantly.

"What do you mean, what's going on?" she said, exasperated, "They're here! Why were you just standing in the road! Why weren't you running?" She spoke so fast, her voice high and anxious as she kept darting between one side of the trailer home and the other.

I was more worried for her than I was myself at that moment, her frantic movements were going to tire her out, make her easier prey for *Them*. That was, if she didn't work herself into such a frenzy that would cause her to pass out first.

She rubbed her face with her hands, angrily wiping the strands of hair from her eyes, "That stupid lake! Juan said it would be fine! He said it would be fine. Then those *things* took Gwen and Maria, they were screaming. I fucking ran, that's all I did, I just left them to die!" She burst into choking sobs, her body wracked by the adrenaline taking over.

I tried to wrap my arms around her, to console her, but she shoved me away, glancing around the buildings, "They were behind me, they saw me run. They'll be here any minute. We have to run!" Before she even finished that sentence, she had crossed the small alleyway and was disappearing behind another home.

"Wait!" I hissed, running after her.

As I turned the corner, I felt a weird sensation in my body, the hairs on my arms rose and a feeling like water slowly rolled down me. This peculiar prickling— I remembered this feeling. My mind didn't catch up with my body in time as I turned the corner to see a group of three of Them standing before me. The young girl was pinned to the ground, struggling in vain. They taunted her with horrible, vile things that she couldn't understand but was no less frightened of. If that wasn't the magic I had felt crawling across my skin, I didn't want to imagine what else they had done.

One of Them looked up at me, a smile creeping across his face as he muttered something to his companions; he took a few steps towards me. I glanced back at the girl, whose face was obscured by her oily hair, I hoped she could see it in my eyes—how truly, utterly sorry I was for doing what I was about to do. I didn't give it another thought as I turned around and ran.

I was still sore, still in pain, but the moment I had met that girl things had happened so fast I didn't have time to do anything but let my anxiety take control, to let fear grip me. Regardless of how Vaelythor had treated me, everything he had done could not erase the horrible memories of what his kind had inflicted upon my own. And it certainly would do nothing to save me now from what They were about to do. These creatures were just like the monsters we warned one another about. I ran for it.

But this one was fast—too fast, and he had easily closed the gap between us. In the blink of an eye, he was sweeping his leg under mine. I tumbled to the ground, my ribs aching with the impact on the cold, hard bitumen. I sputtered, forcing myself up onto my feet but he placed a foot forcefully against my back, pushing me into the ground and holding me there. I tried to squirm, to ease myself out but he held me firm. Kneeling beside me he smirked, revealing sharp canines. His golden eyes were lit with a mischievous glow as he looked me over.

"Well, aren't you delectably dressed," he cooed.

He grasped my hair, pulling me backwards. I grabbed his hand, trying to force his grip to loosen, but it was iron tight.

"You'll fetch a nice price," he murmured, pulling me onto my knees so I was forced to stare into his eyes.

I spat in his face. "Fuck you," I growled.

His eyes glowed with such an intensity, the air around me turned cold as my skin prickled with an invisible tingle of electricity. I knew that feeling of magic now, and I also knew my life was once again coming to a dramatic close.

Until I heard it, that distinct whistling as a bullet zoomed by me and collided with my assailant causing him to loosen his grip on my hair. He stared up into the trees, dumbfounded, red staining his shirt as he collapsed to the ground. There was no way his companions had not heard the gunshot, they would be here within moments, I'd have to take my chances either with the Aerendor or with my new mystery savior.

"What are you doing? Get up!" called a female voice from the trees.

Jumping to my feet I made a beeline for the safety of the shadows, my back barely sheltered from the sun before I was immediately set upon by four men with guns. They wore dark hoodies, their faces obscured by black mouth masks decorated with ambiguous markings, automatic rifles in gloved hands were raised inches from my face.

"Wait." A woman walked out from behind a tree, a rifle slung over her shoulder as she looked me up and down. "Juan, watch her—Michael, Deric, Asif, with me."

"There's two more, back there," I whispered, eyeing the corpse of the Aerendor lying unmoving in a pool of spreading blood.

The woman nodded, and three men moved out of the woods with her, their movements calculated and precise as they maneuvered through the trailer park, guns raised. Two or three of them were obviously military trained, their movements sharp and with purpose. They were all well fed and dressed, their clothes and hair were not what you would expect of those living a nomadic life—they were holed up somewhere good.

Somewhere safe.

"You didn't see a girl there, did you?" The guy standing beside me asked, his eyes on his companions.

"Yeah, I did, they have her," I whispered.

His eyes narrowed, grip tightening on the gun as his friends disappeared around the corner of a mobile home. Several agonizingly silent moments passed, before we heard the gunfire—a quick succession of pops, and then quiet again.

We waited silently as the group appeared from the

side of a trailer home, dragging an unconscious Aerendor with them. Walking beside one of the men was the oily-haired girl from earlier. The girl who had saved my life, just for me to abandon hers.

They hurriedly dragged their captive into the shade of the forest, nodding at the guy beside me. He slung his gun across his back and ran to the girl I had callously abandoned, their tearful reunion interrupted by the woman who had saved my life.

"Let's move out." The others swiftly began moving on through the forest, but she turned to me then, looking me up and down more thoroughly, "You're not going to start any shit, are you?"

I shook my head, exhaustion and pain tugged at my senses. I was getting too tired to really comprehend what I had landed myself into, humans could end up being far worse than the Aerendor. But she seemed content with my reply and nodded at her companions, "Follow us."

The girl from earlier glanced back at me, through her exhaustion and shock I could see the questioning in her eyes—the hurt. My heart ached for her, and I reprimanded myself continuously as I followed them through the forest. I might be welcome now, but I'm sure that once she talked to her friends, the best I could hope for was to be cast back out into the wilderness to fend for myself.

I had to hope the reward outweighed the risk. For now, I followed grimly behind them, my eyes focused on the boots of the creature being dragged through the underbrush.

They took a very long and exaggerated route through the forest, skirting along the roads. Even through my untrained eyes I knew they were purposefully misleading me. But somehow, they seemed to know exactly where they were going, and it wasn't long until their intent was clear.

We came up along a wooden fence line where a board was pulled back, they slipped inside one by one. The woman nodded at the board, and I slipped in after the others to find myself standing in the broad daylight upon the asphalt of a school playground. Two shadows moved in the windows, a moment later they materialized by the open door, coming outside to greet the group. One was man and the other a woman, both around my age with sun-kissed freckled skin and curly black hair. Their eyes lit up when they saw their friends, and narrowed warily when they noticed me and the Aerendor.

"Jax, see to the new girl," the woman who saved my life nodded in my direction, "Sariah come with me and Lynn, Juan, and Michael on perimeter. Asif and Deric bring our new friend to the cage."

The three women ran off to a shed in the corner of the school yard, the men and the Aerendor disappeared inside the school. I found myself beside the guy with the sun-kissed freckled skin staring awkwardly at me. A breeze stirred the dried leaves into a soft frenzy around us and he smiled.

"My name's Jax," he said pleasantly, extending his hand. "Welcome to our school!"

I closed the gap slowly, extending my hand for him to enthusiastically shake, his merry disposition was in stark contrast to every human I'd met so far. It jarred me so much I found myself stunned into silence.

"Oh," he exclaimed, releasing my hand to take a step back, "I'm sorry, I'm just…I don't know, a little excited to meet someone new."

I nodded, "It's okay. I was a bit stunned, was all."

"My apologies! Hey, would you like a tour?" He pointed at the school with his thumb.

I nodded dumbly, following him inside. Like every school, it entered a hallway filled with lockers with adjacent rooms built off it. He prattled on and on about how he used to attend an elementary school just like this with his twin sister, Sariah. We walked slowly through the corridor, Jax's enthusiasm slowly waned as it dawned on him how lacking my contribution to the conversation was, and we fell into silence.

When the monotonous droning of our boots began to bother him, he cleared his throat, "Oh, I bet you're hungry."

"A little," I was famished, and to be honest—I wasn't sure if I wanted to eat or sleep more right now.

"Let's see what we can find," he pushed open the

doors to reveal a small lunchroom, and my mouth gaped wide like a trout. It was stacked floor to ceiling with crates, boxes, barrels, of all shapes and sizes with all sorts of labels. There was such a variety of cans and packets of food I hadn't seen in over a year, and it was all here—this small group had a food supply for dozens of people to last a year, if not more.

"What tickles your fancy?" He asked, opening a box filled with an assorted brand of cereals.

"I—" I stared, dumbstruck.

"Or if cereal isn't really your thing, we have soups? Canned peaches? Oh, oh! Can I get you some jerky?" Jax excitedly went from box to box, pulling out one of everything and setting it aside on a tray, where he then added a table set with forks and knives, napkins, and cups.

"Got you a little bit of everything then," he said pushing the tray in front of me. He quickly prepared himself one before taking the seat opposite me.

"Is it really okay for me to…?" As much as I wanted to think rationally, I couldn't help but relax at this stranger's casual nature.

He waved his hand dismissively, his mouth stuffed with a spoonful of cereal, "Eat! Enjoy!" he mumbled through his food.

Gripping the fork, I gingerly brought a piece of peach to my mouth—and the instant that sugary syrup touched my lips I was hooked. I began shoveling the food eagerly into my mouth, barely pausing to breathe. I only stopped once I realized Jax was staring at me, before throwing his head back and howling with laughter.

"A little hungry, my ass." He laughed, refilling my plate with more peaches. "So, you already know my name, what can I call you?"

"My name's Wren," I said casually, emptying my plate and swallowing it down with a glass of apple juice he had somehow managed to procure without me noticing.

"Wow, that's a really pretty name. I've met a few Robins but have never met a Wren!" He seemed genuinely thrilled by something so simple as my mother naming me after her favorite bird.

"How did you guys manage to find so much food?" I was genuinely concerned, even though I thought I had a lot of food hidden around Cave Junction I was suspicious of how a group could find this much food and keep it safe. If movies taught me anything, then I had a right to be cautious.

He shrugged, "Sariah and I joined them a few months ago, there were more of us back then. It hasn't been a good couple of months." He looked up at the ceiling, and my gaze followed.

Cut out hearts were glued there, dozens of them, names in black marker were signed on every one.

I knew what those meant, it wasn't so different from the names carved on the wall of the Den, "I'm sorry."

"That's just how the world is now, I suspect we have a few more names to add to that wall now," He took our trays with the empty plates and cutlery to a sink in the corner and cleaned them. I stood up to follow, but he shook his head, "it's alright, let's continue the tour shall we?"

It took me a moment to realize what he had just done. "You guys have running water?"

He frowned for a moment confused before glancing back at the sink, "Oh! Yes, I don't know what Asif did, but he used to be an engineer or something? I have no clue, you'll have to ask him for the technicalities, all I know is we get fresh water, and I can take a shower."

I paused, "Shower?"

He smirked, "Come, let's continue the tour."

We continued through the school occasionally stopping for him to point out specific points of interest: classrooms converted into storerooms, the gymnasium where cots were aligned and everyone slept, the locker room where everyone took their showers, and then there was one room where a man stood guard out front, gun slung across his back. He was one of the guys who had been dragging the Aerendor around.

We paused outside the room and Jax indicated the man in front of us, "This is Asif, our Chief Engineer."

Asif quietly regarded me before nodding his head, glancing inside the small window in the door. I could just make out the room, with desks and chairs pushed against the walls and someone pacing inside the room, gun at the ready, but I couldn't see much more as Asif blocked the window.

He was a large, muscular man probably in his early thirties with jet black hair and glasses that were too small for his face. In fact, the oldest person in this group couldn't have been older than him. It seemed to be a trend now, not many humans I came across were younger than their late teens.

"Nice to meet you, my name is Wren," I said pleasantly, extending my hand.

He shouldered his gun before grasping my hand and firmly shaking it.

"Wren was admiring your work with the plumbing," Jax said elbowing Asif playfully.

"More so I was a fan of fresh water."

Asif chuckled.

"Is he in there?" I knew he was, but I wanted to know what they planned to do with an Aerendor captive.

Asif nodded, glancing briefly behind him. Jax become noticeably agitated beside me, as if he was hoping I would drop the subject. But I couldn't, I needed to know what sort of company I now held. Humans were deceptive, and I knew full well how much more dangerous they could be than our invasive monsters.

"What do you guys do with Them?" I tried to sound as casual as I could. No one was a monster sympathizer, and it didn't matter how Vaelythor had treated me— he was still a monster.

Asif and Jax exchanged a look, "We need information, this is the only way."

I tried not to imagine what they did to extort the

information they needed. But war was war, and the Aerendor had done far worse for much less. I tried not to think about it as Jax steered me away down the hall. He was excited to show me where I would stay the night, but nowhere near as excited for what tomorrow would bring. He spoke as if he imagined I would be staying a long while, the others seemed to think so, too—they were eager to share their stories and experiences, eager to welcome me into the fold. I couldn't help indulging them, it had been too long since I had company of my own kind.

But Katie still existed out there beyond these concrete walls, and until my injuries had healed I would regal my new friends with my company. That night was spent in the gymnasium surrounded by strangers yearning for information about the outside world, and I sat there unable to give them the news they so desperately sought.

〉〉〉〉〉〉　〈〈〈〈〈〈

Time seemed to hold no meaning, I was lost in my thoughts, lost in memories that I just couldn't abandon—if I refused to let the memories in, would that mean I had abandoned Katie, too? Time. I'd been with this group for over a week now, and I was still learning names. Jax was a constant companion, telling me stories of his life with his twin sister, Sariah. From their adoption at the age of three to a quiet Mormon couple in Utah, to how they came to San Francisco for college and followed the freeway north after the world went to shit.

I had to admit it was oddly soothing, getting wrapped up in his memories, living them with him. It almost made the wait bearable; one way or another though I had to find my sister, but my own survival was paramount to making that possible.

I barely saw Ashlyn, their leader, or her cousin Deric—one of the guys that had dragged the Aerendor to the school. I learned early through rather unpleasant conversations that Michael was to be avoided, although he was useful as a mechanic, stereotypes existed for a reason and his ideologies could prove dangerous in the long run.

You know when you first lay eyes on someone, from their mannerisms to the way they dressed—you just somehow knew, some instinct in you decided whether they would be friend or foe? The way Michael looked at me, at the women: the sneer, the roving glances, the hair that would raise on my arms and the unsettling feeling in my stomach. I knew it well, it had saved me in the past—this feeling, and I wasn't going to ignore it this time. I was quick to pick up on the fact that he was often posted at the wall as lookout, and only ever with other men. He was never left alone, his footsteps constantly shadowed.

But the others were pleasant enough company—Asif was a mechanical engineer from San Francisco, Juan had just finished the academy to become a state trooper,

Deric and Ashlyn both worked for the military, and Lynn…Lynn just graduated high school and wanted to be a fitness instructor.

But the most important thing I learned about this group was that they considered themselves 'monster hunters,' and this wasn't their first, nor would it be their last Aerendor captive. Tucked behind the utility shed at the edge of the fence line sat a mass grave where they callously tossed aside the corpses of Aerendor no longer deemed useful. A weight settled low in my belly; one I couldn't shake. Even after everything I'd seen and heard, I couldn't help but feel repulsed. I knew those creatures deserved it after all that had happened to us, they had all but ensured our extinction, but a part of me also knew this wasn't right.

I kept my mouth shut though, just like Lynn did. I didn't know her motives, but both of us did what we did out of survival. I was lost in my thoughts often, meandering through the school going about the daily tasks I was assigned, imagining the worst was yet to come. This group had its flaws, but this was the safest place for me to be. It was the best situation I could be in, honestly. I might have been pampered in that Aerendor's company, but I knew I was neither safe nor truly free there.

It felt like an eon had passed before I met the group's illustrious leader: Ashlyn. As head of the group, she spent most of her time away from the school. The group hadn't been very forthcoming with what she usually was up to, but I had an inkling it had to do with following the Aerendor movements in the area.

She walked into the locker room one day interrupting Sariah and me as we scrubbed at the mold gathering on the tiles. I knew it was her the moment I laid eyes on her. Her dark eyes found mine immediately, their keenness set goosebumps along my arms. She had such an assurance in how high she held her head, and how straight her back was. Ashlyn commanded the attention of a room when she walked in. Not like a pretty woman in a sundress when she walks into a coffee shop, but the way perhaps a CEO would when they walk into the office. When she peered down at you, she wasn't just *looking* at you. She was observing. I knew she noticed the way my skin pebbled, and how I drew back from her.

Whatever Ashlyn was looking for in me, it didn't seem to bother her. She announced there was to be a meeting the following night, to discuss the next excursion, before she disappeared. In and out, she wasn't one for small talk. She got straight to the point, like a real soldier.

An excursion, though. That gave me hope, I could learn more about where I was, how much farther I had to go to get to Lake Selmac—to get to Katie. That was how they had found me, a scouting party. After losing three of their friends a few days prior to my arrival, they caught wind of humans inhabiting the trailer park nearby. It was Lynn's idea to sneak in to see if her family was among the group; she didn't find them.

They never found their friends either.

But Lynn still hadn't said a word to me, and I hadn't found an opportunity to take her aside and apologize. She didn't necessarily avoid me, but she was attached to Juan at the hip. Where he went, she followed.

There was nothing I could do, and I resigned myself to the fact I would have to be careful with who I chose to turn my back to. I fell into a fitful slumber that night, caressed by an itchy sleeping bag set on the hard-wooden floor in the gymnasium, and worried about what tomorrow would bring.

CHAPTER
Eight

I awoke stiff and sore, my rib and foot didn't hurt anywhere near as much as they had before, but the floor certainly wasn't an ideal long-term arrangement. I'd been here over two weeks now, and yet, it felt like much longer. It wasn't easy to see that they didn't quite trust me, yet. If I was in their position, I would have locked myself up in a closet away from the others, too. But today somehow felt different, I just couldn't explain why. Perhaps the change in the attitudes of those that flitted by the room I had spent the last fortnight in. They were more hurried, manic even. It felt like we were going to war. But we kind of were, weren't we?

Sariah showed up a few minutes after I had woken with a change of clothes and escorted me to the showers to wash ourselves in silence.

It wasn't unpleasant—her company, but Sariah was a stark contrast to her brother. It was clear her approach to the apocalypse was attributed to her telling Jax not to talk to people. I wouldn't necessarily consider it a bad thing, after having Jax talk my ear off the last few days it was nice to be able to enjoy the silence with someone. Even if it was just the trickle of the water running down the drain.

The silence didn't last long. Once we were dressed and had exited the showers, we were set upon by Jax, Ashlyn, and Lynn at her heel.

"There you guys are!" she exclaimed.

"Making friends, are we?" Jax asked, nudging his sister in the arm. She rolled her eyes at him, shrugging him off.

"That's great—truly, but conference room, now," Ashlyn said tersely.

Ashlyn held a tight leash as we followed her to what I could only assume had once been the teachers' lounge at the front of the school. The couches had been arranged around a large table in the center of the room covered in maps and blueprints.

"So, does our new friend have a name?" Ashlyn asked once we had taken a seat.

It dawned on me that for as long as I had been here, I hadn't really introduced myself to her. I had tried to keep to myself—a low profile. Jax's conversations were the only real interactions I'd had and even then, they were mostly one way.

"Wren," I said, extending my hand.

She glanced at it before unrolling a map across the table, "Well, *Wren*, I won't bother introducing myself. take it you're well aware of who I am."

I nodded.

She turned her attention back to the map, pointing out several locations around the school.

"Should we really be sharing this with *her*?" Lynn interrupted, her pensive glare boring into me.

Ashlyn rolled her eyes, "She's hardly a threat."

I tried not to let her comment get to me—but she wasn't wrong, was she? I was little match for a group of monster hunters with automatic rifles. Lynn's outburst caught me off guard, as deserved as it was (after all I was the outsider who almost got her killed) it made me all the more cautious. I waited, hardly breathing, for her to tell the group what had happened at the trailer park. Waited for her to tell them how I had left her in the arms of monsters, that I had run like a coward when she had selflessly tried to save me.

But the moment didn't come as Ashlyn continued on, "So, Wren, I have to know now—are you joining us on the excursion?"

I didn't hesitate, "Yes."

A smirk, "Good, in that case," she pointed to a location on the map in front of her, "we've been trying to secure this area for weeks. But finding you in that trailer park—that's the first time we've had such a daring offensive from them. Where did you come from?"

"Cave Junction," I saw her finger trace a trail from the elementary school along the Redwood Highway and through the Rogue River-Siskiyou National Forest to the place I once called home.

I was in Grants Pass. The city I was born in. The city was thirty miles to the north of Cave Junction. Had I really closed thirty miles without even realizing it? How had I passed the towns of Kerby, Selma, Wonder, and Wilderville, without even seeing a sign? Was I that out of it to be able to completely miss four towns?

"What was the situation there?" The others leaned in closer.

I was pulled from my reverie, and shrugged, "It was free of them until..." I froze, how long had it been? How long was it from my isolation until those creatures had attacked me in that house on the riverside? How long since I had met *him*? "As far as I was aware, They hadn't traveled up from California through the national forest until about a month ago."

Ashlyn ran her hands through her hair, looking down at the map, "Interesting. Why would They have avoided that area?"

"There's not much out there," I shrugged; I decided to keep the small town where Vaelythor was to myself for now. "But I heard from a traveler that they have an encampment on the shore of Lake Selmac," I was counting on tapping into their need to help others when I quietly added, "and they bring humans there."

Everyone seemed to perk up at that, their voices trying to speak over one another until Ashlyn quieted them, her expression grave, "We've been...aware of the situation at the Lake Selmac encampment for some time."

"That's one hell of a way to honor Sasha's memory," Lynn whispered angrily.

Ashlyn held up a hand, "We've all lost someone."

"What happens to them?" I asked. I knew deep down, I truly did—but a part of me refused to believe it.

The room got quiet, still as a pond on a winter's day. Sariah finally spoke up, her voice was soft, gentle, it reminded me of how someone would whisper sweetly to a sleeping baby. "There's a reason we only see women at their encampments."

My blood chilled in my veins as the implications became painfully real. I desperately didn't want it to be true, the very thought—imagining my sister standing there under those bobbing lights in her thin gown.

"That's why we're staging an operation," Ashlyn said urgently, "We need a reconnaissance team to rendezvous at the Lake Selmac encampment, take note of inventory, numbers, movements—and to finalize location on where the humans are held after they are sorted."

"Sorted?" It hadn't occurred to me that they weren't kept at Lake Selmac, that maybe they are moved to another location afterwards.

That meant Katie could be anywhere.

"We've had travelers feed us information and we believe the most credible source for relocation is somewhere an hour north of us. Any humans that travel that way disappear."

All the people I had ever met that went north of my cave were never heard from again. Were they captured before they could make it past a certain point? Was that where Katie was being held now?

"I volunteer." I was so close to her—there was no way I would give up now. I'd find my sister or die trying.

"As do I," said Jax, nodding at me.

Lynn raised her hand, "I'll go, too."

Ashlyn started shaking her head, "No, Lynn. I want you to rest, I'll send Deric." She looked me over quickly, "Wren, have Jax show you where the dugout packs are, I want you guys ready to go tomorrow morning."

I nodded, mentally clocking out as the rest of the meeting was between the others. They discussed inventory, new guard patrols, and nearby houses that would be converted into safe zones. I honestly didn't pay as much attention as I should have, the prospect of seeing Katie as early as tomorrow left me feeling giddy as a newborn foal. I couldn't focus on anything else and almost missed Jax's entire speech about how excited he was to do the run with me.

"Run?" I said dumbly.

"Yeah, that's what we call it when we leave the school for anything. Anyway, let's get you a pack and hit the sack. We'll be up at dawn." Jax nodded to Ashlyn as she continued to look over the maps, and I followed him out of the conference room.

One of the storerooms he had shown me before had twelve backpacks in a row against a wall, each was filled with several days' worth of supplies. Various foods, a first aid kit, extra pairs of socks, a towel, a pair of utensils, a knife, and small things like string, rope, and a flashlight. Tied to the top of each pack was a sleeping bag and a water canteen hung from the side. All in all, there were enough supplies per pack to last at least a week, minimum—even though it was just a reconnaissance mission, they didn't take any chances. If someone was going to be separated from the group and had to survive for some time alone before meeting back up, they wanted to make sure they had the means to. I had to admire the effort they went to for one another.

Jax procured a map from his pack which had a small keychain of a superhero attached to it, "Every pack has a map. Here, here, and here," he indicated three spots in a vague circle within five miles of the school, "are the meet up locations if something goes wrong. I mean, everything will probably be fine. You'll do great, but... I have to disclose this information just in case, ya know?"

I nodded politely. It made me nervous, but also incredibly relieved knowing they had thought this through enough to have not one, but three back up plans. I still couldn't get over the fact that I had missed Lake Selmac, *by miles*. He went over a few more points of interest on the map before Sariah showed up. Time had flown by and it was so late already, she ushered us to the cafeteria to enjoy a hearty dinner with the others.

After dinner Sariah led me to the gymnasium where everyone else slept. She procured a pair of red and white polka-dot pajamas. While I had slipped behind a screen they had set up for privacy to change, she had also made me up a cot in the corner of the room, complete with an impossibly soft fleece blanket with the image of a black cat playing with a ball of yarn. On the floor by the cot was a pair of jeans, black t-shirt, and steel-toed boots, I suppose that was to be my get up for tomorrow's adventure.

"Is this alright?" Sariah asked quietly, looking over the cot.

I smiled, "Thank you. This is more than perfect." I sat down on the cot, relishing the fact that I didn't have to sleep on the wooden floor in that horrid janitor closet again.

She matched my smile, before retiring to her own cot on the other side of the room next to Lynn and Jax, who were already sound asleep. I made myself comfortable, thinking of everything that might transpire tomorrow. What if I saw Katie? I didn't know what I would do, would I risk Jax and Deric's lives to rescue my sister? She was the whole reason I came out this way, and even if she didn't hear me, I knew that she knew I promised to return. That I would save her. But who could say what tomorrow would bring, so I let sleep take me and for the first time in a while, I stayed asleep throughout the entire night.

We were fed, clothed, packs on, and at the ready awaiting Ashlyn by the hole in the fence early the next morning. Deric and Jax were playfully joking with one another, taunting and jesting about their lives before in an attempt to pass the time until she showed.

Thankfully I was only subjected to their banter for a few minutes until our fearless leader popped her head out of the hole, "I assume you know how to use one of these?" Ashlyn asked handing me a handgun.

I knew nothing about guns, but I knew enough to see that the one she gave me was very different from the one strapped across her back. I just nodded my head, I didn't actually know how to use one, but I didn't want them questioning me. It was easy to be suspicious of how anyone could survive this long in the wild without a gun. I'm surprised I lasted for as long as I had if I were honest with myself. I watched as Jax tucked his pistol in the back of his jeans, so I did the same. Mirroring was how I would survive, at least until I got to my sister, after that I didn't really care. I had no plan for after.

"Good. Are you guys ready?" Ashlyn asked.

"You know it!" Jax said excitedly.

"Ugh, let's just go already," Deric said, hefting his pack across his back. He started walking as Jax and I hurriedly said goodbye to Ashlyn.

I was worried that for all their planning, we would still be forced to walk the five or six hours back south to Lake Selmac. But once we had left the safety of the school behind, the group took a detour towards a small shed behind an abandoned house.

I breathed a sigh of relief as Deric pointed out a row of mountain bikes, telling everyone to take one. A smile crept across my face as I mounted the bike and followed the others out towards a trail extending behind the shed.

What would have been an exhausting six-hour walk now turned into a calm hour and a half ride. Deric and Ashlyn had spent last night setting up a route of trails through the woodlands and farms on the way to the encampment, fully aware that this plan would add an hour or two to our journey, but safety was paramount. None of us were going to complain, certainly not I, my life was worth the extra hour or two of biking across the terrain. I glanced up at the sky, my eyes wary of every movement, my ears of every sound.

The sun had only begun to twinkle over the horizon setting the sky alight in soft pastels of pink and yellow, orange and violet that began to chase away the black and the blue of night. By the time we had made it to the halfway point of our journey somewhere on the outskirts of Lake Selmac, the sun had fully emerged from its slumber to bathe the land in gold.

We paused briefly at the side of an old, crumbling shed to quench our thirst while Deric reviewed the map. A pair of doves sat perched on the awning above us, cooing their sweet song together, not caring about our sudden intrusion.

"Alright guys, time to get serious. On the other side of that forest is a house where I think we can get the best vantage point to see what's up," Deric announced, crumpling his map into his pack. "We'll leave the bikes here."

Jax held his finger against his lips and followed Deric into the woods. I stood a moment longer, steeling myself for whatever I would see. Everywhere we went weeds grew waist high, vines smothered dust-covered cars, and leaves clogged gutters. I dared to admit feeling almost at peace in this overgrown world as the gentle voices of doves in the dawn called to me.

I heard the snapping of fingers and looked up to see Jax signaling to me. I shook myself from the reverie and quickly caught up with him. "No time to be enjoying the scenery," he whispered, shaking his head.

I rolled my eyes before allowing him to lead me through the forest to Deric, who sat on the edge of a rotting log. Before us was sprawled a two-story homestead—colonial-style, it was edged by frenzied hedges and surrounded by the thick, unforgiving forest which we now tried to quietly traverse.

Jax moved towards a window, peeking in before trying it, the window lifted after several hard pulls and the three of us snuck inside. The house had obviously been ransacked; the cupboards and pantry were bare, debris littered the ground and all manner of insects had taken up shop in the dark corners. Cobwebs were spun in every doorway and as we walked up the stairs it became more apparent how much nature reclaimed what was once hers.

A window was broken in the top left bedroom, and a family of swallows had taken to building their nest on the dresser. They squawked angrily at our intrusion, and we hastily left. The adjacent room was stripped of most of its belongings, what was once a library or home office now housed a derelict collection of moldy books and a simple, wooden desk covered in a thick layer of dust.

We set our packs up by the door and looked out the windows, towards the shore. The room we were in had the advantage of peeking right through the gap of two large pine trees, revealing a myriad of weird, spiral-shaped buildings in the distance. I hadn't noticed earlier that binoculars were in every pack, and I set myself up next to Deric and Jax, surveying the encampment.

"Holy shit," Jax exclaimed, his binoculars turning this way and that.

Lifting mine to my eyes I followed his gaze to the shoreline and despaired. Set upon the marshy land by the shore were great stone structures, like towers topped, not with parapets or roofs, but cone-like structures that reached even higher. Upon their very tops was a crow's nest structure, patrolled by several Aerendor in peculiar outfits. Long dark cloaks hung like a cloud over shiny, metal armor fashioned outwards from their chests like the wings of a bird—beautiful but unmistakably deadly.

"Notice anything?" Deric asked.

It took me a moment to realize that he was referring to something in particular, "They're not holding weapons." It took me by surprise, and Jax too, as he mumbled in response.

"There are no walls either."

"Why wouldn't one of their main encampments be fenced or guarded with weaponry?" I wondered aloud.

We saw it at the same time, a large boat intricately

curved to resemble wings, like the breastplates of the lookouts, was gliding smoothly across the water. Not just one, four followed suit, gently drifting to the shoreline to be greeted by a mass of guards in their peculiar armor. Still, no one had weapons.

"Look at the flags," Deric said.

Draped graciously over the side were pennants with a familiar symbol; my eyes traced the curve of the leaping creature's back where wings sprouted outwards to its graceful, extended neck upon which sat a horse-like head adorned by two sets of horns, one set curling towards the face and the other set branching outwards into a pair of heavy-set antlers. It was the crest, the same one on the cloak that Vaelythor had placed upon my shoulders that day in Cave Junction.

"There he is," Deric whispered.

Part of me knew the instant he said it. I knew exactly who he was talking about, and at the same time I had hoped he was wrong. My eyes frantically scanned the arrivals as they stepped off from the boats, and sure enough, standing regally at their head was Vaelythor.

He looked every inch the royal draped in a majestic crimson robe cinched by a golden vest and swathed by an ivory cloak. His ivory-colored hair was adorned by a golden circlet and at his waist was an intricately whorled belt supporting the weirdest sword I had ever seen. I'd honestly never seen them with weapons before, even if they had that strange power I'd witnessed, it made sense to not carry a weapon. But sure enough there he was, with a sword that was no doubt just as deadly as any magic he could wield.

I had to wet my lips and gather my thoughts before I managed to squeak out, "Who is he?"

If Deric and Jax knew who he was, then I had to be very careful with what I chose to reveal.

Jax wiped the sweat that had begun to bead on his forehead, "He's like a king, I think?"

Deric spoke up, "From what we can gather, They're a highly patriarchal society with a sort of monarchy. Like our monarchies, a single-family rules, and they have dukes and earls and barons, but this guy...I've seen him everywhere around Grants Pass. Unlike the others, he's very active in his role and judging by the way the others react to his presence he's high up there in the chain of command. I don't quite think he's the king, though."

"Looks like his cronies are with him today," Jax said.

I glanced towards the row of buildings Vaelythor was now striding through, and sure enough on his flanks was Yaern and Raekhan. Their attire was distinct from the other Aerendor around Lake Selmac.

Yaern was wearing an emerald tunic and burgundy cloak, his russet hair left free to be caressed by the gentle breezes that lifted from the lake. As much as I didn't want to, I let my eyes fall on Raekhan, even if you were unaware of his position—you knew he was a warrior. From his intricate, dark-stained leather chest piece adorned with a bandolier of glinting knives to his cloak draped over one shoulder highlighting the sword at his hip and the bow and quiver slung across his back, he was born for battle.

"How many guards?" Deric asked.

Jax didn't hesitate to answer, "two per tower."

"And the ground?"

"Looks like they're leaving," I quickly spoke up, my eyes frantically searching for Vaelythor. He had made his way through the camp to the other end, barely visible through the trees. Those horse like creatures they were so fond of were all tied in a row beneath a strange building that curved upwards towards the sky, but from here it almost looked like half of a watermelon.

"They have stables, too," Jax said excitedly. I wasn't sure how that was good news, any creature associated with the Aerendor couldn't possibly mean good news for us.

A few moments of silence passed as we sat there watching Them. Vaelythor, Yaern, and Raekhan mounted their steeds and bid farewell to the other Aerendor before meandering out of the encampment and down the road out of our sights. A thought had occurred to me, and I didn't know if the others considered it as well, but it was considerably bold of Them to be out in the open without a regiment of guards if They were *that* important to their people. I felt slightly nauseous as I entertained the idea of maybe—just maybe, they didn't need guards to protect them.

"Alright, I'm calling it now, we're following them," Deric said, packing away his binoculars and hefting his bag onto his shoulder, he was out of the room before Jax and I could reply. He seemed quite fond of that habit.

Jax and I exchanged a look, he seemed as confused as I was, but we both quickly packed up and ran after him. We were surprised by how quickly we found our quarry following them as quietly and as far back as we could amongst the trees. Every time a twig snapped under foot we'd collectively freeze, watching and waiting. The Aerendor gave us no indications that they heard us let alone even knew they were being tailed.

We followed them back to our halfway point, the main road cutting the forest in half before us. We waited as they turned northeast, following the road, talking to one another in hushed voices. From this distance I couldn't understand anything they were saying.

We followed silently behind, at the edge of the forest, unseen, unheard. Almost two hours later we began to understand, their destination became clear as we reentered Grants Pass. We huddled beside a chain-link fence, the barbed wire hovering menacingly above us. We watched as they disappeared behind the metal doors, two guards stationed out front shut it behind them.

Deric pointed to a sign hanging on the fence further up and we moved closer.

Rogue Valley Youth Correctional Facility.

"What could They possibly be using a youth facility for…" I didn't know why I even had to ask aloud, but it became all too clear to me when one of the doors leading to a yard opened and a mass of humans exited led by several guards. They milled about the yard huddled in groups; they weren't chained but were dressed in those billowy, ivory gowns I'd seen Katie in.

We pulled our binoculars out at the same time, pressing ourselves as close to the ground as we could.

"I only see women," Jax whispered.

Deric nodded, "This is it, this is where They keep them."

A chill ran down my spine, I could barely breathe. This was where They kept us, housed in cells, like animals. I shuddered, pulling my jacket closed. If Katie were in there, I had to save her. I had to do everything I could. But it was getting dangerous now, it was about more than just saving Katie. This was about saving humanity.

"They've been this close to us the entire time," Jax muttered, his voice held a bite to it. "Let's head back to the school, there's nothing we can do right now."

Deric waved at us dismissively, "You two head back, I'm going to learn as much as I can—we're going to save them."

CHAPTER
Nine

Deric joined us in the conference room sometime before midnight; the moon heralded his return by bathing the world in an ethereal glow. We all sat huddled together on the couches, listening intently as Deric relayed everything he had learned.

He described minor and major details of the encampment at Lake Selmac and the location of most of the prisoners at the youth facility. Ashlyn's shadow loomed over the map as she placed down markers, silent except to beg clarification from Jax or me.

"So, we can't go in the front door?" Asif spoke up, a dangerous glint was in his eyes.

Ashlyn deliberated for a moment, "You know, that might just work." She placed a marker at the front of the prison, one on the northern side and then another on the western side.

"We're going to split into three teams, North, West, and South. I'll iron out who is in which team later, but for now I want us to prepare. West team will be situated by the county jail next door, their job is to cut the fence and place explosives all along the western side and bait the guards from further in. The Northern team will come in ten minutes after the initial explosions, cut across the parking lot and ignite charges on the perimeter at this first building here," she tapped one of the buildings.

"You will also serve as a distraction to pull in the rest of the guards. Rendezvous points will be set up to the North and West for your teams, meanwhile the South team will be coming in from the forest over the train tracks here and pull as many prisoners as you can from the buildings here," she pointed to the building of the facility on the southern perimeter of the prison.

"From Deric's reconnaissance it seems the majority of prisoners are being held on this end of the prison; we'll have a rendezvous set up for the South team in a nearby house geared with supplies. All prisoners will be escorted to this location before you make your way back west to the school. North and West teams will take a longer, exaggerated route."

"I expect they'd swing closer to the city center?" Juan asked.

Ashlyn nodded, placing more markers on the map, "North will swing towards this hardware store before meeting with the West team in this cul-de-sac, here. I'm going to send out ground teams to load supplies into the rendezvous points and nearby safe houses."

Asif inched closer to her, whispering, "Does this mean I get to do what I do best?"

She smirked, "I expect nothing less."

Asif clapped his hands in excitement, and I watched them wearily, wondering exactly what his specialty was. Jax tapped me on the arm and I leaned in, "he used to be an engineer for a defense contractor with the military."

"What he means is the Arab likes to blow shit up," Michael interjected loudly.

We glared at him.

Ashlyn chose to ignore his remark, "Alright everyone, go get some food. Rest and relax. We'll convene later tonight for team selection."

Everyone muttered their thanks and began to leave; Sariah pulled me aside as I walked out the door. The others walked past without a glance, except Jax who paused briefly before Sariah dismissed him. The door shut with a clang, and I turned to her with a questioning look.

"I thought perhaps you'd like to go for a walk with me?" she asked shyly.

"Sure."

She had never been so upfront before and I confess I was slightly concerned. Sariah was well loved by everyone here, she seemed to be the type of girl who wouldn't harm a fly, if anything I felt safest when in her company. But I'd be lying if I didn't admit I was a little concerned about leaving the building after learning just how close the Aerendor were to the school.

I let her take my hand, leading me through the playground, out the hole in the fence, and along a back path into the forest. We walked along a lightly trodden path edged by weathered bricks, the forest came alive around us—the pines quaking high above, brittle leaves snapping under our feet.

"Where are we going?" I tried not to entertain the idea that maybe I was wrong about her.

I could hear the smile in her voice as she replied, "My favorite place."

A few minutes later we hit a wooden fence line, following its length we came upon a door that Sariah pushed open, revealing a small garden. She shut the gate firmly and went to sit down on a concrete bench at the garden's center, a statue of a Roman goddess sat as a centerpiece of a defunct fountain, draped in a fiery red vine. Trellises were set up nearby to overhang the beautiful statue, but the plant had other ideas, nearly smothering the goddess.

Sariah noticed me staring and pointed upwards. I followed her hand to where deep purple fruit hung low from the vine, she plucked several and offered them to me.

"They're grapes."

I stifled a gasp, "I haven't seen grapes in…a very long time." I greedily plopped a few in my mouth, savoring the sweet juiciness.

She laughed and pulled a few more from the vines for herself. We sat silently by one another on the bench enjoying this quiet moment together.

"Are you worried about tomorrow?"

I paused, "A little."

"I am," she admitted, looking up at the moon.

It was exceptionally bright, and now that there were no streetlamps or vehicles to pollute the sky the stars were so myriad and fantastical. Reds, and blues, and yellows, and oranges. Every color you could imagine danced across the night sky, creating a display unlike anything I had ever seen. Even when we went camping or hiking when I was a child, I'd never known this sky. This was a foreign sky, dawning over a brand-new world.

"It's beautiful, right?" She gestured to the garden bathed in moonlight, her eyes were so soft, so full of hope. I realized it then, that look she had. It was the exact same one my mother had as she said goodbye to me at the cave, that one last time—when I had lost both my mother and father. I could feel the tears at the edge of my eyes, but I fought hard to keep them at bay.

"We'll be fine, you know," I said softly.

I glanced at her, tears shone in her eyes too as she replied, "We've never done anything like this before. Even before everything…Jax and I were good kids, stayed out of trouble. Our mom and dad adopted us when we were three. They were Mormons and tried to raise us that way, we didn't really believe any of it, but we went along with it to make them happy. They were good parents, sometimes a bit strict but I mean, who doesn't have parents like that?"

I nodded, she went on, tears in her eyes, "When we graduated high school, we had applied to so many colleges in California, we wanted a fresh start. A future. Our mother was the most disappointed, she wanted us to stay and help run the bed and breakfast that had been in their family for generations. But we got accepted to Stanford—*Stanford,* God you'd think she would be ecstatic! It had, like, a five percent acceptance rate, and we *both* got in. We left a month later, and as soon as the summer ended this all began. We haven't seen or heard from them since, and after what the news had said about Salt Lake City..."

She grew silent, her eyes teary as we both sat there remembering the day we heard—the day the world stood still. Dugway, Utah, was the entry point into the United States for Them, which really disappointed all the Area 51 fans. After Russia led the charge, everybody wanted a slice of this new world we had contacted. China, Germany, India, Brazil, the U.S.—ironic that although we were the last to make contact, we were undoubtedly the most responsible for humanity's destruction.

I wrapped my arms around her, bringing her head to rest on my chest, "I promise we'll be fine. You'll see, all this worry will be for nothing."

She sniffled, wrapping her arms around me.

"Jax is all I have left."

A tear rolled down my cheek, disappearing in her soft, curly black hair, "He'll survive. You'll both survive."

She tried to shake her head, but I held her still, and we sat there holding one another for what seemed like hours. The world moved around us, the trees shook in the cold breeze, an owl called out nearby, and the moon continued her ascent to the heavens.

"We should head back, before the others come searching for us," I finally spoke up.

Sariah nodded before reluctantly breaking my embrace. It was a slow and quiet walk back to the school, but the moment we arrived we were ushered into the conference room where Ashlyn took a long and hard look at each one of us before sighing.

It seemed she had chosen the teams; I couldn't deny the hopefulness I had. I was desperate to be on the team coming from the South, the team that would be rescuing the prisoners—only for the selfish reason of wanting to see my sister's face first.

"Know that what I am about to ask of you is going to be difficult, and I deliberated long and hard with who should be on what teams. But I believe each one of you is perfect for the role I have assigned."

She pulled three papers out from beneath the map, placing one North, South, and West. She flipped them over and read each aloud, "West Team: Asif, Juan, myself. North Team: Michael and Deric. South Team: Sariah, Jax, Lynn, Wren."

Sariah hugged me tightly and I smiled up at her. We were all together, we could keep each other safe. I glanced over at Lynn. She still hadn't said a word to me and I'd been with the group long enough. Time seemed irrelevant, but in that time, I never got the chance to speak to her. And I never got to see our Aerendor captive. I frowned; sometimes, at night, I'd swear I could hear the Aerendor speaking soft nothings into the cold emptiness that was his prison.

Ashlyn carried on through my self-reflection, and after explaining a few minor details to the North and West teams, she dismissed us for the night. In the morning, the North and West teams would venture to their posts and prepare their rendezvous points and plant the bombs early. By this time in a few days, we would be neck deep in the prison. I glanced over at Lynn uneasily, waiting for the others to leave. As she made for the door, I gently grabbed her arm and she spun on me, her eyes wild.

"What?" she growled. Taken aback I released her; hostility flared beneath those chocolate eyes.

"I-I was hoping we could speak really quick?" I tried to make my voice as sincere as possible, but she was obviously not in the mood.

"I have nothing to say to you," she said curtly.

"I just wanted to apologize," I said quickly. She paused with the door held slightly open, staring out into the black of the night.

Without turning she simply said, "I don't accept it" and walked out.

The dawn came swiftly, the North and West teams were long gone before I had even awoken. Sariah and Lynn had disappeared after breakfast to try and recover extra linen and pillows from the nearby houses, which left Jax and me to hold down the school. It was eerily quiet in the halls as my boots echoed across the concrete floors. One of the windows was left ajar, a cool draft settled around me as I made my way down the hallway. Jax sat in a chair at the end reading a cover-less book.

"Bored?" I asked.

He didn't look up as he lazily flipped a page, "Yup."

"Want to get some fresh air?"

He glanced up briefly, then looked at the door he guarded.

"I'll watch it," I offered.

He only deliberated a moment before dropping his book to the floor and stretching, "I have literally been here since dawn hoping someone would tell me that!" He gave me a hug before disappearing down the hallway, calling back, "Don't worry by the way, all it does is sleep!"

I sighed, taking a seat and staring up at the ceiling. It was a boring job, I found myself beginning to fidget before I felt it—that shiver up my spine, the caress along my arm. I heard it then, the whispering.

The Aerendor was awake.

I glanced nervously down the hallway, other than the branches of the trees outside shaking in the breeze there was not a single noise. Whatever Jax was doing it was far enough away that it couldn't hurt for me to look inside. I don't know why I wanted to go in, or what possessed me as my hand tightened around the doorknob. I ducked inside, pulling the door quietly closed.

Two blue tarps were thrown haphazardly against the windows, black tape blocked out the sun and the air. It was stale and cold, a single lantern hung precariously over a metal cage in the corner farthest from the door, casting an ominous shadow across the pale walls. Shadows spread across the room, sharp and angry, cutting through the light.

I slowly walked up to the cage, my heart hammering in my chest as I stood before it. It was a brutal contraption; unlike anything I had ever seen before. I wasn't even entirely sure it was made by a human, the metal had an unearthly sheen to it, with gnarled spikes driven into the sides to anchor it to the ground. Distracted by the cage I didn't notice the pale, golden eyes watching me from within. They held none of the shine or luster from when I had first seen him, from the intensity of an autumn maple leaf to muted sand, his alabaster skin was dull and marked by splashes of purple and blue. A ragged cut ran from above his right cheek down to his chin, dry blood was crusted to his face.

"A new human to torture me, how delightful," he whispered, almost inaudibly. His spirit was broken, just like a human, just like ours. He had given up, accepted his fate.

"I'm not here to torture you," I said simply, sitting on the ground in front of the cage.

He eyed me warily, clearing his throat before asking weakly, "You can understand me?"

"Yes."

He moved slightly closer to the middle of the cage, his eyes fixated on me as he asked, "How?"

Should I lie? What if he told my new companions what I told him, that I could understand their language? We had taught the first arrivals our languages, and their kin were quick to pick it up, but as far as I knew, no human understood the Aerendor dialect. But even if he did tell them that I understood, would they believe me over one of Them? *No, they wouldn't.* The Aerendor were lying, murderous monstrosities, my word was worth way more than one of theirs.

"One of your own gave me the ability."

His eyes narrowed as he looked long and hard at my face, I cleared my throat before continuing, "I'm not claimed."

I could almost see the thoughts running through his head, behind those pale golden eyes, suspicion no doubt mounting. Several moments of silence passed as he watched me carefully, until it became too much for me.

"What?" I asked, annoyed.

"You don't realize what a gift you have been given."

I shrugged, "So, now I can understand you. How is that a gift?"

He shook his head, "Who gave it to you?"

I froze, remembering now what Deric and Jax had said back at the lake. Vaelythor was some part of the Aerendor royalty, some very powerful and dangerous part. Would that be in my favor? Knowing this *gift* I was bestowed came from someone so highly regarded among Them? I contemplated, my eyes downcast.

"There's only one reason he gave you that," the Aerendor said, his voice darkened as he regarded me carefully. "Only one reason he could."

"Pshh, and what reason would that be?" I asked dismissively. I knew he noticed that hitch in my voice, the slight tremble.

He cocked his head, like a hawk observing its prey. It was easy to forget as I sat here watching this broken creature how dangerous They could be.

The Aerendor smirked, "No, child of Man, I don't think I will tell you. I will let it haunt you, because once we know you can speak our tongue, we will know why it was done. But you—you won't."

He leaned forward against the cage bars, his teeth glistening in the flickering candlelight. A chill ran up my spine as I mustered the strength to not express the fear that was building up inside, I couldn't give him the satisfaction of knowing his words affected me. But he had won, he knew it, and there was nothing I could do. Vaelythor had told me it was a simple spell, for me to understand him. But was it?

The memories hit me hard as I shut the door behind me and slumped to the floor. Vaelythor. That day in the clearing he hadn't said a word, but when he had met me again by the Visitor Center—he spoke to me in our language. In English. In the Before, we had taught them our language, several of our languages in fact, but They hadn't taught any of us *theirs*. It was a hotly debated topic on the evening news, every station had their own opinion, everyone wanted their voice heard as to why our new visitors were keen to learn of us, but not to reveal too much of Them.

Why would he need to spell me to understand him if he could understand me? Unless that wasn't all he did. It was terrifying, the day of the invasion—no one understood Them, not the government and certainly not the military. I don't really think any of us did, and if I really wanted to understand Them there was only one way I ever could. If I wanted to know why me, and what it meant, there was only one being I could ask.

But could I face Vaelythor again? Knowing what I knew, knowing that there really was an ulterior motive? Right now, it didn't matter, the only thing that did matter was finding my sister, and if she wasn't in that prison—what then?

She was the only thing that was important, I didn't care for anything else.

CHAPTER
Ten

Dawn was on the horizon and a thick fog clung to the air, shrouding the school in a damp, suffocating blanket. The world was quiet and cold, the only thing that existed was what was within the short few feet around us that we could see. We hefted our packs on our backs, our guns tightly gripped in our hands, our journey was much slower as we followed the main road east before striking out into the woods and across the overgrown farmlands. Not a word passed between us, and there wouldn't be.

We were as silent now as we were at breakfast. Those who stayed behind cast us fearful glances when we left. Nine of us started out from the school with no idea how many of us would return. Ashlyn went over plans A through Z, there was a backup plan for every backup plan. The North and West teams had converted dozens of houses within ten miles around the prison into rendezvous points. If anyone found themselves in trouble, there were opportunities to recover. But each of us knew what we had to do if we failed, if we were being caught: the sacrifice of one to save the many.

It took much longer to make it to the dirt path at the southern edge of the prison than we had hoped, the fog had made our journey difficult as we placed extra packs at the base of the tree line and waited, all eyes on the prison.

Ashlyn spoke up first, "I have full faith in each one of you. I'm not one for long, sappy goodbyes. So, let's get in and get out."

Everyone silently went from one another to give a strong, steady hug—except Lynn, she was quick to dismiss the embrace I offered as her arms firmly grasped Juan. Not a word was said as Asif, Juan, and Ashlyn departed with their bag of explosives to the west side of the prison. Once the fog had swallowed their presence, Michael and Deric quickly disappeared into the forest, They were headed north to set their explosives to go ten minutes after the West team had let theirs off.

The world was quiet once again as Sariah, Jax, Lynn, and I sat tentatively at the edge of the woods. Jax was here mere hours ago to plant his explosives on the southernmost building, it was easier for him to sneak in, as although the humans seemed to be quartered closer to here, there weren't that many Aerendor in the vicinity. We never paused to question it, and even now, sitting here in the cold and wet—I pushed it from my mind.

I was one step closer to seeing my sister, one step closer to rescuing her. I didn't care about what that Aerendor had said, I didn't care about Vaelythor, and I certainly didn't care about Lynn.

We sat hunched over, barely able to breathe, as we awaited the sounds that would signal the time for us to move closer. The fences around the prison had long since eroded or been scavenged, giving us surprisingly easy entry onto the grounds. In front of us sat what used to be a large shed, the roof had since collapsed and whatever was inside had been destroyed by the elements. Nature had worked her magic on the grounds, smothering the manicured lawns with a thick knee-high carpet of weeds. Five hundred feet beyond that shed stood the closest of the prison buildings. Hidden behind three layers of barbed wire and concrete fencing, about two dozen humans slumbered as prisoners.

Today was their lucky day.

Hopefully.

Huddling together in the dirt, we sat quietly, the wind whistling through the holes of the rusting shed in front of us, fog billowing past. Almost half an hour later we heard it, a series of explosions that parted the fog to the west and lit up the sky with vile black smoke and angry crimson flames.

"They must have hit a pipeline," Jax said uneasily, but he shook his head and moved out from the cover of the trees. "Let's move."

We followed closely, darting from the safety of the trees through a small door left hanging on its hinges. A few rusting vehicles sat inside the shed, barely holding the collapsed roof aloft. We moved between them, making for the other side. Our hearts collectively skipped a beat when we heard the unmistakable sounds of gunfire to the west.

"Jax," Sariah said uneasily.

I watched as she cowered by Jax's side, her eyes wide. She really should have stayed behind at the school, but she refused. There was nothing to be done about that now, we were too far in, we would have to see this to the end. Jax pulled the detonator from his backpack, holding it in his hand with an iron grip, the skin stretched tight over his knuckles.

He glanced at Sariah before clearing his throat, "You stay here, sis. Lynn, I need you to cover me from the fences up ahead and guide the prisoners to Sariah."

They both nodded.

The fog had still not abated, the world remained a mystery beyond us. As much of a hindrance as it was to us, we hoped it was equally annoying to Them. All we could see in the distance was the twinkling of the sun against the harsh, acrid smoke rising higher and higher. We could only see the roof of the building we were aiming for, there was no way to really know what stood between us and the humans on the other side.

The ground shook as a series of explosions rocked the northern half of the prison, a devilish fire joined the black smoke that rose from the west. The sound of gunfire echoed across the compound as we burst from the shed as one, running towards the first set of fences. These, too, had been scavenged or eroded by nature, a vine snaked its way over the barbed wire, a morbid yet beautiful scene. We had to move quick, Jax removed wire cutters from his bag and began cutting holes in the fence. After the first set he moved onto the second, and then the third before he signaled to us to halt. I could just see Sariah sitting in the fog beyond, huddled just outside the shed. Lynn nodded at Jax as she crept back to sit by the hole near the second fence.

He brought the remote to his chest and stared at us, counting down. Jax and I huddled together, and I placed a hand on his shoulder as he pressed the button. The wall two hundred feet from us exploded sending concrete and debris into the air. As soon as the rocks had fallen from the sky, clattering to the ground like a rain of ashes, we rushed forward into the prison. Another series of explosions rocked the west side of the compound, a safety measure in case the Aerendor decided to come back to guard their human cattle.

Inside the prison we followed the corridor to a series of grated gates which we were surprised to see already open, leading into a concrete box filled with red doors left ajar. As soon as our feet passed the threshold over a dozen pairs of eyes stared back at us, wide and scared. All were women, all were human, and all dressed in identical ivory, linen gowns. The faces that stared back at us told stories we couldn't imagine, although not a single one was marred by scars or bruises. They were well fed, well kept, and their ages ranged from young teens to some being at least forty.

My eyes met each and every one, my heart beat so fast I could hardly hear the questions they asked, but my excitement turned to dismay as I realized Katie was not among them. They paused only briefly before running down the stairs towards us, so many voices rose at once, before they were lulled into silence by the sound of nearby gunfire.

Jax pointed down the hallway, "Follow Wren, she'll get you guys out."

One of the women stepped forward, "There's another group of us in the block over."

Jax nodded, "I'll get them."

Another group? I almost jumped at Jax, trying to wordlessly convey my need to be the one to get to them, but he was having none of it. He held me aside, his voice heavy with conviction as he convinced me that we would be lucky to have five minutes before the Aerendor showed up. I surrendered to him easily, if Katie was in that other group, I only prayed Jax would be able to find her.

I dawdled only long enough to see him disappear down another hallway before turning my attention to the group of girls watching me intently. Their wide eyes were full of hope as I waved them all forward towards the hole in the wall. Lynn was waving frantically from the fence line and the women streamed out towards her. I waited as each one passed me by before moving out into the open. Lynn had already started moving the women on towards Sariah when a whistle sounded to my right.

A lone Aerendor stood mounted, silhouetted against a series of bouncing balls of light that cast an eerie glow within the fog bank. His eyes narrowed as his lips pressed against a wooden object, another whistle pierced the silence, all around us whistles answered back. He didn't move, his eyes fixated on me like a hawk just before it caught a mouse. The whistles continued, a haunting sound that chilled me to the bone. It oddly reminded me of a British hunting party sighting a fox—just before they released the hounds.

Jax appeared in the crater he had made, crying out wordlessly as something whistled by my face, crashing into the concrete with a sickening thud. I took a step back to gaze down at a long, metal spear. My brain caught up with my body as I made a mad dash towards the fence line. Lynn stood by the shed, ushering the last of the prisoners towards Sariah as she funneled them into the forest.

Another spear whistled by my face, the wind caressing my cheek before it crashed into the ground. I heard gunfire behind me as I watched Jax provide cover for the second group of prisoners which had just erupted from the prison to disappear into the fog bank. I knew I should have kept running, but I had to stay behind long enough to distinguish their faces. The fog had swallowed them whole. I watched a group of Aerendor emerge from the shadows, mounted on their horned steeds. A whistle sounded while their mounts reared and charged towards me.

I turned and ran, crawling through the holes in the fences and sprinting towards Lynn and Sariah, guns at the ready to give me cover fire. But the fences were enough to hold back the Aerendor as I ran through the door of the shed, Lynn and Sariah on my heel.

We quickly met up with the women in the forest, handing out extra packs and instructing them where to go if we got separated. Voices rose from behind and we turned to see the Aerendor emerging on our side of the fences riding towards the forest.

I looked desperately among the faces of everyone. Their expressions echoed the fear and adrenaline I felt. We couldn't outrun Them, and we all knew that. I pulled the gun out and looked at Sariah and Lynn. They both copied me and in unison, we aimed—and fired. The Aerendor's steeds reared up, snorting wildly as they scattered into the fog. We shouted for the women to run, Sariah leading the charge. They filed behind her, while Lynn and I held the rear. We couldn't help glancing back towards the prison, and the black smoke that rose high into the golden sky.

We jumped the train tracks, running through the suburbs towards the Rogue River. Someone had secured boats to the edge of the river, and we jumped aboard, sailing across to the other side to seek shelter in the forest. The moment our feet hit the Rogue River Highway we knew we had made it, but none of us were eager to dawdle. We took shelter in the safety of the forest, hacking and slashing our way through.

Time passed slowly, the smoke rising high into the sky above us. The forest thickened around us, towering redwoods and pines smothered by a thicket of bushes and ferns. We came to a stop, we realized then our mistake. We couldn't see anything beyond what was right in front of us. We were an easy target. Old, gnarled trees we hadn't seen on our journey to the prison suffocated the air around us. Sariah pulled the group together and we drank from our water bottles, everyone silent—we were on edge, jumping at the slightest sound.

We heard it at the same time, brandishing our guns towards the wild fervor coming through the underbrush. Deric and Asif burst from the forest, soiled by dirt and blood, they looked relieved when their eyes met ours. Deric ran forward and hugged me before turning to everyone.

"We met Jax on the way down with a group of prisoners, there's a whole battalion coming through. His group and Michael are going to swing more westward before heading south."

"Have you heard from Juan or Ashlyn?" Sariah asked quietly.

Asif and Deric shook their heads.

"Let's get everyone to the school first, before we ask more questions," Lynn said promptly, ushering the women to their feet.

It wasn't long before we were found, dazzling balls of light illuminated the fog around us. We instinctively froze, but it was too late. Spears whistled past, striking trees and dirt, sending us into a panic. Chaos ensued as everyone ran into the heart of the woods, the fog swallowing them whole. I found myself in a thicket with Lynn by my side, and two other women. We ran vaguely southwards, the sun had been swallowed, choked by smoke and fog, its light unable to guide us as we stumbled blindly through the forest.

We burst into a small clearing where a yellow house sat abandoned, caressed by weeds. A chicken pen occupied the backyard, a frenzy of feathers lay heaped before a hole in the wire. I grimaced, pausing at a metal gate as the girls and Lynn ran past me. A branch snapped as two Aerendor rode out from behind the house, their steeds tossing their heads, the antlers glinting in the unnatural bobbing light that floated nearby.

Run.

The girls saw Them almost as soon as I did. We backpedaled into the forest, jumping off the crudely beaten path to carve our own throughout the underbrush. We hoped their mounts would find difficulty in navigating the thick flora that sprouted around us, using that to our advantage. I slowed myself, taking a moment to catch my breath. The blood rushed through my head. My heart felt like it would leap from my chest if given the chance. The bush beside me trembled, and I saw his golden eyes as he tackled me to the ground.

Struggling with him atop me, as soon as I pried my arm free, I aimed at his chest and pulled the trigger. He slumped to the ground with a thud as I sprang to my feet, trying desperately to catch up with the others. My eyes darted to every shadow, every leaf caressed by a gentle breeze—one more Aerendor ran free through the forest. I could hear him, somewhere to my right, but I could not see him. I kept my eyes on Lynn's back as she chased after the two women we had found ourselves with, her gun poised as her eyes nervously scanned the forest.

We burst out onto a dirt road the same time the Aerendor did, he held his spear aloft at Lynn and just as he pulled his arm back a gun shot rang out and the Aerendor fell to the ground. Behind him, at the edge of the forest stood Juan, his left arm hung limply at his side, a gun in his other.

"Juan!" I cried out. He nodded weakly, slowly ambling toward us.

Lynn ran towards him. Ignoring his protests, Lynn tossed his arm unceremoniously over her shoulder, propping him up with her petite frame. We slowly continued through the forest along the dirt path. There was no way to know if the way we were headed was the right one, but one way or another we knew we had to just keep on moving.

We were exhausted; we still had plenty of food and water but after we drank and ate our fill the fatigue took hold. The adrenaline had subsided, we were running on fumes, making it hard for us not to stumble on every loose rock and tree branch. After a short while the dirt road dipped, and we found ourselves deep in a forest of conifers and oaks. The underbrush was near impossible to hack our way though, and the fog had yet to abate. My arms burned with every hack of the knife I wielded to make the descent through the forest easier for Lynn as she half-carried Juan. The girls who walked beside us were quiet, their gazes solely focused on putting one foot in front of another. They were traumatized, and I couldn't blame them. I didn't know how much more I could handle myself. Our progress was painfully slow, and my movement became sluggish and uncoordinated.

Until, mercifully, we stopped. I had been so focused on placing one foot in front of another I hadn't looked up, and as soon as I did a wave of emotion hit me. I didn't know if I was in shock or locked by fear, but in that moment, I knew I felt both. Standing before us swathed in an ebony tunic that was such a stark contrast to his ivory hair, his waist adorned by glinting silver blades was Vaelythor. His golden eyes were sharp and bright, focused solely on me, his familiar green cloak with that mystical crest fell from his shoulders.

I tried to push past the others, but Lynn didn't give it a second thought as she raised her gun and took a shot, everything in my being stilled as I watched. In the blink of an eye Vaelythor dodged the bullet and rushed her, disarming us of our guns and allowing them to disappear into the underbrush in a single swoop before separating me from the others.

"Run!" I yelled at them, pulling the knife from my pocket. I angled around to put as much distance between him and the others.

"Wren, you can't—" Juan tried to say feebly, but Lynn nodded, her face tight as she forcefully dragged

Juan away. The two women watched for just a moment before Lynn ushered them onward into the forest, they disappeared like shadows into the fog without a glance back.

I didn't know what he wanted, but I knew what I did. I didn't want to talk; I didn't want to play his silly game. I rushed at him, taking a swipe with my knife. He easily dodged me. Again and again, I ran at him, and again and again he dodged each swipe. I yelled out in frustration as I ran at him again. Now I feigned left and pushed forward, tackling him to the ground and rolling into a ditch. I immediately raised my knife, his hand shot up—grabbing my wrist, and in the blink of an eye I was on my back as he towered above him. His grip was strong, absolute, and I cried out in anger, trying feebly to free myself.

Something happened I did not expect, his eyes widened as the leaves and rocks floated around us, the sound hit a moment later. The forest exploded, a bomb had been set off somewhere. Black smoke quickly mingled in the air as trees fell and flames licked the dry trunks setting the forest ablaze. Gunfire sounded nearby. Vaelythor leaned over me and the ground shook again due to another series of explosions, one after another.

The forest floor beneath us moved and I watched as Vaelythor fell into the yawning darkness below. My last-ditch effort at survival allowed me a moment's grace as I gripped the root of a tree, suspending me above the chasm. I cried out for help, my ears ringing, the world was just a blur of dust and debris. A vibration rattled through my very bones as a sharp pain exploded in my stomach, a wetness spreading through my shirt. I flinched, unable to suppress myself as I tumbled into the darkness. Hitting every root and rock on my way down, I fell further into the abyss, surrounded by smoke and fog. Consciousness fettered and I used what little time I had left awake to watch as a crimson flower floated by on the breeze.

CHAPTER
Eleven

Cold.

Damp.

The smell of earth, the taste of copper, warmth spreading from my abdomen, as it emerged it began to rapidly cool and solidify. A hard, unmovable mass that tugged at my raw flesh. I shivered; my breath tight in my chest—the pain was excruciating. It took everything I had to open my eyes, to behold the predicament of whatever horrible fate was now before me.

But there was no light to behold, no world to interpret, the darkness was absolute. I tried to roll over, but a sharp pain shot out from my stomach and leg, and I cried out. A few feet from me a light emerged, dim at first, before it brightened and swirled.

An Aerendor light.

I sighed—this was it for me. They had found me, either way I was as good as dead. Several more dazzling lights joined the first until they had illuminated the entire area in a soft, creamy glow. Rocks above and rocks below, I was underground. Somewhere in the forest south of the prison lay the cavern I now found myself trapped in.

"We meet again, little bird," crooned a familiar voice from the darkness.

I spat into the distance, not knowing where he was. I was unaware of what injuries I had but I knew I couldn't risk moving. Whatever danger he posed to me meant nothing, I was unlikely to make it out of here alive. I knew it the moment I felt the pang in my abdomen it could only be one thing: I had been shot. By whom, and why, was anyone's guess. Was it an accident? A bullet gone astray? Or was it meant to spare me from the fate of becoming Aerendor property? I supposed I'd never know.

Pebbles shifted nearby as Vaelythor crawled into the light, gently cradling his left arm. Even in the light I couldn't see the extent of his injuries, but I knew it wasn't the only one he had. He crawled past me, laying down to my left so I could see him. I watched him closely, my eyes narrowing as he procured my backpack from the darkness.

I glared as he pulled out my water bottle and brought it to my lips. Shoving his arm away weakly, I turned away.

"Now is not the time for games, human," he said tersely, bringing the bottle back to my lips.

"Who's playing?" I asked acidly.

He was resilient, forcing me to open my mouth and accept the water. I drank it angrily, my throat burned, and my head ached. I could barely keep myself awake as he propped my head up with a spare jacket from my bag. His eyes roamed over me, no doubt taking in my injuries.

"Why are you humans so stupid?" he asked, his voice tight in frustration.

"It was worth it," I replied weakly.

"Was it?" he remarked, pulling my jacket from my shoulders and going over the cuts and bruises on my collarbone and arms. His left arm sat in his lap as I watched his eyes tighten, I wasn't the only one in pain.

"They're free now," I said smugly, I felt hollow as I tried to bring as much stale air into my lungs as I could.

I saw him frown, his golden eyes darkening. He waved his right hand over me before resting it on my forehead, "You're cold."

I snickered—what would he care? I shivered, trying to shake his hand from my head. He awkwardly unclasped the cloak from his shoulders with one hand and draped it over me, tucking it in at the sides before muttering a word under his breath. It was a gentle whisper that instantly spread warmth through me, just enough to rouse me slightly.

An eternity seemed to pass before he noticed me move my head to look at him. "I see you have been busy since we last met. Did you find what you seek?"

My heart skipped a beat.

Katie.

Some irrational part of me tried to jump to my feet and I cried out in agony, clutching my stomach as I curled into a ball on my side. Vaelythor moved to my shoulder, trying to pull me onto my back, I was far too weak to resist him.

Before I could understand what he was doing, his hand had pulled back my shirt, the blood separating with a sickening wet plop. I cringed, trying not to call out as he gently poked and prodded the small hole in my abdomen.

Those golden eyes darkened, "It seems you are more injured than I originally thought."

"Hardly seems problematic for you," I replied simply.

He bared his fangs, and my heart stopped as I winced in pain. He glowered at me, placing his hand over my wound he gently pressed down, I squirmed in agony as blood oozed over his fingertips.

"Just kill me!" I cried, tears rolling down my cheeks. My breath came in gasps as I tried to get him to release me.

"No," he said tightly.

"What do you get from letting me live? The torture?" I glared at him defiantly. "That's it, isn't it? This is all some sick game to you." It had to be. The reason that other Aerendor had mentioned, maybe he wasn't so different after all: not a killer—but a torturer.

He leaned menacingly over me, "Do not presume to know me, human."

"Then why won't you let me die?" I asked pathetically.

He regarded me, and for a moment I thought he'd finally answer that question that had been plaguing me since I met him. But he leaned away to prop himself up against the rock next to me and stared up at the small stalactites that hung from the ceiling.

Time seemed to move immeasurably, hours or minutes could have passed as I drifted in and out of sleep. I felt that call of the void, at the very fringe of my existence, beckoning me to my demise. I stubbornly held on, my body growing weaker and duller as time ticked by. I despised the situation I was in, to think what could easily be my last moments alive would be spent in a pit under the world with this creature as my only company.

"Are you awake?" he asked gently.

I nodded my head weakly.

"That bullet is festering your blood, if you don't want to die, you'll need to let me remove it," he said.

I heard him fishing around in my backpack and pulling something out, a pop later and I could smell the sweet, irresistible aroma of canned peaches permeating the air around us. My eyes shot open and I watched hungrily as he fished a peach out with a fork and held it over me. I leaned forward to grab it and he pulled the peach back.

"Let me remove the bullet, and I'll let you eat," he said.

I glowered, the hunger and humiliation enough to make me momentarily forget the pain I was in.

"I can turn it into a game if you'd prefer. For every question of mine you answer, you will be rewarded," he smirked.

I glared at him, but the peaches called to me, and I was far too weak to think of any rebuttal, so I curtly nodded. I'd be lying if I said I wasn't worried about what information he wanted, but no matter how hungry I was I wouldn't tell him about the group, about the prisoners, about the elementary school, about Katie. I knew deep down, as much as I despised the circumstances—letting him help me now was the only chance I'd get to see Katie again. I still had hope that she was in the second group with Jax, and I wouldn't know unless I let him remove the bullet.

He seemed pleased with my response and leaned closer, whispering indistinctly, the orbs floated towards me, suspending themselves over my abdomen. He leaned over and began to gently press around the bullet hole, no doubt trying to find where it was.

"What is your name?"

I frowned, trying not to wince with each prod. He watched me carefully, his eyes smoldering. I sighed, I'd humor him, "Wren."

He stopped prodding me long enough to fish a piece of peach from the can, placing the bite in my mouth. I devoured it instantly. As he went to ask another question, I held my hand up and he paused, waiting.

"What is your name?"

He smiled, answering instantly, "Vaelythor."

I nodded, my eyes trying to focus on something—anything. I watched the depths within his eyes twist and twirl, transfixed. He put the can down to prod some more, his hands pausing. I felt it as soon as he did, he found the bullet.

"Where are you from?" I couldn't tell you the relief I found myself feeling, that he would attempt to distract me with such trivial conversation while he did what he did.

"Cave Junction."

The orbs swirled slightly as he pulled a knife from his waist, the blade sparkled in the light as if imbued with tiny specs of glitter.

He nodded, "The town I first met you in?"

"Yes." I gasped as he gently pushed the blade through the bullet hole, a cold sweat broke out across my brow as I tried to remember how to breathe.

"Your arm is better?" I cried out, I had only now noticed he was using both his hands, and I struggled to focus on anything but the pain.

He nodded and without missing a beat asked, "How long have you lived there?"

I knew the answer, and yet it took me so much effort to answer through the pain that seemed to have seized my entire body.

"My entire life."

I stopped him, this was my chance to have my questions answered, "Where are you from?"

He deliberated for a moment. When we first met Them, when communication was being established— there was very little they shared with us. As far as I knew we were never graced with the name of their country, their people, their world. But our leaders, the ones we relied on to protect us—they didn't seem particularly concerned at the time. Everyone jumped at the opportunity to meet *aliens*, but who could blame them? We had finally done it, answered the age-old question that had plagued humanity since the beginning—are we alone?

"My people hail from a world much like your own." He whispered something under his breath as he pushed the knife in just a little bit more. "I miss staring up at the night sky, the moons comforted me."

"It sounds pretty," I said, simply. Just like before, his people dodged the question, the only hint I got was the presence of multiple moons.

"Your turn," I breathed. The world around me seemed to slow as I focused on each breath I took.

"True." He thought for a moment, "What did you do for entertainment?"

"Before or after the end of the world?" I asked sarcastically. I didn't expect him to reply.

"Both."

It was getting harder to be angry with him, I really wanted that—to maintain that dignity, that anger. But even as I lay there in agony because of him, I couldn't. "Before...I liked going to the museum, the gardens, the zoo. I liked watching, I liked the serenity, the learning."

"What are those? Museum? Zoo?" He slowly began guiding the bullet towards the tip of the knife. I could feel every movement, no matter how gentle he tried to be.

"Museum, it is—*was,* a place where the knowledge and history of humanity was stored. You could see artifacts from old civilizations or creatures that once existed but no longer do."

Even mentioning it now, I could almost smell the musty, brightly lit white halls of the California Academy of Sciences in San Francisco, walking up and down it with my camera and group of friends during the summer. I couldn't count how many times we made the trip down south just to see a new exhibit.

"And the zoo—it's where you'd go to see animals from all over Earth, ones you probably would never see in your lifetime otherwise." Although I'd been dozens of times to the one in San Francisco and Eugene, Oregon, with my friends, whenever I managed to go alone was my preferred option. I often found myself sitting in front of any random exhibit for an hour or more just watching the animals play with one another.

"Where I am from, museums sound very similar to our Archive Halls, and zoos are very much like our Menageries. Although neither of them is open to just anybody." He nodded at the can of peaches on the ground, but I shook my head.

"Knowledge is power," I said simply.

I watched as the balls of light brightened slightly before returning to normal, then Vaelythor slowly flexed his left arm, only slightly wincing. It must have still hurt, and yet he was trying so hard to ignore his own pain to save me from mine.

"Are you healing yourself?"

"Yes," he replied cautiously.

Interesting. Was it that they had regenerative qualities like a lizard re-growing its tail, or was it tied to this mysterious power they seemed to have? "Is it difficult to do?"

He thought for a moment, "Sometimes. Depends on the circumstances."

"How do you do it? It's not technology, I don't care what you sold our politicians," I added the last part quickly. I was in pain and I was at his mercy, the least he could do was tell me the truth.

He smirked, "Your leaders were always rather easy to manipulate. No, it is not what your kind considers technology." He flexed his left hand and his skin began to glow dimly, the veins from his fingertips to his wrist shone in an eerie bioluminescent glow. "It is…an energy, we learn to harness it, to mold it, from a young age. Our world is alive with it; it hums in the air, breathes in the sea, toils beneath the ground."

He looked around the cave, "Your world has it too, it's—*different*. Harder to control. Here it is wild, untamed, and your people have smothered it for too long."

"It's magic, then," I said simply.

He made a face, "I remember another saying something similar—I suppose you could akin it to your ideas of magic."

A hot searing pain erupted from my abdomen as he used the distraction of my reverie to pull the bullet from my wound, letting it clatter to the ground. I cried out, choking as a sob rattled me. The orbs circled around me, one illuminating my sweat-soaked face. His eyes narrowed as he washed his hands clean of my blood with the water from my bottle.

"I need to close the wound." His words sounded powerful, "But there is only one way."

I felt the tang in the air, the energy coalescing around him. But he waited, he paused.

"What do you need to do?" My thoughts were jumbled as I quelled the panic attack that was threatening to overwhelm me. I couldn't help the shivering, the very quaking in my bones. I was panicking, I was in shock.

He placed the back of his hand against my forehead briefly before slipping a hand inside his vest, a dainty silver chain was grasped firmly in his fingers. He watched me intently, dangling the bauble above me. At the end of the chain sat a wire cage shaped like a teardrop enclosing a swirling iridescent gem. The orbs moved with precision, surrounding the amulet. Their light seemed to be absorbed, coalescing within, casting a cascade of shimmering colors across the cavern walls.

"It's simple, little bird. I need you to wear this."

Mesmerized—almost hypnotized, I reached out my hand just to pull it back, "What's the catch?"

He cocked his head sideways, "Catch?"

"Don't be coy with me, what are the conditions?" I said, annoyed.

He smirked, shrugging, "Only that you have to wear it until you have healed, or you will undo all that I have done so far to save you."

"Why can't you simply heal me with your magic?" I asked incredulously.

He regarded me a moment, choosing his words carefully, "There are rules to magic as there are to technology. A delicate balance must be struck, if you teeter too far, you risk throwing yourself off the edge."

I deliberated for a moment, it had to be a trap. There had to be something else. Somehow... "Do I have to be *claimed* to bear this token from you?" There was venom in that word, unavoidable and not unwarranted.

He noticed, but chose to ignore it, "No."

"What is it anyway?" I asked, reaching my hand out to just barely touch it. The light still bounced around the walls, like a shimmering parade of jewels. It was beautiful, a sight that I could not honestly say I had ever seen before. It was almost enough to make me forget the pain, the blood pooling around the hole in my stomach.

"An amulet. It has been in my family for a long time," he shrugged.

"An heirloom? I don't want to take a precious family jewel from you—" He held up his other hand, stopping me.

"If that concerns you, simply return it to me when you have healed." The kaleidoscope of colors burned so bright, beckoning.

I weighed the pros and cons, considered the debt I would have to incur to save my life. But was I not already in his debt, several times over? "What will it do to me?"

"It'll give you the same healing properties I possess," he flexed his arm to show me.

I sighed, "What even is the point?"

He frowned, "The point?"

I shifted, releasing the weight of the stones pressing into my back, "Of prolonging this life."

He pulled the amulet back from me, the light around the room shifting as he knelt beside me. "Your people need you."

Now it was my turn to frown as I tried to consider the meaning behind his words, "What do you mean?"

"I know they mean something to you," he said nonchalantly.

I scoffed. "They survived before me; they will survive after."

Darkness gathered at the edge of the lights, shadows shifting across his face, as if he held some inner dialogue between good and evil. "We know your people are at the school."

A small spark ignited in my very core—the *school*. I looked up at him, fear erasing the pain and little rationality I had, "You knew?"

He knew I feared, he watched it plain as day on my face, "We were happy to let you keep that location, but your attack today cannot be overlooked."

"Please," I begged, my voice cracking. I didn't care how pathetic I seemed then, all I cared about was that they could be saved. "Please, warn them, help them get away. They don't deserve this—"

He shook his head, "I can't do that. Only you can."

I balled my hands into fists, holding back from letting out the anger. The hatred, the raw uncontrollable urges that would end in regret. It wasn't his fault, he didn't have to tell me, he didn't have to save me. And as much as I hated to admit it, he was right. He couldn't save them. The memories of that group flitted by in hasty images: Jax making me food the first time I met him, Sariah in the garden at night; they quickly morphed into memories of my family: my mother and father serenading one another in a vain attempt to lift everyone's spirits, my sister—

"Katie," I whispered, and I instantly regretted it.

Katie.

She was still out there.

"Wren."

I heard his voice, but I couldn't see him as I lost myself in the memories of that night, I found her wandering the road. "Let me save you, so you can save her," Vaelythor knew what he was doing, he knew what strings had to be pulled, and I hated him for it.

The dilemma that yawned before me was a simple one: reject his help and maybe I survived, maybe I walked out of this cave to wander the woods until I died of sepsis. Or accept his help, survive, find Katie and the others, live the rest of my days content that I did all I could for them and accept the price that had to be paid later. If I died, that would be the end—but I wouldn't be at peace. I didn't even know if Katie was with Jax's group, I didn't know if she was safe. I had promised her, if I hadn't seen her that day on the road—if I hadn't known she was still alive, I would be so content.

I could die.

But I couldn't now, could I? Not just because of Katie, if what he said was true—everyone we just liberated, was in danger. All this could have been for *nothing*, and now I was given an opportunity to fix it.

To save everyone.

"Vaelythor." I hated the way his name sounded on my tongue. I extended my palm, "Save me."

He dangled the amulet over my palm, slowly dropping it to rest on my skin. I felt that electricity, the tang in my mouth, the energy coursing through my veins. I could feel the pain receding as whatever power Vaelythor now wielded took hold within me. The light the amulet had cast upon the walls disappeared, the jewel in the silver cage shimmered before dimming as the orbs that hung in the air between us drifted to different corners of the cavern.

For that instant where the amulet had just touched my palm, I felt as if a veil had lifted, and a voice softly called through it. I strained, trying to discern what that sweet, honeyed voice was saying. It disappeared as soon as it had arrived, the darkness swallowing it whole. I shook my head, convinced I had imagined it.

I clasped the amulet around my neck, releasing a deep breath I hadn't noticed I was holding.

Minutes passed as I felt a surge of warmth spread through my veins, my very soul. I felt myself becoming me again—*becoming alive*. I stared up into those golden orbs that were so intensely focused on my broken body. They flared with such an intensity, I was lost in the fieriness, my mind overcome by the energy that flowed through me.

"I can breathe," I whispered, my fingers gingerly poking my stomach. The hole was still there but the bleeding had stopped, the pain had ebbed, and my body somehow felt whole again.

"You will be okay," he said to me, standing up to look around us.

A sweet, sticky aroma called to me and I glanced down at the open can of peaches beside me. Not sparing a second thought, I devoured the rest, my parched throat and empty stomach momentarily soothed. Without the burden of pain and hunger, I gingerly staggered to my feet. Holding my hand against the wall until I caught my bearings and surveyed the cavern. In the corner where Vaelythor had ventured was a slit in the wall big enough for a person to walk through, and as I approached, I felt it—a cool breeze. Wherever it led, there was an entrance that would bring me topside, bring me back home.

"You coming?" I asked as I entered the tunnel, the orbs of light bouncing around me. I heard him murmur something as his shadow loomed over me.

We walked for what could have been hours or days, time meant nothing in the darkness under the earth. The orbs bounced along the tunnels as I followed the cool breeze. Vaelythor walked quietly beside me, not a word exchanged between us.

It was hard not to consider him almost human in the light. His expressions were like ours, his mannerisms, if not for the pointed ears and unusual ivory hair I wouldn't have been a fool to consider otherwise. But soon enough it was easy to see the difference, where he had yet to break a sweat, where his feet had yet to stagger, his posture yet to slouch—I had begun to tire.

"Perhaps you should rest," he said.

I swayed, catching myself on the wall of the tunnel. There seemed to be no end in sight, the breeze had marginally become more noticeable as we went on, the size of the tunnel narrowing and widening. Debris momentarily halted our progress. Still the only light I could see were the orbs that floated around us, the world above knew nothing of the world below, and there was no way of knowing where the tunnels led.

My body might have healed to where I could ignore my injury, but my mind had not healed. Mentally, I was exhausted. *Just a few more steps, just a little while longer.* That's what I kept telling myself as I put one foot in front of the other. But there was only so much you could take, before you fell to your knees in the dirt.

"Maybe I should," I said begrudgingly, pushing my pack up against the wall of the tunnel and leaning on it.

Vaelythor sat a few feet away, watching me.

"What?" I asked.

"I'll stand guard, if you want to sleep." The orbs that hung in the air above us slowly dimmed, and I watched as they swirled slowly above me. They were hypnotic, calling to me.

He was right, I should sleep. My eyes did feel heavy, darkness tugged at the edge of my vision. It would be so easy—so simple, to just close my eyes for a little bit.

CHAPTER
Twelve

I drifted listlessly in a brightly lit world, aware of the crunching of leaves beneath my bare feet and the gentle caress of an invisible wind in my soft, unbound hair. Sunlight warmed my face, the sweet scent of honeysuckle lingered in the air and yet—through all the sensations, there was nothing for me to behold. My eyes were shuttered to the calamity, my brain held me in a dreamlike state. I could feel another world tugging at my senses, begging me to come back.

Is this heaven? I asked the abyss, not expecting an answer.

No, child. The abyss answered.

My mind felt foggy, the light slowly fading from an intense orchestra of golds and oranges to the dull pastels of a summertime meadow.

It is time to return.

Wait! I called out, I tried to run towards the unseen voice, but I didn't move. I couldn't move, I was unable to do anything, except throw my thoughts out towards whoever it was that accompanied me in this strange place. I felt the presence waiting, *who are you?*

It chuckled, a beautiful soothing sound.

We will meet soon enough.

The golden hues flickered, and poof—darkness, and silence.

I felt his arms slowly release me, I knew straight away who it was, as my back was placed amongst the leaf litter. The ground was warm, comforting, the sweet scent of the dirt enveloped me as a gentle wind blew strands of my hair across my face.

Weakness still gnawed at my very soul; my eyes were unable to open. This time the darkness did not demand my life—but simply my consciousness. Boots shuffled around me, disturbing the dirt, the sweet smell of petrichor filled my lungs. The creaking of the trees above were suddenly interrupted as another set of boots shuffled across the leaf litter. They paused several feet away, and I could feel the unseen eyes on me, watching me.

Vaelythor didn't seem too concerned with our intruder as he patiently listened to him speak in a hushed, hurried tone—a sense of urgency underlined the words I could not hear. Vaelythor knelt beside me, his hand gently brushing the hair from my cheek. A streak of warmth followed, and I rolled my head to follow, my eyes blinded by the light as I tried to look up at him. I had so many questions, we were above ground—somehow. He had carried me from our underground prison, he had saved me again. My hand went to the amulet around my neck.

"You're safe, little bird."

My mouth felt numb, my throat dry, as I tried to rasp—tried to beg, for him to stay. I had too many questions, he couldn't leave now. He couldn't.

"Wait!" I struggled, squinting into the bright midday sun.

His companion's footsteps began retreating as Vaelythor whispered in my ear, "Your people will be here soon."

I reached out with my hand, grasping his boot, "Thank you." They were the only words my mind could string together.

I could feel the tensity in the air as he whispered, "You have a job to do now, Wren of Cave Junction." I heard footsteps in the distance, the crunching of leaf litter, and snapping of branches. Voices rose and fell, their words indiscernible. "We will see each other soon enough, little bird."

Before I could muster the energy to respond the boot beneath my hand withdrew. He and his companion disappeared into the forest, leaving me alone in the dirt. The voices in the distance grew closer, more urgent, calling. The snapping of branches as boots stomped through the underbrush paused briefly in the dirt a little way from me. I heard the sharp intake of breath so clearly as a familiar masculine voice called out my name. He sprinted towards me, sliding into the dirt to scoop me up in his arms.

"Wren, you're alive. She's breathing!" He yelled out, rocking me back and forth.

I think I managed to smile as I replied, "Nice to see you again, Jax."

His breathing was erratic, and his heart sounded as if it would beat right out of his chest; he cuddled me close. Several other people came crashing through the forest, breathing heavily, as they slid in beside us. Their voices mingled to one, it was hard to discern anyone except Jax.

"She's still alive. She's breathing. We have to move her now, quickly!" A swarm of protests from the others but Jax clearly was having none of it as he scooped me upwards and picked his way through the forest. I struggled to open my eyes against the mottled light I could feel bathing my face, but they refused, and I lay there limply in his arms listening to the world around us.

"Sariah is going to freak when she finds out," Jax said into my ear.

A smile spread across my face, my eyes glistening as I imagined what had been going through Jax and Sariah's minds while I was gone. I had promised her we'd be alright, that neither I nor Jax were going to leave her. A pit formed in my stomach as I imagined what she must have gone through. I didn't know where I was, how long they had been searching for me, or if the prison break was even successful. I froze—the prison. The entire reason I was even here, that I nearly died.

"Jax?" I croaked, my voice felt weird—unusual, as if it didn't belong to me.

His gait didn't falter as he leaned closer. "Where is she?"

"Who?" His brows furrowed and he leaned back.

The shadows of the trees melted away, and the full warmth of the sun lit my face and warmed my body. The sound of stampeding feet rushed towards us followed by voices raised in concern. Jax called out, but his words were as indiscernible as those who now crowded around us. Whatever energy I had managed to grasp to stay conscious was slipping away.

Now that I was safe, now that I could hear the happy voices of my own people, that I knew they were alright—it was safe for me to slumber. The last thing I remember before I embraced that tug of mercy was the caress of a warm blanket across my chest and a soft hand gently stroking my cheek.

"Are you awake?" The words roused me from the absolution of my dreamless slumber. My eyes fluttered open to behold soft beams of light shining through the open window, illuminating the bouncy charcoal curls and golden freckled skin surrounding the wide, sincere smile of Sariah.

Her caramel-colored eyes immediately teared up as she held herself back from everything she wanted to say, instead simply saying, "Hi."

I couldn't help but match her smile as my eyes began to water. "Hi."

She let the tears slide down her face as she embraced

me in a hug that was a little too tight, a squeak escaped me. She jumped back, wiping the tears from her face with the sleeve of her sweater, "I'm sorry, I'm sorry, I'm just so—you don't understand! I was so worried, they told me you, I just, you understand, right?"

I nodded my head sympathetically, grasping her hand with mine. "I'm here now, Sariah. I don't plan on leaving again any time soon."

"Don't even think about it, because I certainly won't be letting you out of my sight again!" She pouted.

We both smiled at each other like idiots, but her mood suddenly changed as she glanced around at the empty room we were in. "Wren, you've been gone awhile. Lynn said she saw you—and those *creatures* were right there. And then the bombs."

A knock sounded at the door as Ashlyn entered instantly, Deric hot on her heels with a plate of food. He placed it down on the table beside the makeshift bed. They both glanced at Sariah, obviously indicating she should give us space, but Sariah was having none of it, ignoring their looks and subtle hints.

Ashlyn's smile was forced as she looked me up and down, her eyes belying her true feelings. She was wary and I could see the hidden questions forming in her mind. Deric tried his hardest to look anywhere but at me and resigned to picking at a loose thread on his jacket.

"Sariah," Ashlyn started, but Sariah shook her head, her curls bouncing defiantly.

"I already know what you're going to ask her, so just do it," her voice was almost laced with venom, and I couldn't help but flinch. A lot must have transpired while I was dying in a hole in the ground, because this was not the Sariah I knew.

Ashlyn sighed, wiping the sweat from her brow, "Listen, I'm not going to beat around the bush, Wren. We're all happy that you're alive and well, but," she looked me up and down, "I need to know what happened out there."

Deric took a step closer, his head hung solemnly, "That explosion...we lost a few people, some of the women we saved. You were in the middle of it."

"Those monsters slaughtered us like pigs, and we didn't kill a single one," Ashlyn ground out. "Guess they figured if they couldn't have the girls then we couldn't either."

"The gunfire, you didn't kill any of them?" I asked.

Ashlyn shook her head, "It was supposed to just be a distraction, to draw their attention."

I felt sick. We had lost people. The very people we went out to save.

"Did we lose anyone, from the group?" I barely choked out the words.

"Asif is in critical condition," Ashlyn said with little emotion.

"He was so stupid, that dummy. He drew an entire squad out into the open to buy you guys more time," Deric sighed.

My head swam with the images of those women, clad in their white linen robes; they no doubt thought of us as their saviors, the cavalry that had come to spare them from the hands of our oppressors. But that wasn't what had happened. So many of them had died and it was all because of us. I didn't even take a moment to consider the repercussions of what we had done; I don't think any of us did. I remembered what Vaelythor had said: what we had done could not be overlooked. We weren't safe here, and They knew exactly where we were. Could I trust him, though? Trust that he was telling the truth? He had saved my life, multiple times now, for reasons I still had no answer to. But last time was different. I was dying, teetering on the brink of darkness, and he had brought me back so I could help my friends. Whatever true motive he had; it couldn't be all that bad.

"I'm sorry Wren, but I need to know what happened," Ashlyn said, interrupting my thoughts.

Sariah rolled her eyes, but bit back whatever it was she wanted to say.

There was no way I could tell the group what had transpired between the Aerendor and myself. I would be killed on the spot, the animosity the group now held after their losses, they would think I had been turned. No, I'd have to lie—but I'd have to stick as close to the truth as I could. I glanced at Sariah, before taking a deep breath. Not to mention the one thing that had been in the back of my mind the entire time, who had shot me? Was it a mercy bullet? Or was it to insure my death? Was that why Ashlyn was insistent on my side of the story?

"I don't remember much." Memory loss wouldn't be hard to fake, and believable with an explosion that big. It was the best thing I could come up with on such short notice.

"I know…I was in the forest, it was Juan, Lynn, and two of the girls from the prison, I don't know their names. Juan was injured, there was an," I caught myself before I called him an Aerendor, and part of me for a reason I could not fathom, felt uneasy calling him anything other than what he was, "one of those creatures cornered us. I told them to run, I stayed behind."

Deric nodded, "Not just any, it was one of their royals. He's basically a prince. You stood before the highest-ranking creature we've seen, and you lived to tell the tale."

"A prince?" He'd said it before, when we were at Lake Selmac, but it was still hard to comprehend. That explained their concerns. So, they were suspicious of me, thinking I had been claimed. "Juan? Lynn? The girls. Did they…?" I couldn't bear to finish the question.

"They're here, they're safe," Sariah reassured me, taking my hand in hers. I smiled up at her, relief spreading through me.

"I remember the explosions; it wasn't just one—there were several. The ground disappeared. Next thing I know I woke up in the forest and Jax was there."

Deric and Sariah exchanged worried glances, before

they turned their gaze to Ashlyn.

Ashlyn's gaze hardened, "You've been gone nearly a week, Wren."

I couldn't contain the intake of breath, or the confusion riddled across my face as the impact of what she said sunk in. *A week.* There was no way I traveled those tunnels beneath the earth for almost a week. I absently fingered the amulet around my neck, they hadn't removed it. No wonder they were so suspicious, but no one mentioned the gunshot.

"A week," my voice drifted.

"You don't remember anything else? No weird dreams? No voices? You were still wearing the same clothes you had left in that day. Jax carried you here, you were covered in dirt and blood. There's no way you survived almost a week without food or water unconscious in those woods." I could see all the different scenarios playing out behind those dark, pensive eyes of hers.

"I know what you're saying, Ashlyn, I really do, but I have no other explanation for it. I don't know what to say or even what I can do to convince you otherwise, but that's all I remember."

"Come on, Ash, we'll have time for this later. We have a lot we need to get done," Sariah said quickly, glancing outside the window.

Deric nodded, "The new girls are still being rather difficult and we're really short on supplies. We can't have a scouting party, supply run, guards, and then having to worry about one of our own being a spy or whatever it is you're trying to get at."

Ashlyn glowered at him. She glanced back at me, "Sariah, I want you to stick with her for now. But we need you two up and ready to help the new girls."

"The girls." I nearly jumped out of the bed. Everything I had been fighting for, sacrificing for.

The three of them looked at me curiously as I limped out of the bed and down the hallway, Sariah hot on my heels.

"What's going on, Wren?" she called, worried.

"Where are the new girls?" I asked breathlessly, fatigue gnawing at me.

"Uh, they're out on the blacktop. Juan and Deric installed a new pump so we could wash clothes."

I was at the doors to the playground, yanking them open only to be blinded by the sunlight basking me in warmth and a gentle breeze that brushed the leaves from my path. I strolled forward to behold six women bent over a basin filled with soapy water—their hands tirelessly scrubbing at the dirty clothing soaking within.

They all looked up, bewildered. I searched every face, my heart clenching tighter and tighter, the last girl didn't meet my eyes as I ran towards her, pulling her back as her golden hair fell from her face. Sariah ran up beside me, a hand on my shoulder as I finally let out the breath I had been holding.

"She's not here," I said, defeated, the girl staring at me in confusion.

"Who?" Sariah asked. "Who are you looking for?"

I shook my head solemnly, "It doesn't matter."

She wasn't here. Maybe she was never at the prison to begin with. I took a step back, taking every ounce of energy I had to remain standing as my world came crashing down. All the struggles, the hardships had led here, to this single moment in time. She was supposed to be here.

Unless...

She had been.

I didn't even want to consider what that meant. My heart felt as if it would shatter—what if she was one of the few causalities Ashlyn had mentioned, what if we had freed her only for her to lose her life when we fled. I froze, my world continued to crumble around me. There were only six girls here—*six*. There were what, over a dozen, maybe two? At the prison, we rescued so many women, and out of them all, there were only six left.

"Wren Delilah Harper. The last time I saw you cry was because of that asshole, Jake," said the most familiar voice. I spun around immediately, "when he broke up with you."

Her soft, fine golden hair delicately framed her sharp cheekbones, bangs gently hugged her brows, trying to hide her sharp turquoise eyes. "It was a stupid reason to cry back then, and you probably have an equally dumb reason to be crying now."

I didn't even breathe as I launched myself at her, squeezing with all my strength; I let the wracking sobs take control of my body. I lost it. I didn't care what anyone thought, I didn't care. She was here, she was alive, and she was just the same as the sister I had known.

"Katie," I wailed, pressing my face against her shoulder. She gently stroked my hair, a smile playing about her lips, her cheeks held a rosy tint as I knew she held back tears. She wouldn't cry, and I didn't expect her to. She was always stronger than me, stronger than our mom. She was very much like our father, an unyielding force that didn't have time to be emotional, she always thought everything through before she committed to it.

"I was wondering when I'd see you again," she said simply.

I pulled back to look her up and down. Like the other women she wore that ivory dress that hung from her athletic form, and unlike me she had the body of a dancer. She had grown out of her baby fat long ago; I was stubbornly holding onto my lanky teenage form, even into my twenties, and chubby cheeks, no matter how hollow they were from malnutrition. But like all the other women from the prison, Katie was well fed—all of them had shiny, clean hair, their nails were immaculate, their skin unblemished. Not a part of them looked violated, as if they were treated like slaves.

"How are you…?" I wasn't sure how to word my question without coming across as if I were blaming them.

But I know the others from my group noticed, if not—they would soon. It wasn't something easy to ignore. While we defiantly fought against the Aerendor incursion, these women had been pampered. One glance and the stark contrast between the two groups was apparent, the weathered, work hardened skin and dirt smudged faces of my friends and the shiny locks, smooth-skinned faces of the girls from the prison.

"It doesn't matter, we're together again, and that's all that matters," she said hugging me close. I pulled back and watched her gaze trail to the amulet around my neck. An expression, so fleeting crossed her face—it was gone before I could decipher it.

A pit formed in my stomach. Before I could even consider asking further questions, Juan appeared from the hole in the fence line, his face grave. Sariah hurried past me, her fervent whispering back and forth and worried glances told me all I needed to know. Something was wrong. I pulled back from Katie's embrace as Juan jogged past us. Sariah called to me as she ran to maintain Juan's post on the other side of the wall.

I paused, my eyes on Katie, not wanting to leave her even for a second.

She rolled her eyes and nodded in Sariah's direction, "I'll be here when you get back. I promise."

Sighing, I joined Sariah at the other side of the fence, following her eyes to the upturned earth in the small path that encircled the school grounds. It took me a moment to realize what it meant, what it was that had gotten Juan all worked up: hoof prints.

I froze, as Sariah looked up at me. "These weren't here when we carried you in."

"There's no way Sariah. This is right against our fence line. We would have seen them or heard them."

The mounts the Aerendor use, with their giant antlers—whoever was on guard duty would have seen them long before they even got to the fences. We had cut the bushes out from the forest close to the fence line specifically for this reason.

"There were a few hours," she started saying, and I frowned, glancing nervously at the forest surrounding us—the light from the sun cast ominous shadows that could hide anyone and anything from our view. "When we had found you, everybody was up and running around. Maybe…"

There was commotion on the blacktop, and a moment later Jax, Deric, and Ashlyn strode out from the hole in the fence to stand beside us. Ashlyn knelt down, frowning. Deric did what I did, his eyes scanning the woods.

"How long has Juan been on guard?" Ashlyn asked.

"Twenty minutes, tops," Deric said.

Jax cleared his throat. "There are more tracks over here," he said, following the prints westward to the edge of the blacktop's fence.

"Let's not freak out. There's got to be a logical explanation, a wild horse. Deer?" Sariah squeaked.

That pit in my stomach suddenly got heavier as I

remembered the warning Vaelythor had imposed. We couldn't be allowed to get away with what we did, I thought we'd have some time—maybe enough for me to properly reunite with my sister and for everything to settle down.

"I'd like to consider that, but the fact of the matter is we just got Wren back and suddenly there are prints right at our borders," Ashlyn replied, her voice cold. "I want a scouting party established immediately. Deric, Jax, Wren," the look in her eyes was suspicious at best and a chill ran down my spine, "we need eyes on the encampment at Lake Selmac. I want to know what's going on. Lynn and I will scour the nearby homes; Juan and Sariah, you two stay here with the new girls."

A shadow by the hole in the fence loomed over us and we all turned to watch Katie walk towards us, her head held high, her eyes solely on Ashlyn. "I want to join the scouting party at Lake Selmac."

My heart skipped a beat, admittedly I was beyond excited that she wanted to join us. It meant that if something went wrong, we would have each other at the very least.

"I don't quite think—" Ashlyn started.

"No offense, but I oversaw the women when we were under Their control, I know what to look for. Am I wrong in my assumption that perhaps none of you do?" Her voice maintained that eerie calm she always had, she was a natural born leader, and I could read the emotions playing across Ashlyn's face like a book.

"Fine. The four of you grab your supplies, I want you out immediately."

CHAPTER
Thirteen

We decided to take a different route to Lake Selmac this time, Ashlyn was convinced now that we were being watched, and it'd be far too dangerous to take the same route as last time. We avoided going straight south like before; patrols might be scouring Reeves Creek Road and their presence would be hard to avoid on Lakeshore Drive. Instead, we avoided the roads almost entirely, except to cross at Parker Lane, jumping from house to house, everyone nervously scanning every nook and cranny.

At the edge of one of the houses' property lines we were greeted by a wall of spruce trees, a year of being left to nature had caused them to grow wildly, blocking our movement and our view. We paused at the edge, laying our bikes against the side of the house, before taking a moment to drink and pull out our binoculars to survey the surrounding area. Jax and Deric decided to risk scaling the side of the house to sit on the roof, their gazes drifting southwest.

"What do you know about the Lake Selmac encampment?" I asked Katie, trying to keep my voice low.

I wanted to ask her so many things, but in private—away from the watchful eyes and suspicious glances of the others. The safest thing I could do was ask something the others wouldn't think twice about, I knew they were just as curious as I was. Although I was certain they had already asked each of the girls about their time with the Aerendor.

It was odd seeing my sister dressed in jeans and a plain shirt, it was always a dress or a skirt for her, she loved the way they moved when she danced. But I was ready to accept anything other than those linen dresses the Aerendor had forced them to wear.

She kept an eye on the woods as she whispered, "They use the encampment to ferry supplies from the private airport south of here to their operations in Northern California and across the mountains in Klamath."

"Seems like an odd choice, I don't imagine it's that much more efficient for them?"

"They haven't established a foothold in Northern California or Southern Oregon, I suppose they assumed utilizing Grants Pass was the way to go," Katie shrugged.

It was an interesting theory, but it still didn't make sense. As Deric pointed out, they had royalty camped up here, not in one of their hotbed hubs like San Francisco or Los Angeles. But in our tiny county, and They were expanding north across the national forests.

We had assumed They weren't fond of the cold or the wet, but it had been a year since Their dominion over the world had become almost absolute. The internet, electricity, plumbing—if you didn't have a generator or were self-sustaining it had all disappeared by the time they had made landfall in San Francisco. So why would they only now be focusing on Northern California and Southern Oregon? It reminded me of the stranger I had met in Cave Junction, he did warn me that even the north wasn't safe from Them. Before even the radios rang silent, the farthest north they had established was Nevada and Utah—maybe what was left of humanity still lived normally in Washington or Canada? Russia could easily hold the last semblance of civilized humanity and we would be none the wiser.

"You guys need to get up here," Deric interrupted my thoughts, not taking his eyes off whatever he was intently focused on through his binoculars.

Katie and I scaled the house, perching ourselves precariously on the edge of the gutter, using our binoculars to see what had Deric so spooked. I didn't even have to zoom in to see what it was that concerned him so—from here the once-clear view across the wetlands to the lake was obscured by dozens of new spiraled buildings. The encampment was abuzz with movement.

Zooming in, I watched as what could only be hundreds of Aerendor moved through the encampment, all were armed, and some helped to set up buildings or moved supplies from the incoming boats to covered tents around the shoreline. Deric pulled my binoculars to the left slowly, where a group of a few dozen black-clad Aerendor stood in a uniformed line, their presence demanding as they stared dead ahead—waiting.

"What does that look like to you?" Deric asked.

"An assault force," Katie replied for me.

The three of us put down our binoculars to stare at her, she simply shrugged, "I've seen them before. They're what we would consider a SWAT team. They accompany the higher ups. When one of Them is threatened—they're summoned."

"How many times have you seen them?" Deric's voice was tight. It was easy to put two and two together, he wasn't subtle.

"Twice before, once when I was in San Francisco, during the initial assault." I remembered the day Katie got her acceptance letter to UC Berkeley. She was beyond ecstatic; dancing was her entire life and she had what it took to make it big.

"And the second time?" Jax asked.

"In Happy Camp, soon after."

My heart lurched. *Happy Camp*? That was six hours north of San Francisco. Why would she have been in Happy Camp?

"Is that where you were captured? You were in Happy Camp this entire time?" I couldn't help myself, I had to know, we thought we had lost her in San Francisco.

We mourned her constantly; Mom never came to terms with it. If Mom and Dad had known Katie was a mere forty miles away, on the other side of the border, we would have never stopped looking. She was so close this entire time, and my mother and father died thinking their eldest was long gone.

"When we were told to evacuate after what happened in Los Angeles, a few of my sorority sisters convinced us to hold out at one of their parents' houses. We thought we'd be safe in little Happy Camp, a town that small couldn't mean much to Them."

Her face seemed so—impassive. As if what happened couldn't be helped, as if she had come to terms with her fate. It was the first time since seeing her again where a part of me became concerned that maybe I had lost the big sister I once knew. War changes people, I knew that just as well as everyone else here—but beneath our dirt smudged faces and oily, unkempt hair—deep down we were still us.

Deric leaned forward, his face inches from Katie, who refused to budge, "So why are you telling us this now, when Ash asked you the same thing a week ago? Multiple times in fact."

"Deric!" I exclaimed, annoyed.

"I know she's your sister, Wren. That much she has told us. But neither she nor the other girls have told us much. I'm even more concerned by the fact she has been with *Them* for what, a year now? You're telling me you've been with those things for an entire *year* and yet not once have any of you had anything negative to say about your time there."

I grabbed at his arm, trying to pull him back, "Deric, that's enough."

"No, Wren. In fact, it's actually really good that she begged to come with us. Because I will be far more lenient than the others—than Ash, or Lynn, for that matter." Katie raised her eyebrows, her form unyielding.

"Jax?" I looked to him in exasperation, it was bad enough Ashlyn was on the war path, but I couldn't be fighting everyone as the fragile peace our group had established crumbled once more. Whose side would I take? Whose side *could* I take?

"I'm sorry, Wren. He has a point." I could see the pain in his eyes as he reluctantly allowed Deric to continue.

I hated how right he was, and I hated how much— deep down, I, too, had concerns. They were right to be concerned about my absence for a week unaccounted for, but for Katie to be gone an entire year under the watchful eyes of *Them*—no, I couldn't blame them at all. Because I felt the same.

But something gnawed at me, and I let that little voice drift to the surface to be heard: if she was in Happy Camp, why would they transport her to Grants Pass? Why go through the national forests? And why go on foot in that small town north of Cave Junction?

Mercifully, a horn sounded in the distance and we instinctively flattened ourselves against the rooftop, our binoculars scanning the shore of Lake Selmac. At the very top of one of the spiral guard towers a lone Aerendor stood, a long blood-red horn draped in ornamental tassels in his hand, its sharp note bellowed out across the shoreline. Every Aerendor stood at once with their right hand over their left breast. They collectively turned to bid farewell to the group of elite black-clad soldiers as they began to depart the encampment.

"You see him?" Deric asked, scanning the encampment again.

"Who?" I asked, my eyes darting between every face. Was he looking for Vaelythor? He had to be here, a royal guard without the royal didn't make much sense.

"They stopped," Katie whispered.

We all turned to watch as an Aerendor dressed in a charcoal robe and fitted forest-green vest with a golden belt around his waist strode towards them shouting orders. My heart lurched as I beheld his flowing black hair—it was Raekhan.

"It's the Hunt Master," Jax said, his voice cold.

I heard the sharp intake of breath beside me and glanced over at Katie. She had such an intensity in her stare, as if pained. She refused to take her eyes off him, following his every move—her body tense and rigid against the shingles.

What did he do to you? I felt sick remembering how he had approached me in the town north of Cave Junction outside the motel.

"We need to go now, if we move fast enough, we should be able to beat them to the school," Deric said, jumping down from the roof and grabbing his pack. Jax followed soon after, but my eyes never left Katie.

"Wren, come on," Jax said, waiting for me as Deric strode towards the next house—scouting ahead. I nodded at Jax, making my way off the roof.

I turned to follow him, but Katie hadn't moved at all, her gaze still rest southward. I hissed at her that we had to move, *now*. She slowly lowered her binoculars, sliding off the roof beside me as we hastened our steps towards Deric.

As Jax and Deric disappeared around the side of a shed, I noticed Katie stop dead in her tracks, removing her binoculars from her pack to stare through the last opening in the trees towards the encampment.

"Katherine!" I hissed, running back to tug at her arm.

She shrugged me off, her body rigid. I tore the binoculars from my pack and followed her gaze. The guard had mounted themselves on their horned steeds, Raekhan at their head. She was unmoving, unyielding, her mind in another world.

"Katie, what's going on? Did he do something to you?" I felt disgusted asking, we were almost certain we knew what They did to the humans they kept.

The men were either enslaved or murdered, and not a single woman I had seen under Their care didn't look well cared for. The women outside Cave Junction, the ones in the prison, the girls who stayed at the school—their hair was shiny, long, and flowing, their skin was blemish free, nails immaculate, and always dressed in clean, well-made clothes.

I lifted my binoculars again, as the guard slowly left our view Raekhan paused, pulling his mount around to face our direction. The hairs on the back of my neck stood up as I watched him turn his head to stare right at us. Startled, I dropped my binoculars to look at Katie—and I regretted it. My entire world stopped as I saw the tiniest smile that lifted the edges of her rosy, pink lips.

She lowered her binoculars without a word, tucking them into her backpack before following Deric and Jax. I cringed at the eerie thoughts that began to cloud my mind, racing after her. I tried to ignore it, I tried. But I could not ignore what I had just seen, what she had just let me witness.

"Katie?" My voice was barely a whisper as I followed her.

Katie dodged me at every step as I tried to separate her long enough from Deric and Jax to ask what happened. But it would have to wait for now, because as we rounded the corner we collided with Deric and Jax who immediately pulled us down to the ground next to them. Directly in front of us, across Parker Lane where we had to cross to return to the school was a group of three Aerendor.

They weren't clad in black, rather—they were adorned in the usual riding leathers, daggers at their waists, gloved hands tight around the reins of their mounts. We sat there in the bush across the road, watching, waiting.

Why where They here? Could they have been the same ones that left the hoof-prints by the school? If so, that meant we were followed, or at the very least being watched. They probably followed our footprints this way and lost us when we crossed the road.

Deric poked each of us, tilting his head northward. He obviously wanted to go around them. We couldn't risk wasting such valuable time, especially not with Raekhan and the royal guard on the way—everyone we left behind was in danger.

With exaggerated slowness we backed up to the other side of the shed and made our way across Parker Lane, bursting into a sprint as we cleared the long grass to the other side. Each one of us glanced back, waiting to be caught. But there was no one there, no pounding of hooves, no shrill cries. We moved as fast as we could, following Deric as he led us around and across Davis Creek Road down a beautifully overgrown road smothered by the overhanging branches of elderly oaks.

At the very end of the lane, a forest rose to choke our path. It was impenetrable, we had no choice but to go around. This route was infinitely slower, but it was safer—the Aerendor's mounts would have no way to navigate the tight spaces with their horns and we'd be hidden from the major roads. We knew it'd take at least an hour before we would emerge somewhere behind the school. Especially since we had to abandon any chance to retrieve our bikes.

The world was eerily quiet as we neared the school, our senses on high alert. We didn't give ourselves the chance to breathe an audible sigh of relief until we made it to the fence line and Juan's smiling face poked out to greet us.

We mumbled our hellos, rushing to Ashlyn to report our findings in the conference room. Every map that choked the table before us was smothered in pins and rocks denoting important information such as safe houses, depleted houses, resource dump locations, and last known Aerendor camp locations. She made quick adjustments from our reports.

I noticed Lynn was present, standing behind Juan's protective bulk; she cast quick glances at me. Sariah stood next to me and on her other side, Katie. She was quiet, lost in thought, her eyes avoiding mine. My heart beat erratically, my hands shaking, there had to be a reason— *any reason*, other than the one prevalent in my stupid head right now. I was in chaos, wondering if my sister was a double agent and if Lynn's reaction was because she was the one responsible for shooting me. It was hard to hear anything over the constant roar inside my mind.

"Wren?" Ashlyn asked.

I looked up at her, confused, "Yes?" Glancing around the room I noticed all eyes were on me.

Michael scoffed, "Get your head out of the clouds, girl."

Ashlyn ignored his comment, repeating what she had said, "Can you and Sariah round up the girls?"

Sariah was already at the door, looking at me. I nodded at her, casting one last furtive glance at Katie. Her circumvented gaze told me everything.

"While you were gone, Ash had us collect everything we had and keep them in go bags in the storeroom. I

229

think she anticipated this," Sariah whispered. I could tell she was scared; I couldn't blame her—I was scared too, perhaps more so than her. She didn't know about Katie, and she didn't know that someone from our group shot me.

We found the girls in the cafeteria, calmly discussing siphoning some of the coconut oil to help keep their hair shiny. I frowned, holding myself back from berating them for such a careless thought. We weren't rationing yet, even with the extra people, but soon we might have to flee with whatever we could carry, and I knew there was no way we could bring everything we had stored here. But I had more pressing matters to concern myself with.

I never really paid attention to the girls before, all I had cared about was Katie. When I looked at the six women sitting on the benches before us, I noticed something. It wasn't just that they all had long beautiful hair and dressed identically in those harsh white linen dresses—they were all around the same age as Katie. She would be turning twenty-six this year, in the autumn, and each one of these women were closer in age to her, than me. And they were gorgeous, tall, athletic, their very beings could have been torn from the pages of the Iliad.

Sariah waved to the girls, "Hey, so earlier today Ashlyn came and talked to you about us maybe having to leave. Well unfortunately the time has come, so if you guys can grab what you can from the gymnasium and meet us at the storeroom as soon as possible, that'd be great."

I tried to contain my smile; Sariah made everything a suggestion rather than a command. But the girls seemed to collectively agree to what Sariah had said, they stood up and exited without a backwards glance.

I watched until the last girl left, "Do they seem odd, to you?"

She took a deep, shaky breath, "I didn't want to think about it, honestly. They've been through a lot and I've just tried to put myself in their shoes and think about how I would react if the same had happened to me."

I couldn't really argue with that logic, but it didn't make me feel any better. Every part of me was screaming. You know when you have that gut feeling that drowns out any other feeling you have? It was trying to tell me I was right, that there was something to be worried about—but I just didn't know how worried I should have been.

Fifteen minutes later, everyone was fitted with a pack and whatever additional supplies they could carry. I looked from face to face as Ashlyn outlined which houses we were going to hit first. Ashlyn, Deric, Michael, Jax, Sariah, Juan, Lynn, myself, Katie, and the girls whose names I didn't yet know—stood in a circle on the blacktop, rummaging through our packs and confirming whatever Ashlyn called out from a ragged list she had stuffed in her jacket pocket.

"Alright, this is it everyone, we can't take any more, not right now anyway. We could possibly come back later to get the rest, but for now we must make do with what we have. We have enough canned goods to last each of us a few weeks if we ration. As for bullets, we're going to have to do the same. We don't have much, so if you have to use your gun, make it count."

She hoisted her backpack over her shoulder, tucking her gun into the back of her jeans. We all mimicked her before walking out into the alley along the fence line, pausing as a familiar voice called out.

We all turned to see Asif leaning against the fence, his face haggard, his skin sallow. He did not have long; it was clear to everyone the wounds hidden beneath his clothing would prove fatal. But it was wrong, so very wrong—I couldn't believe I had forgotten about him, the injuries he had suffered for us to live, for my sister and the girls to be free. I had been so distracted by my sister I hadn't taken a moment to remember the people who had made that possible. We all crowded around him, murmuring, Ashlyn placed her forehead against his.

"Thank you, for this," she whispered, her voice hoarse.

We said our goodbyes, and we meant it. We knew that's what it would be—a goodbye. We would never see him again, and as the others moved ahead of me, I took a moment to loiter to say my farewell.

"The gift you have given us, given me," I shook my head. "You gave me my sister back, and I can never repay you for that." A life for a life. "Are you sure you can't come with us?"

He smirked, "We didn't get much time to get to know one another, you and I. But I admired the strength you had to survive as long as you did, by yourself. It mustn't have been easy, and I don't know if I could have done it."

I shook my head, ready to interrupt him, but he held up a shaky hand, "No, listen. I want someone to know this. The group doesn't know, day that I met them, I know no one told you, but they found me in a house they were raiding. It was my house, the house I had grown up in. It was just me then, and only me. My sister had just died, in the next room, she couldn't take it anymore. I was sitting there, Wren, in the living room—with a gun in my hand. The gun she had used to kill herself. I was going to do it, even though she begged me not to follow her. I was going to do it."

He swung his arm up to cover his mouth, coughing violently, shoulders shaking as he pulled his arm back— blood soaked the sleeve of his jacket. "Ash convinced me to live. If they were an hour earlier, my sister would have been alive, too. I have carried that weight this entire time, but I am ready to see her again, to see my parents again, too. I don't regret my decision, Wren. You get to see your sister again in this life, and I get to see mine in the next."

I stood a moment, memorizing his face—the tired brown eyes, the shaggy black hair, the way when he smiled the right corner of his lips would raise higher than the left. He was right, we didn't get the opportunity to get to know one another, but if there was one thing I could do for him, it was that I wouldn't forget him or what he had done. I embraced him firmly, letting out a deep sigh, there was nothing that could be done except let him have his dying wish.

I walked away; Asif's face the last thing on my mind when a gun shot rang out into the silence. I flinched, he knew what he was doing, using that gun to end his suffering—and give us as much time as possible as every Aerendor in the area flocked to the school. He could finally have peace, and we got to keep our freedom.

Pausing at the gap in the fence line, my eyes narrowed in on a fresh pile of dirt behind the shed. I hadn't given it any second thought, the fate that would befall the Aerendor prisoner in the classroom. I knew he wasn't their first captive; I remembered that mass of graves when I first came to this school. I wasn't okay with the idea then, and even now it still didn't sit right with me. But it was the most likely outcome, he knew too much about us, his freedom would mean our enslavement.

I caught up with the others quickly, falling into stride beside Sariah. They tried to ask what had happened, but the tears in my eyes told them enough. We continued on, the plan was to hit one of the stash houses southeast of us in a nearby campground then continue southwards. Unfortunately, Juan and Deric were quick to report back: it was too dangerous to consider going east near the town or south back towards Lake Selmac. That left either traveling west towards Redwood and Wilderville or north, into the middle of Oregon.

Everyone was quiet as we followed single file through the unkempt properties in a southwestward direction. It was dangerous going south to begin with, but we figured if we avoided Lake Selmac by staying primarily west, avoiding all the roads we could, and never allowing more than one person to cross at a time, we would be safe. If we really were being watched Ashlyn would break off to taunt them long enough for the rest of us to escape. It was a horrible idea to consider, leaving one of our own—*again*, but I couldn't argue with the rationale she had. She always thought of everything, considered every possible scenario; she was in the military before the world went to hell. She knew what was required of a leader, she knew what sacrifices had to be made, and I was inclined to listen without question.

We finished crossing the last road before the first stash house, Ashlyn called everyone back to huddle together in the thick bushes at the very edge of the property. Deric volunteered to run out to check the surroundings, make sure it was safe enough for the group to approach the house. We couldn't be too careful, there were fifteen of us now and doing something as simple as moving made us extremely vulnerable.

He had been gone five minutes before rushing back, eyes wide as he ushered us to keep moving south. Ashlyn looked at him questioningly, but he shook his head—his eyes relaying what he would not verbalize.

As we picked our way through the forest, Ashlyn marked the stash house with an x and showed us another house on the other side of the 199 that had three check marks against it—meaning the last three times the house and surrounding area was checked it had been clear. But we learned it wasn't that simple as the highway yawned before us. We stopped at the edge of the comforting shadows the trees cast. Our eyes collectively scouring the empty road. Not a soul in sight, not a sound to be heard, the sun shone brightly, but barely brushed the tops of the trees behind us. Twilight was fast approaching.

We took the moment to take a drink and rest while Ashlyn obviously grappled with the idea of letting us risk crossing the 199 in the light or wait until dark. I had too much time to think of things—to let my mind wander. Katie sat with her group of girls as they silently drank from their water bottles, eyes occasionally glancing up to sweep the woods nearby. Michael sat at the edge of the group, shaking his head as he stole glances at the girls nearby. Deric and Ashlyn sat far enough away from the group that we could not hear them as they poured over the map, pointing and looking around us for landmarks. Jax and Sariah had taken a seat beside me, passing a piece of chocolate between the three of us. Sariah smiled up at me, her hand gripping my knee in support. She could tell I was worried, but she had no idea the worries that plagued my mind.

Thankfully, mercifully, Ashlyn and Deric wandered back to the group before the worst of my inner monologue could take hold and derail me into a nervous wreck. They both knelt beside us, pulling out the map again to go over the route to the stash house on the other side of the highway.

"We decided as soon as the sun is fully behind those trees, we are all—as a group—going to make a run for the tree line. Juan and Lynn went on a scout of the surrounding area and unfortunately those creatures are heading right for us, if we wait until nightfall, we might end up surrounded. We can't defend ourselves here in the open, we have a much better chance if we make it to a house."

I hadn't even noticed Juan and Lynn had disappeared, my heart lurched slightly thinking about the fact that they could have been in trouble this entire time and none of us had noticed. I glanced at Jax and Sariah, who looked equally concerned. Katie came forward and put her hand on my shoulder.

She turned to address Ashlyn, "We're ready."

The girls stood in a circle, turning in anticipation when my sister approached them. You could almost compare their wide eyes to sheep greeting their shepherd. More things I wish I didn't notice; it was making it hard not to come to conclusions or think anything but ill towards my sister. After I had just gotten her back, after a year of thinking she was dead—thinking I had no family left. But no, now was not the time nor the place to be thinking the things I was. Our very lives were at stake, I could afford such irrationality when we were safe and sound.

Ashlyn was the first to run out across the highway, leading us in a mad dash towards the tree line. Every person that made it turned around to watch the others, our eyes scanning even the skies for the slightest hint of trouble. But there was nothing, only the birds and wind to comfort us. We moved through the trees, that opened into the backyard of a large house. As one unit, tightly packed together shoulder to shoulder, we followed the fence. Juan broke off from the group to investigate the house, Michael took up the rear, his gun raised high. A few minutes later he had rounded the other side to meet us by the driveway, shaking his head. The house was either empty or held the remains of the last occupants. It wasn't worth the risk.

Ashlyn nodded, ushering us to follow Juan as she walked beside Michael, her eyes scanning every nook and cranny as we scampered past. Occasionally one of us would bend over and grab something that looked useful. It amazed me that supplies still littered the properties and woods, but I wasn't one to pass up good luck when I was given it. Sariah found a derelict can of pineapple that was somehow magically still within date (according to Jax, and I wasn't entirely sure how he knew what month it was let alone day) and Deric who found several unused bungee cords.

"Where is this next place?" Sariah asked, breaking the silence.

Juan unfurled his map again, checking a nearby street sign as we maneuvered around a fallen tree, "Just up here."

I breathed a sigh of relief, the nerves of moving everyone at once with Aerendor on our tails didn't make for good serenity. We stopped outside a small blue house with a large fenced-in yard. It sat further back on the property line from the road, giving us great views of the surrounding area. Although the trees were fewer here, we were secluded—sheltered.

Juan jumped in through the back window while we waited outside, our eyes and ears straining. There was the shuffling of feet from within, a simple click and the front door opened. We rushed in, immediately throwing our packs on the floor in the living room and mercifully resting on the sofas and chairs.

Ashlyn walked up to where Sariah and I sat at the dining room table, "I need you two on guard duty for a few hours."

With binoculars, canteens, and a small drawstring bag in hand, we went outside to see what we had to work with. Although the house was small, the property was large enough that the previous owners had decided to have their very own vegetable garden, complete with a fenced-in chicken coop. Sariah went to investigate the garden while I scouted the coop. I smelled it long before I saw it. That undeniable stench that permeated the air. The decomposing corpses that lay atop one another, the bones haphazardly jutting out of the mud, a fate that had befallen so many of our beloved pets. I didn't need to see any more.

"Wren, I need help! There's so much," Sariah called out, running up to me. I followed her back to the vegetable garden, not as hopeful as she was. It was hard to not be so cynical all the time, but nowadays I found it easier to think the worst than the best. Besides, there was more of a chance she'd found enough food for one or two people, hardly enough to feed us all.

"Wow," I said simply, surveying the out-of-control garden.

Without the tender green thumb of whoever had lived here maintaining it, nature had taken control and vegetables had grown uncontrollably, riddled with weeds. Lettuce, spinach, kale, cabbage, carrots, leeks, onions. There was so much. In the raised bed nearby was a simple herb garden saturated with thyme and basil, oregano and chives. There were even poles bending under the weight of an assortment of pea plants. We loaded as much as we could into our bags until they threatened to burst, I handed mine to Sariah, telling her to relay the good news.

After all, we were supposed to be on guard.

I waited for the door to shut before I continued my walk along the property. There was a small man-made pond in the back paddock, probably made to feed whatever animals had once occupied the space. Luckily whatever they were, they had managed to escape the confines of their prison. It brought me some solace, finding torn down and broken fences in paddocks. I tried as hard as I could to imagine the animals out in the world exploring and living life unfettered.

They were unclaimed, just like us.

The sky darkened above as the sun disappeared, making it harder to pick my way across the paddock. Somewhere in the distance, a dog barked, and I instinctively felt for the cool, hard plastic grip of my gun. I hated them: *guns*. I hated the fact they existed and hated the fact that at the end of civilization I was beyond grateful that I had one in my hand.

A twig snapped in the darkness, a soft voice cowered before a deeper one, I instinctively flicked on my flashlight—shining it into the trees. Michael stood hovering over one of the new girls, her disheveled black hair tumbled across her shoulders, one of the straps of her tank top was hanging limply at her side.

"Jesus, Wren. Chill, you nut, it's just me and sweet little Marie!" Michael grumbled; his hand grasped firmly around the girl's wrist.

"What's going on here?" I looked between Michael and Marie.

Marie's eyes were wide, red-rimmed, as if she had been crying. She begged me with those eyes, those wide scared eyes. I took a few steps forward, my flashlight focused on where his hand still gripped her wrist.

"It has nothing to do with you, so if you could kindly fuck off," he growled, raising his arm to shield his eyes from the light.

"Marie?" I asked, my other hand hovering over my gun. Her mouth moved over and over, repeating the same phase. My heart lurched when I realized what she had said, what she kept saying.

Help.

Michael took a step towards me, his bulk shadowing Marie as she tried to pull herself from his grasp. I raised my gun, pointing it towards him.

He snorted, "Like you're going to shoot me." He closed the gap between us, the gun against his chest. "Do it, I dare you," he taunted, pulling Marie's arm upwards. She cried out, panicking, struggling in his grip.

Trying to find the conviction to pull the trigger, my hand shook, and Michael laughed, "Pathetic. Run along now, and your pretty sister won't be next."

He threw Marie to the ground, unbuckling his jeans as he stood over her. I cocked the gun, ready to pull the trigger—but I didn't have to. Another shot rang out, and Michael slumped to the side, hitting the ground with an audible thud.

Marie and I turned at the same time, Katie strode forward. The other girls stood behind her, the group behind them—everyone watching. She paused before us, helping to pick Marie up from the ground. She nodded at me as she walked past, the girls disappearing with them into the house.

Jax came up to me, his eyes questioning.

"I couldn't do it; he was right there, about to..." I couldn't even voice it.

He wrapped his arms around me, cradling my head against his shoulder. "We saw the entire thing, Wren. It's not your fault okay, just come inside."

I glanced at Michael's corpse, where it lay in the dirt. Ashlyn met us at the back door, placing a gentle hand on my shoulder, "Let him rot."

CHAPTER
Fourteen

I tossed and turned, until I was awoken from my dreamless slumber by a loud thud against the side of the house. My eyes were greeted by a flash of light in the window that disappeared as quickly as it had appeared. I pulled my jacket over my shirt and put on my shoes, flashlight in hand, and made my way to the back door. Everything seemed quiet. High above, dark clouds rolled across the sky, only letting the strongest of the stars shine through. On the ground, a slight mist had gathered in the paddock. Michael's body lay where we left it.

Everyone else was fast asleep, we had tried our best to forget what happened. To move on. Deric was assigned guard duty when he lost arm wrestling to Ashlyn, only after losing to my sister as well. I hadn't seen most of us laugh as much as we did at dinner. Sariah and one of the girls (Sophie, I think her name was, with the shorter blonde hair) had prepared the vegetables into a delicious skillet for everyone to enjoy. Marie had sat silently in the corner, surrounded by the girls.

I opened the back door to call quietly to Deric.

I repeated his name: once. Twice. Three times.

"Deric, now's not the time to be playing games," I berated the cold, still air, walking out onto the porch to glance over the sides.

As I descended the stairs, my eyes scanned the barely moonlit grounds as I rounded the side of the house facing my window. There was a shuffling of leaves, and the snap of a twig. I immediately turned my flashlight on.

"Stupid worthless humans, I knew he couldn't be trusted. Promised us women, and now he's dead. Pathetic." A stranger's voice barked out, "I guess you'll just have to join him."

"Help," croaked Deric. He lay on his back, his wide eyes begging, while an Aerendor in black clothing sat on his chest, his knee in Deric's neck. He was choking him.

I dropped the flashlight and ran at him, ramming the Aerendor with all the strength I could muster. He flew off Deric as we both tumbled into the bushes, branches snapped and tugged at me as I wrestled with an assailant I could no longer see. The shadows thickened in the shade of the trees. I could hear Deric composing himself somewhere to my left, coughing and spluttering as he tried to breathe.

I saw movement out of the corner of my eye and turned just in time to avoid something sharp and shiny whistling past my face. I surged towards my attacker, striking out before me, unaware of where he was—but I was desperate to avoid being caught unguarded. My fist collided with his face. I felt his knee rise to strike me in the stomach, sending me reeling into the dirt desperately gasping for air. He had caught me in the exact spot I had been shot.

A rough hand pulled at my shoulder, forcing me onto my back as I stared up into his golden eyes. That menacing snarl, tight eyes, bloodthirsty scowl I was expecting to see wasn't there—his brows furrowed as he stared at my neck in confusion. Releasing my shoulders where he had pinned me to the ground, his chest still heaving with the adrenaline as he glanced back at where Deric still lay coughing under the window.

Confident that we weren't going to be bothered and that I was unable to defend myself, he turned the intensity of his stare upon me. "What are you?" The agitation in his voice set a pit in my stomach.

"I've been claimed," I replied quickly. His reaction confirmed my suspicion that Vaelythor had done something to me. If he had lied and claimed me without my knowledge, I was in luck. No way would a simple rogue stand in the way of a royal's claim. Right?

Barely a whisper, he said, "You are not claimed." He pulled back, his eyes never leaving the amulet as I gently fingered it.

I wasn't claimed.

I was still me; I was still free. If Vaelythor really hadn't claimed me, then what had he done? What could he have done that would cause one of his own to react in such a way? Whatever it was that happened back under the earth, that mysterious voice that I heard when the amulet had touched me, that sultry siren in the world of blinding light—she had something to do with it. That I was now sure of.

"What does this mean?" I asked, my hand twisting the amulet.

He stood up, his eyes roving over me, perplexed. He opened his mouth to speak, and the shot rang out before his body slumped to the floor. Deric stood leaning against the house, a gun in his outstretched hand. I ran to support him before he collapsed, blood pouring from a wound in his thigh and from a cut above his brow. I wanted to be angry at his ill timing, but there was no better way for this scenario to play out.

"That was so fucking stupid of me," he groaned as I threw his arm over my shoulder.

We stopped at the backdoor when everyone else came running out with guns and flashlights. Ashlyn immediately grabbed Deric's other arm, dragging him into the living room to set him down on the couch. Sariah ran in with a bottle of alcohol and bandages, cutting open his pant leg to work on his wound. The blood had already begun to coagulate, I breathed a sigh of relief—an artery hadn't been nicked. He squirmed uncomfortably as Sariah took a wet washcloth and wiped away as much of the blood as she could.

"What happened?" Ashlyn asked, sending a sidelong glare at me.

"I got jumped," Deric answered, crying out as Sariah poured the alcohol over the gash in his leg.

"Convenient then, that you were there just in time," Ashlyn looked up at me.

"I saw the flashlight, I heard a noise—I went to check

it out," I muttered quickly. I didn't think I still needed to prove every little thing I did to Ashlyn, not that she was wrong for being suspicious. Apparently, I did have some sort of repertoire with an Aerendor royal, but that was another issue for another day.

"She saved me, Ash, chill." He groaned, "It was Michael, this entire time. It was him; it was his fault. He offered the creatures the women, *our* women."

Her lips puckered disapprovingly, but she dropped it, rallying Juan and Jax outside. Katie walked up beside me, a gentle hand grasped my shoulder and I turned to her, grateful for the support. From behind her the other women peeked sheepishly out of a doorway, their eyes wide—not in fear though, but in curiosity.

"Are you alright?" Katie asked me. Deric cried out, squirming from Sariah's not so tender prodding of his temples.

"I'm fine," I muttered.

"Can I see him?" she asked, suddenly.

"See who?" I was bewildered.

"The creature."

Why would she want to see the Aerendor? Why would she want to be anywhere near another Aerendor? That day by Lake Selmac flashed before my eyes, and I quelled it. I couldn't deny her though, not within earshot of everyone else without rousing their suspicions. It was bad enough that Ashlyn thought ill of me, and Lynn for that matter. If they were also to become concerned with Katie or any of the women who followed her...no,

I couldn't let that happen. I waved my hand dismissively towards the door. She left without a word, returning shortly after to retreat into the bedroom with her girls.

Once Deric had settled down Ashlyn gathered us all into the living room, pulling out her map. Juan and Lynn stood by the windows, their eyes glued to every shifting shadow.

She looked up at us, "I'll move his corpse by Michael's. He might have been useless to us in life, but in death the least that dick could do is buy us some time. Unfortunately, we can't wait until the morning, we must leave now. The next safe house is..." her finger paused on a small property at the edge of the national park, it was marked aggressively by a giant red X.

Ashlyn continued, pointing out three houses: north, south, and back the way we had come—west. "Obviously the west and east locations are compromised, we can't risk doubling back. If Michael really was in league with them, then who knows what he's told them. So, we either go north or south."

Deric and Jax looked over the map, both muttering the pros and cons of going either direction.

"We can't go north. We know they have hit the trailer park before, which means anything beyond that could be ripe with patrols," Jax muttered dishearteningly.

"But we haven't had a scout in the south for months," Deric replied.

"Well, it's only down the road, not even a mile," I replied.

I didn't know why they were insistent on staying in the built-up areas. If it were just me, I would have convinced Katie to come back to Cave Junction. We knew the ins and outs of that area, of most of the forest, and I was certainly confident in my ability to know every inch of the woods surrounding the Den.

"There are three houses on that property and a lot of open space," She replied. "It's really risky."

"How long until daybreak?" I asked.

Juan checked his watch, it was an overly complicated gadget that did more than just tell the time: he'd proudly announced the weather and phase of the moon with it before, as well as what direction we were facing. "We have three hours."

"It's cloudy, too, we may have extra time," Juan said. "That's two gunshots now, from this location. It's clear Michael told them about this house; they'll swarm all over here soon enough."

"He's right, it might bide us more time if it rains," Lynn whispered. I glanced out the kitchen window, even under the cover of the patio you could see the heaviness those clouds carried, the threat of rain. I knew better now, though, if the Aerendor really were determined—it wouldn't stop them from following us.

The furrowed brow, the puckered lips—Ashlyn was not happy with this plan. But what else was there for us to do? I wouldn't dare suggest heading to Cave Junction, I knew Lynn wasn't on my side, but now I was beginning to suspect Ashlyn might not be either. The property to the south of us backed up into the national forest that bordered Cave Junction if things didn't go well…at least Katie and I knew our way around those woods.

"Fine. Everyone packs up, we're leaving in thirty minutes. Juan, Jax, scout out the highway, I want to make sure we don't walk ourselves right out there into an ambush." Ashlyn went to distribute the fresh food into everyone's packs while Sariah and Sophie tended to Deric, discussing how he was going to be supported.

I disappeared to the bedroom, helping the other girls load their backpacks with the new food and refill their waters. Everyone was quiet, moving with speed but not efficiency. We were all exhausted and on edge, as much as we went through the motions—none of us really were trained soldiers.

Not even Ashlyn. She was in the National Guard, prior to a year ago she had never seen real combat, never had to shoot someone. Still, running this long on adrenaline and lack of sleep made everyone jittery and clumsy. A lot had happened in such a short time. We had to abandon the one place they had called home, a friend lost his life, and another had to have his taken from him. Everything that had led to this point flooded my already exhausted brain, distracting me. It took me several attempts to clip my backpack around my stomach. Luckily the blow from the Aerendor earlier hadn't reopened my wound, it was tender and would cause discomfort—but I would be fine.

We stood there in a row on the front lawn, watching as Jax and Juan returned. The coast was clear, as far as they could see, and we began our journey southward in the darkness. Even the stars above wouldn't guide us, as a low and heavy cloud system moved in, dampening the air. Our breaths grew heavier, and each one of us peered uneasily into every house and behind every tree we passed.

Rows and rows of trellised bushes dotted the field before us, remarkably nature hadn't reclaimed it too much, and we made the decision to cross rather than walk around it. Sariah raced to a nearby vine that grew out of bounds of the run-down wooden support that held it and began plucking the mystery berries that hung from it.

"Should you really be doing that? How do you even know what they are?" Ashlyn asked, watching Sariah drop one of the berries into her mouth.

"They're grapes, Ash!" She replied cheerfully, dropping another handful into her mouth.

"You're sure?" Lynn asked, gingerly poking the fruit on the vine next to her.

"I'd hope so," Jax said walking up to us, "Our grandparents owned a winery in Utah, it was part of their Bed and Breakfast."

Everyone seemed to have the same idea: we pulled out our small knapsacks, snapped off entire bunches of grapes, and filled them to bursting point. Whatever couldn't fit we would plop into our mouths as we began moving through the vineyard. They were juicy and sweet, perfect. A rare moment of peace. In the dark I could see the smiles on everyone's faces, even Marie perked up. Sariah and Jax playfully threw a few grapes at each other while Juan and Lynn straggled behind, feeding grapes to one another. Katie said a few words to the girls who followed her before leaving to walk alongside me.

"Do you remember when we were younger," she whispered into the night, her voice cutting across the marching of our boots through the soil and broken sticks, "when the rains would begin in the spring, Mom and Dad would drive us down to Napa Valley?"

A fleeting memory bathed in light, although it had rained every year we went. I remembered it all too fondly, my mother's golden wispy hair brushing her delicate cheekbones as a crisp wind would roll in, she would always shiver but insist on dragging us out across the different farms with a cardboard box to load with as many fruits as we could possibly pick. Dad would usually stand by the gate of the establishment talking to the owner, enjoying a cigarette while discussing the latest sports news. I always remembered glancing back at him, and he would be ready to catch my eye with a wave of his hand.

Daddy is always here.

That's what he would say.

Every time.

"Yes," I said, trying not to choke on the memory.

There was a reason I tried not to reminisce, why I did everything I could to fight the memories. Even such beautiful, joyful memories—all they were now was a distraction. An unnecessary pain.

"I haven't had grapes since the last time we went, before the shutdowns. The curfews, quarantine—before the world stood still." She paused to let the girls, Juan, and Lynn walk by before continuing her story several feet behind them, "That was the last time I saw Mom and Dad, too."

Ice had gripped my heart as I steeled myself for what was about to come. I could see the glistening of tears in her eyes. "We never stopped thinking about you."

It was the truth, but it felt—hollow. There was nothing we could have done, when the roads were blocked, we were stuck in Cave Junction, and she was in San Francisco. We tried to move on, to accept that she was most likely dead. Mom always carried her favorite photo of Katie with her, when she thought no one was watching she would take it from her pocket and stare longingly at it. I let her go to the grave with that photo, the only thing she had left. It was the one Dad took of the two of them on our family trip to a winery on her twenty-first birthday. I remembered that day fondly, because although I tried, my parents wouldn't agree to letting their sixteen-year-old have a sip of wine. A smile crept onto my lips as I remembered when Mom and Dad were distracted inspecting the wines on sale, Katie let me have a sip of her merlot.

"I don't blame you," she said, "any of you. There was nothing you could have done." She wrapped an arm around my shoulders, "If you had been there in San Francisco, or Mom or Dad—I think things would have turned out far worse."

I wanted to ask, I needed to know. I hadn't come across anyone yet who had survived the invasion in San Francisco or the annihilation of Los Angeles. But my sister had somehow escaped, and to Happy Camp of all places! But somehow, somewhere—she had ended up with *Them*.

"When did they die?"

I knew that question would come eventually, I feared for it every time she spoke to me. It didn't help stop or lessen the pain I felt when she eventually did ask. Another thing I had tried to forget, for both their deaths were painful memories I would rather have forgotten. I had numbed myself from the good for so long, it helped me almost forget the bad. The horribly unfair ways in which they had died, all the good they had done in life, everything that had made them who they were— wiped out in a matter of a few hours. In this world, there was nothing to leave behind to be remembered. Asif and Michael's corpses would disappear into the breeze, nothing left to tell anyone of the type of people they were, who cared for them, who hated them. Their accomplishments, and their failures.

"Dad died six months ago." It amazed me to realize how long it'd been since I left the Den, since I had left the graves of the only other people who meant anything to me. I'd been gone almost three months, so much had happened since then.

"Mother?" Katie pulled me back to look into my eyes.

I took a shaky breath, "Two months before that."

"What happened?" I saw a tear slide down her cheek, matching mine.

I pulled back from her gentle grasp, indicating that we should keep walking as the group began to pull too far ahead.

"Cave Junction was safe, for such a long time. There was a group of us. We decided to shelter together during the curfews. We modified the fences and roads, opening up our houses so it was like living in our very own gated community," I nearly trembled at the thought that the one place other than the Den in Cave Junction that I felt safe, the blue house at the edge of the river, almost became my undoing, "You remember Beth and Jack?"

Katie smiled, "How could I forget them? They were practically family."

Although they weren't—it never stopped us from referring to them as our aunt and uncle. We had known them our entire lives, Beth had gone to school with our mother and Jack worked with our father at the lumberyard. As soon as we knew the world was changing, Beth and Jack were at the door.

"Some other neighbors joined us; I can't even remember their names. I can see their faces and remember what jobs they had. Remember that one guy who would wake up at six in the morning every Saturday to mow his damn lawn and cut sheet metal in his garage?"

She chuckled, "Yeah."

"He was there, too, a police officer joined us later, Ron I think his name was?" We glanced both ways as we crossed the highway, the group occasionally pausing to look back at us. I waved them on.

"The first to go was perfectly manicured lawn guy— he died in his sleep." Ironically, for all the ruckus he had caused the neighborhood, he arguably had it the easiest of everyone.

"Do you remember how Beth would wake up every morning with her cup of coffee and sit out on the porch, reading one of her books, and Jack would sit out there with her, just watching the sun rise? One morning, neither of those happened. We waited; it was past noon before we went upstairs to check on them. We thought they had wanted to sleep in or needed some alone time. Hell, even Mom and Dad disappeared every now and then. It wasn't a big deal at the time. Until that cat lady, Mary, I think? She came screeching out of the bedroom."

It was so hard not to walk myself through the memories—to be back there again, "Beth and Jack were in their Sunday best, lying on the bed, a note on the nightstand. They had taken some pills. I don't know what it was, but they looked so peaceful, so serene."

"Mom took it the hardest, she barely smiled after that. That's when we noticed several of our neighbors had disappeared. Ron went to investigate, we all waited for him at the diner. That's when we saw *Them*, the first time I had seen an actual one. We were all as still as we could be. There were three of them, clad in their dark clothing, walking across the road, mere feet from where Ron hid. Mary though, her screeching would come back to haunt us. A spider of all things had landed on her, she yelled, ran out onto the street—all three turned. We lost four people that day."

"That's when Mom was injured." The moon twinkled above through a break in the cloud cover, casting a brief light in the utter darkness. The world was eerily beautiful as Katie and I walked side by side, the sounds of the wind in the trees and the relentless crickets that chorused on and on.

"We left the town. There was this cave on the other side of the river from the campgrounds, completely hidden. We turned it into our own camp. Ron, the police officer, he went to patrol one last time, see if there were any more survivors. He wanted to save everyone; he was such a good guy. A genuine person if I ever met one. He encountered a scout on the outskirts. He bled out in Dad's arms."

I was stalling, just for this moment. I steeled myself, "Mom died that night. She was so pale, and she shivered horribly. In the end, it was just us three. Mom's death broke Dad. I saw him cave in; he became a shadow of his former self. He barely ate, barely moved, all he wanted to do was chop those damn trees."

My throat threatened to close. The memories felt so fresh, so raw, so much more like it was mere days ago rather than many months. "He butchered so many in a fit of rage. He died two months later, in my arms, clutching his chest. And then I was alone, for the next six months."

Katie ran a hand through her hair, a veiled attempt at trying to disguise how subtlety she tried to wipe away her tears. We continued in silence for a few minutes before she spoke again, letting the weight of what I said sink in.

"What about Pippa?" I frowned, of course she would mention that dog, that impossibly loyal all the way to the end dog.

"Broke her leg three months in," I said dismissively.

It wasn't fair what happened to that dog. Her death was a stupid stereotype: dogs always had to chase cats, right? Right off the deck, that was all it took. She snapped the bone in her front leg. Dad didn't blink when he picked her up in his arms and took her out into the forest away from us.

A single gunshot shattered the quiet and stillness followed after. He returned for a shovel and then disappeared for an hour before coming back. The last image of her I had was writhing in pain in my father's arms, the pitiful whimpering as I knew what fate had in store.

Katie hung her head solemnly. As much as that dog had clung to Dad during our hikes, Pippa held a special place in Katie's heart. It was Katie who had found her wandering the highway. It was Katie who had taken her home, hiding her away in her bedroom while she came up with a story to convince Mom and Dad to let her keep the dog.

I had trudged myself through the thick mud that was my mind, bearing myself once again to still raw wounds. We arrived at the safe house, the group ahead disappeared down a driveway that edged the national forest. We walked in silence along the gravel, listening to it melodically crunch beneath our boots. Large paddocks stood on our right, although many of the fences were broken and decayed, open for the livestock to wander as they pleased. I could still see in the distance a herd of cows slumbering peacefully in the scattered moonlight. A few raised their heads to watch as we passed by, it had probably been a long time since they had seen a human. They were not bothered by our presence, choosing to return to their slumber.

Several of us broke off to investigate each of the three houses, settling on the one in the very back, the largest of the houses on the property; the shingled roof, which sat three stories up, was eclipsed by the towering trees whose lowest branches shadowed it. It was an older colonial—blue siding with white wooden posts, your stereotypical American dream home.

"Mom would have killed for one of these," Katie said as we stood by the front door, her hand gently stroking the curves in the beveled glass of the French doors.

"She did always tell Dad that if he died before her,

she'd take his life insurance and buy a colonial on a hundred acres in Colorado, so I believe it," I smirked.

There were enough rooms and beds for everyone, but Katie chose to share a bed with me. Even as kids we had never shared a bed, but she needed this as much as I did. The moment my head hit that musty pillow and I saw Katie breathing deeply beside me I was gone. Such a fierce and deep slumber overtook me, if I did dream— I would not recall it.

I rolled over into the sunlight warming the empty half of my bed, where Katie should have been. I tried not to panic, boots shuffled and pans clanged downstairs— I managed to convince myself to be calm, that everything was okay. She always was an early riser, and I was the younger sibling who slept in until lunch every day.

The moment I opened the door to the bedroom Sariah was there, "Wren! We have water! There are baths!" she exclaimed excitedly, grabbing my hand and dragging me through the house.

The easiest way to describe what she so excitedly called baths was a mudroom converted into what vaguely resembled a roman bathhouse. In the very middle of the room was a sunken concrete basin that would easily fit six adults, and the reason I knew that was because, ignoring my protests, I was unceremoniously disrobed and forced to be one of those six adults.

Water flowed from a pipe in the opposite wall, and although it wasn't hot, it mercifully wasn't cold either. Sariah and I sat there with four of the girls who clung to my sister like a queen. I never found the opportunity to get to know them. In the sunlight trickling through the skylight, I finally took a moment to relax.

We took turns introducing ourselves. The girl on my right was named Erin, gorgeous wavy brunette hair, dimples, freckles—she was soft spoken and shy. I had yet to see her keep eye contact with anyone. The girl next to her had jet black hair and impossibly clear skin—Seri, she was an exchange student at my sister's university. Next to her was a girl with the grace of a ballerina and the air of nobility, she held her head high, her shoulders back, shiny black hair was carefully given strategic blonde highlights that framed her face elegantly. Siham, she had come to the United States to be a doctor, as per her family's request. The last girl sat beside Sariah, her bright blue eyes rivaled even my sister's, but she had a fiery untamed crimson mane; Keira, one of the girls from my sister's sorority. She looked like she could have been Nicole Kidman's younger sister.

We exchanged pleasantries and stories of before the end of days, what we missed the most: from hair dye to nail polish, bread to ice cream, and cheese! I felt guilty, reminiscing of that day in the silo house north of Cave Junction, when Vaelythor had presented me with a tray of goods all the girls here longed for. Keira leaned over and said loudly enough for anyone outside to hear how much she missed deodorant, before glancing at our naked bodies and staring down at her own.

"Not to mention, a razor!" Erin blushed ear to ear at Keira's blatant digression, the other girls simply smirked.

Seri discovered a box of soap and shampoo, the conversation ebbed as we eagerly scrubbed ourselves almost raw. I lost myself to the sweet lavender-scented soap and rosewater shampoo, it was likely something the owner of the house had made themselves—in an unmarked white bottle that simple said shampoo and uneven bars that had the image of a flower carved into them—but I certainly wasn't going to complain. I couldn't remember the last time I had a normal bath like this, with soap and shampoo, and people.

We must have loitered a bit too long, as Katie and Marie appeared at the door with a few piles of fresh clothes for us to change into, beckoning us to the dining room for lunch. Once dressed in seemingly identical pairs of jeans and shirts we filed out into the dining room sheepishly. In the kitchen Lynn had managed to make everyone oatmeal with the grapes we had picked, bowls delicately placed on the island bench. I went to stand by the bay window, the view panned out over the giant redwoods, but the real star of the show was in the room itself: a piano.

Siham dusted off the seat and sat down, straight backed, her slender fingers lifted the key case to reveal pristine keys underneath. Without pause she slowly began playing a soft, lilting melody. She was the picture-perfect example of poise and elegance. She wore the same clothing that we all did, yet somehow, she made the jeans and a shirt look sophisticated. Her body swayed gently as she played, her eyes closed, a ray of sunlight pierced through the cloud cover, illuminating the room.

It was surreal, how clear and beautiful the sound was—some of the girl's eyes began to water as we sat there in silence, bowls of oatmeal in our hands listening to Siham finish her song. That sound, something I had always taken for granted. Music was simply a distraction for me, like television—I enjoyed the background noise but had never been able to truly appreciate what it had to offer. Not like Katie, music and dance fed her soul. I appreciated it now, though. When it was too late. We reveled in the silence that permeated the empty space as Siham's hands stilled.

The serenity was short lived, static filled the air, and a voice came over a radio attached to Lynn's belt. She fumbled with it, startled by the peaceful revelry that she found herself lost in.

"We have a problem," Ashlyn whispered hurriedly over the radio.

"I'm here," Lynn replied, running to the windows at the front of the house. We followed behind her, hugging the wall. From our position we could see the cows grazing contently in the paddocks, the dilapidated second house, but everything beyond that was hidden.

"Where's Ash right now?" I asked worriedly.

"The first house, the closest to the road. Jax is with

her, and Juan is in the second house." Lynn replied.

"They're coming up the road, six of Them—on foot, and armed. They're not stopping to check houses or properties, they might pass?" Juan said through the radio.

"Juan, maintain position—Jax and I will rendezvous with you," there were a few audible clicks through the radio before Ashlyn's voice came through again, "Everyone get your packs ready; we might need to leave."

"Copy that," Juan replied.

"Marie, Katie, can you help me get Deric ready?" Sariah asked, they nodded, ascending the staircase to the bedrooms.

We dispersed to the other bedrooms, pulling shoes on, securing backpacks to our backs and guns in our hands. We met a few minutes later in the sunroom at the back of the house, it opened right into the forest, the perfect escape route. Lynn stayed at the window with the radio in one hand, gun in the other.

The sound of a gunshot echoed; Lynn grappled for the radio calling out for Juan. One, two, three more shots echoed out—Lynn yanked open the front door, running out towards the second house. I ushered the girls out of the sunroom along a small stone path into the forest. Sariah and Marie carefully supported Deric as he limped his way through the underbrush. Mercifully the forest path wasn't choked with bramble or tall weeds, most of it was suffocated by the canopy of the redwoods, ferns occupying the open spaces between trunks. Two more shots rang out behind us, we hurried to put distance between us, surrounding a fallen tree. Katie dragged me to a small vantage point—a series of boulders that gave a clear enough view of the property that we could see the tops of all three houses.

Juan, Ashlyn, Lynn, and Jax ran from the second house towards the one we were just in, each one took turns turning to shoot at the group of Aerendor that stood further back, using the first house as cover. I waited until I saw Ash's head in the kitchen window and let out a whistle—she turned towards the woods, pointing in our direction. The four of them emerged from the sunroom, joining the others behind the fallen tree. Katie and I rushed down to join them, looking one another over for injuries.

"They had to have known, they ignored every goddamn house," Ashlyn growled, kicking the tree, the wood splintered beneath her heavy boots. "Come on, what are you guys staring at, we have to move."

No one said a word as we headed deep into the national forest. Every now and then I paused to stare back and noticed the others did as well—the Aerendor were on our trail now. They knew we would have escaped into the woods. Whether they followed or not was another story. Who knew how far away the royal hunting party was. Katie and I knew our way through this forest, hopefully better than their hunters.

"Fuck, fuck, fuck!" Ashlyn said over and over as she perused the map. Jax led us as Juan secured the rear.

"Where do we go now?" Jax muttered as we came to pause in a small thicket of ferns.

"I don't know," Ash said in frustration, her brow furrowing.

Everyone took this moment to drink from their canteens and eat some of the grapes they had leftover in their knapsacks. Katie came up beside me, nudging my arm, "Cave Junction isn't that far from here."

I nodded. It was worth a shot, better than blindly stumbling through the woods until dark. Katie and I approached Ashlyn, Deric, and Jax, their voices hushing as we came closer. Deric leaned heavily on Jax as they parted to show us the map.

"What?" Ash grumbled.

"There's a town a few miles to the west," I replied simply. I didn't want to supply more than she was willing to accept.

"A town, in the middle of the woods?" She was already skeptical.

"Not the middle of the woods. It sits between two National Forests," I said.

She raised her eyebrows, but Deric pulled the map to himself and traced our route west, tapping on a small smudge, "There it is. It's better than nothing."

I stifled my excitement. *Better than nothing*. It was my *home*! My gaze drifted to Katie. *Our* home.

A deep sigh, "Fine, whatever. Let's get moving, I want us in town with plenty of light left over." She hastily folded the map into her pack and trudged past us.

Katie fell back to walk alongside me, "We're finally going back."

"We're finally going home," I replied.

CHAPTER
Fifteen

We barely stopped. Traversing the rugged, uncharted terrain of the southern Oregon wilds. Even with Deric's leg as it was, he never said a word in complaint. Occasionally he and Jax would lag, and someone would come up to relieve Jax in helping Deric, if only for a moment. We never stopped being on edge as we picked our way through the woods. Every snap of a tree branch, every breeze in the canopy had us jumping, ready to defend ourselves. There was no way to know how far away our pursuers were, or even if they were following us.

The dirt before our feet began to part, mixed with white stones. When we heard the gurgling in the distance, we knew we had made it through. The river cut through the forest before us, crystal clear and gentle— it mirrored the bright green foliage that surrounded it and the darkening sky above. We had heard the rumbling halfway through our journey. It would rain soon, and hard. The sky to the east above the town was the deepest black I had ever seen, the wind blew cold against our cheeks, in the very distance the rain blanketed the horizon in a vertical sheet.

"Where to now?" Ashlyn asked, coming up beside me to glance up and down the river.

Several of the girls rushed forth to fill their canteens in the river. Did I lead us to the Den? Or did I risk navigating the town in the rain to find a house that could easily be occupied by Aerendor scouts?

"We can't make it to the town. It's too dangerous, I have a campsite we can stay at until the storm passes." I started walking, following the river north. I expected some sort of refusal or questioning, no one said a word as they followed closely behind.

>>>>>>> <<<<<<<

Everything was how I had left it; I checked every trap leading up to the Den, removing the decaying remains and fixing the wires and strings to set them back up. I made sure to show everyone what I was doing. The Den itself was untouched, the reed mat at the door, the bed within in, the plants in the pots growing wildly. Everyone piled in, finding a comfortable place on the floor to claim as their own, moments later a gust of wind rushed in. The rain had come. Thunder boomed, rattling our senses, and flashes of light lit the sky. The *drip, drip, drip* of rainwater down the wall into the potted plants was oddly soothing. We sat there in silence, huddled together, contemplating the sequence of events that led us here.

Eventually Sariah and I got up to prepare meals for everyone, a simple soup made from canned veggies heated over the crude fireplace in the corner of the cave.

It was surreal kneeling there before the pot, dishing out a spoonful of soup in cups to everyone. It was a painful memory, watching Sariah divvy out the soup. It reminded me of a time when someone else had done the exact same thing almost a year ago. Back then, instead of Sariah, it was my mother helping to dish the soup into bowls.

I saw Katie staring longingly at the cave wall, her eyes shadowed. I knew she too must be suffering with memories as she read the names of everyone I had carved into there: Mom, Dad, Beth, Jack, Ron, even Pippa.

"Where are they?" she whispered.

"A grave, at the bottom of the cliff." It took me hours to dig, but it was the only thing I could do to distract myself from the crushing numbness I had felt.

Several of the others had started up conversations now, their words a dull drone in the background, mingling with the splashing of the rain outside. Sariah stoked the dying embers of the fire to keep it going. Ashlyn helped to re-bandage Deric's wound, while Juan and Lynn napped by the cave entrance, guns close at hand.

Katie traced our parents' names, "Both of them?"

"Of course." I peeked at her from my peripherals.

She smiled at that, "At least in death they can be together for eternity."

I nodded, dumbly. Nothing could be said that would ever change what had happened. Sleep didn't come easy that night. I drifted in and out, lulled to the darkness by the endless droning of the rain outside, and brought back to consciousness by every twitch of my sister beside me. I was present through two guard switches, I kept my eyes shut, begging for sleep to take me. I heard the whispers of those that lay on the floor beside us. The darkness took me as I felt my sister's arm wrap around me and hug me close.

"You hid stashes throughout this entire area?" Ashlyn asked, looking over one of the guide maps of the hiking trails in the Rogue River-Siskiyou National Forest I had hidden beneath my mattress. Blue circles, red Xs, and green plus signs dotted seemingly random points in the forest and the town of Cave Junction. Supply was running low. Although a hare was caught in one of my snares this morning, it was certainly not enough to feed fourteen people.

"In case I needed to leave," I replied.

"And these?" She picked up a stack of folded papers with crudely drawn lines on them, studying them carefully.

"Floorplans, of houses in the town." Ashlyn raised an eyebrow, "in case it got too late for me to return to the Den."

"We were raised here, it might have been a while, but even I remember these trails and the houses," Katie spoke up, walking over to look through the floorplans of the houses I had roughly made. "They look just how they were before." Her voice ended in a whisper; her hand froze on a floorplan: the one I was caught in, our parents' house. The house we had grown up in. Her finger softly traced the upper bedroom, *her* bedroom. I saw the memories she did, as if we shared the sudden recollection together—the late nights we spent together painting our nails, talking about boys, reading magazines, and watching television. She even tried to teach me to dance in that room.

"How many of these stashes are left?" Deric asked from his guard position at the cave mouth.

"Assuming no one found them," I slowly counted the blue circles, "in the town—five. In the forest—eight."

"The red Xs?" Ash asked.

"Empty."

"And the green pluses?"

"Places that had supplies other than food." Most of them were houses that hadn't been ransacked, filled with medical supplies, linen, tools. Anything that could come in handy.

"And how long ago were these stashes last checked?" She circled houses on the northern side of Cave Junction, avoiding those along the river, where I had last encountered the Aerendor, where my parents' house was.

Where I had first met Vaelythor.

I fingered the amulet, it was starting to become a habit, the firm weight and warmth of it in my hand soothed me. Would he be there again? Had he returned to that small town up north? Or even now was he leading an army across the forests to take back what was his? I tucked the amulet inside of my shirt.

I shook my head, remembering Ash's question, "Um, about two months."

"You mentioned before that people used to stay in the campground, you were attacked in the town center—is there a possibility that both creatures and humans currently reside in the town?"

"It's possible," I said simply. "I'll go down there by myself if you want."

Cave Junction was the safest option, there'd be no reason for the Aerendor to make a permanent camp here. But the town up north, where the Aerendor had completely taken over, where their supposed prince had made residence in a converted mill house. I still struggled with whether to tell them that's likely where we would find him. Just up the road from Cave Junction, barely a blink away. But what good could come from that? He had spared my life, multiple times, he was the real reason I stood here beside my sister. I couldn't betray him, at least for now.

Her eyes twinkled, "You and I will go on a scouting run. We'll grab what we can and send a supply team later."

I nodded, suspicious of being alone with her. "I'll get ready."

Crossing the river, we found ourselves walking side by side along the empty main road into Cave Junction. Ashlyn had chosen the same route I had taken hundreds of times. It was weird to hear the crunching of the leaf litter under two sets of boots instead of one, hearing two sets of breath. Since finding my sister again I thought I would walk this route with her, there was time for that—I wouldn't dare leave Cave Junction without visiting our parent's home together one last time, even if it would end up being our last.

"How much farther to the Visitor Center?" Ashlyn asked, her eyes nervously scanning the thick woods on either side. The redwoods towered high above, swaying in the gentlest of breezes. The sky was dark, rain could come at any moment, but it would be worth it if we found enough food for everyone.

I turned to answer her, but she had stopped, throwing her hand out in front of me. I would have panicked before I saw what had captured her attention. A doe had cautiously peeked its head out from the underbrush, walking out onto the slick asphalt. She sniffed the road, her ears up and alert, her eyes bright and curious. Her fur was a shiny tan color that blended beautifully with the bright ocher shades of the towering redwoods.

"She has a lot of meat on her," Ashlyn whispered, her hand gripping her gun. I regretted not having my bow, I gently placed my hand on her wrist.

"They'll hear that gunshot for miles." That doe could have fed us for the next week. But the reward did not outweigh the risk. She would live to forage another day; our only hope was that the stash I had left behind at the Visitor Center was still there.

The doe flicked her tail at us, crossing the road, the tap, tap of her hooves on the concrete disappearing as she melded into the woods towards the campground. Ashlyn sighed deeply, disappointment written across her face. I felt it too, it had been a while since we'd had real meat and it was showing, in all of us—our jutting collar bones, sallow skin, and overall fatigue. We needed protein, and that rabbit earlier did little to satiate our starved cells.

The trees pulled back ahead to reveal the Visitor Center rising in a mess of weeds. We stopped at the northern edge of the parking lot, hidden behind the toilets. All was quiet, save the buzz of insects around us and the swaying of the trees above.

"Where is the stash?" Ash asked, her eyes narrowing.

"Behind the front desk, there's a facade in the rocks."

She nodded, waiting a few moments before dashing out across the parking lot. I followed closely behind her, our boots thudding in rhythm as we raced across the wooden walkway to the front door. She paused, distracted by the mural on the outside wall. I understood the feelings that she had because I had the same. The tranquility of the painted landscape where the river met the rocks, the rocks met the trees—but I couldn't let her revel in the simplistic beauty of it. We were completely exposed, I nudged the door open, tugging at her sleeve.

The inside, the Center was just as I had left it. I hurried to the facade, pulling the rocks loose to reveal the small nook loaded with cans of food. We stuffed our backpacks up to bulging point, I hefted it over my shoulder and stood by the door, waiting for Ash.

With the click of a gun, I turned to stare down the barrel.

Ashlyn watched me carefully. "I'm sorry, Wren, but I have to know—tell me what happened in the woods that day."

I dropped my backpack to the ground, holding my hands up, "I told you, Ash."

She took a step closer, "No bullshit this time, Wren. Tell me the truth."

"What's going on?" I stood there in a daze, why would Ashlyn suddenly turn on me? Did Lynn say something? Ash had been increasingly hostile since the day they had found me; her suspicion was warranted, granted.

But not for the same reason I kept it from her.

"Because I saw you, Wren. I saw you go down in that goddamn hole, with that *thing*." Her voice wavered slightly. It was unnerving to see Ashlyn anything but calm and collect.

But then it dawned on me.

"You're the one who shot me."

She nodded sharply, "Now tell me, how did you survive?"

"I told you what happened, Ash, I wasn't lying," I didn't lie to her. I *didn't* remember what happened, at least—not anything after Vaelythor had saved me. I just omitted details that I knew the others would not have been able to comprehend. There was no way I could tell them an Aerendor had saved me, or that I had spared his life. Ashlyn especially would not have understood. And Katie? Imagine telling your own sister who had been held captive by Them that you were a sympathizer. It left a bad taste in my mouth.

"I find it hard to believe that you survived a bullet to the stomach and spent an entire week in the same caves as the leader of those monsters and you didn't see him at all." Her arm shook.

"You honestly think he would have let me leave alive if I had seen him?" I growled at her, "I sacrificed myself so the others could escape, I stayed behind to *die*, Ash."

I could see the impact my words had as her grip loosened, her stance becoming less hostile. I had to drive the message home, I pulled my shirt up to reveal the ugly red scar on my stomach, "This is what you did to me, Ashlyn. I don't know how I survived; I shouldn't have."

I lowered my hands and took a step towards her, "But I did, and I forgive you."

Several moments passed before I saw the resolve spread across her, she tucked the gun in the back of her jeans. "I believe you," she said simply before throwing her backpack over her shoulder and standing beside me, her arms wrapped around me.

"I didn't want you to suffer," she whispered, her voice barely audible.

I nodded my head, hugging her tight, "I know."

She pulled back, her eyes glistening, "Let's get back to the others."

In our absence, the group split themselves into various tasks. Some were set to collecting wood to fashion into spikes, dug into a perimeter around the cave with strings of empty cans strung between them—an early warning system in case someone or *something* tried to sneak into camp. A canopy of leaf litter was scattered over raised platforms of tied branches over tarps to disguise the cave and its immediate area, providing extra cover for us to store supplies outside. They were quick to utilize that space, storing extra bundles of wood and constructing a fire pit to boil water. Sophie, Erin, and Sariah were divvying up the food supplies into buckets and baskets that I had left behind, making far better use of them than I ever had.

"Where's Jax?" I asked Sariah, handing her my bag.

"He and Juan built some fort on the cliff." She pointed to the northern side of the cave.

A rough staircase had been dug into the dirt atop the cave leading up to where a bramble of sticks, rocks, and tree branches had been arranged strategically to make a small fort that looked surprisingly innocent.

"It seems you guys have been busy in our absence," Ashlyn said as Jax poked his head out from the fort.

"It was all Deric's idea," he replied, a giant grin stretching from ear to ear.

"Good, because I have a feeling we're going to be here for a while. There are more stashes available, with food and supplies that should help us survive until we come up with a plan. The traps have always helped, too. But I don't know well we will persevere through winter."

For the first time, I felt hopeful. We sat down with Jax, listening to the grand plans Deric had conjured up for the Den. Even when injured, Deric just couldn't relax. I couldn't help but admire his tenacity.

The next few hours I spent wandering the woods with Lynn and Marie, showing them the different kinds of traps and how they worked. Only the funnel traps in the river managed to catch anything that day, and Marie was quick to reset them. She gathered the fish and crawdads, returning to camp, leaving Lynn and me to work alone.

I watched Lynn dig in the dirt, preparing a small pit. I wasn't sure where to begin, or even what I was going to say. This could easily be my only opportunity; I wasn't going to waste it. "I'm sorry, about what I did before, Lynn."

She didn't pause in her work, "I know why you did it." She pulled the sharpened sticks from her bag, embedding them at the bottom of the hole, pointy end upwards. "I'm not perfect either—no one else knows this, but I did exactly what you did. I've done it before; I stood there having to make the choice between the death of one or two people." She turned to look up at me, "That's why I'm here now, and she isn't."

I placed an arm on her shoulder, and she raised her hand to squeeze mine tightly, "I was irrational, I know I was. But I've had plenty of time to think it over, to learn from it—and I don't blame you, Wren. What you did in the forest, you sacrificed yourself for us. We would all have been dead if it wasn't for you, and I can't thank you enough for giving me and Juan that chance to live."

I smiled, gently squeezing her shoulder. We moved on, building several more pits along the riverside. They weren't enough to be a danger to a human or even an Aerendor, but it would be enough to capture rabbits, squirrels, even birds, or mice.

We returned to the camp to find Sariah and Marie descaling the fish and crawdads. I felt a nagging at the back of my mind as I surveyed our camp. Everyone was accounted for, except my sister. I walked up to where Sophie and Siham sat weaving baskets from bark and sticks, they looked up at me smiling.

"Have you guys seen my sister?" I sat beside them, watching as Siham's hands moved fast to gently bend and fold the sticks between one another. She was a natural, already on her third basket. Her skills never ceased to amaze me; I was beyond grateful.

Sophie glanced uneasily at Siham; it was so fleeting, but I didn't miss it. "She said she was going for a walk."

"Alone?" I felt the prickling at the back of my neck as I tried to keep my anxiety under control.

"She said she needed some space," Sophie replied simply, slowly bending a stick to thread through another.

"She should be back soon, she does this often," Siham said, offering me a reassuring smile.

I knew I couldn't relax, not until I saw Katie with my own eyes. I threw myself into helping around the Den, trying to distract myself as the sun moved across the sky.

She finally appeared at the entrance to the Den around sunset, carrying a basket of assorted greens. She placed them by the pots of the small herb garden before coming up to hug me. I begrudgingly gave in before whispering, "You were gone for a while."

She took a moment to respond, "I lost myself."

I glanced at her basket, it was filled to the brim with all sorts of forest flora, to the point that some even hung over the basket, barely managing to stay inside. She did have that habit, when she was nervous or anxious and needed a distraction, she would lose herself in a task—dancing was usually her distraction of choice. I had never known her to have a green thumb, but a lot had changed in a year.

"Dinner's ready!" Sariah called from outside. Everyone dropped what they were doing, making their way outside.

I pulled Katie back, "I was worried, you know."

She smiled warmly at me, "I was worried when you and Ashlyn left, too. You weren't the only one who needed a distraction."

I took a deep steadying breath, why did I not even consider that? She had sat here not knowing whether I would make it back or not.

I smiled, hugging her tightly, "Let's eat."

Sariah and Marie had managed to turn the fish, crawdads, and a few canned vegetables into a meal that seemed to cover almost every nutritional necessity. Sariah's pride and joy was somehow managing to make an edible cheese sauce from a nondescript powder she found amongst my supplies. It wasn't a Michelin Star restaurant meal, but it was the best I'd had in a very long time. That voice in my head had to interrupt the moment, reminding me that the Aerendor, that Vaelythor, had fed me better. I squashed the thought as soon as it tried to bubble to the surface, not now, and not here. I was with friends, I was with family, and I was the happiest I could ever be.

It was the first time, sitting down at the outside campfire, and looking from face to face, that I felt the atmosphere of our group genuinely relax. They all smiled, they all laughed. Jax started singing a catchy tune, and we all joined in on the chorus.

The moon twinkled high above, dark clouds occasionally smothered her light, but they couldn't smother our enthusiasm as we regaled to one another our favorite things from the past. The comforts of a time soon to be forgotten, where before it was hair dye and shaving supplies, now it was the comfort of books, the simplicity of a cup of tea.

I was basically home, I had my sister with me, I had friends with me. We had survived, and now—we would thrive.

CHAPTER
Sixteen

Wind howled through the camp, heralding a bitter cold rain. A dense fog settled over us and Ashlyn jumped at the opportunity. Under the cover the fog provided, she decided we would head into the town itself. I immediately volunteered Katie and me to be part of the team—after all, we knew the town the best. Jax, Juan, and Keira suited up and met us at the makeshift gate Sophie had weaved from sticks at the entrance to the undercover area outside the cave.

We took the same route Ash and I had taken the day before. Avoiding the campground and circling the Visitor Center, we hugged the side of the road as we descended into town. The fog made it difficult to see between the buildings, and we huddled close, taking every precaution, stopping at every sound, guns at the ready. Each time we had to stifle the laughs, to think we would expose ourselves to being surprised by a family of raccoons hiding in a dumpster, a cat jumping from a tree to greet us, and a bird flying away from its nest in a gutter.

We skirted the area north of the cafe where dozens of mobile homes sat, ducking inside the first two I remember placing stashes in. The first one was empty—I had no way of knowing how long ago it had been raided. It was a smaller stash, but it did have more unconventional goods like bags of pasta and cereal, things we hadn't eaten in a very long time. It was a disappointment, but one that could be overlooked.

The second mobile home was down the road, a simple two bedroom with a scattering of potted plants out front, I had loaded the living room with crates. Walking up to the front door we knew from a glance that the stash was probably gone—the door lay crooked on its hinges. The inside of the house was ravaged, as if a fight had taken place. The crates were upturned, some lay smashed, walls were broken, and bullet holes tattered the furniture.

"Should we..." Keira started to ask.

We raised our guns, splitting up. Jax called us from the backyard, and we ran to him, hearts beating. He stood above the corpse of an older gentleman, a knife jutted from his back, his face obscured in a pool of dried blood. Juan and Jax dispersed to scan the other mobile homes nearby, Keira and I stayed by the body, our backs to one another. The boys came back a few moments later.

"There's another body in the house next door, same thing," Juan said nodding at the old man.

"Where's the next stash? We shouldn't stay here too long," Jax said nervously.

"Shouldn't we go back?" Keira whispered.

"We can't go back empty handed," I said looking south, "we need to find something. The gas station down the road, there are some barrels outside, I hid food in all of them."

Katie came out of the house we were in before. In all that commotion I hadn't even noticed my own sister had disappeared. I ran to her, embracing her firmly before pulling back. She glanced at the body of the old man, before showing me what she had grasped in her hand: a piece of paper with a hastily scribbled note on it.

"What's this?" The others crowded around us as Katie stretched out the paper.

It had three words on it in smudged, black ink, with drops of blood splashed across the parchment:

They're here.

Run.

We took a step back, looking around uneasily. The Aerendor had been here and judging by the body—it was recently. Although the blood was dry, his body was remarkably fresh, and I hated that I'd seen enough dead things to be able to discern that. We couldn't be sure they were still here, or how long ago it was, but one thing was certain, it was best if we got what we needed and left as soon as possible. Luck was on our side with the dense fog, as much as it hid them from us it also hid us from them.

"Let's go," I said, walking off towards the gas station.

The cat from earlier appeared again, trotting along beside us. Katie bent down to scratch between his ears, letting him affectionately rub against her legs. I saw the barrels rising up out of the fog at the back of the gas station, behind a wall of sheet metal. We moved quickly across the road ducking down the alley.

The barrels were untouched and we each pried off a cover, stuffing as much as we could into our backpacks. Each barrel had been filled to the brim with assorted goods I had taken from nearby homes. It was dangerous to have my largest stash out in the open like this, but it paid off for us and this stash alone could easily feed us for the next three months. More canned fruits and vegetables, packets of coffee and tea, powders and spices, dried herbs and preserved goods.

Keira pried open a bag of dried jerky, sharing it with everyone as we slowly made our way back towards the camp. Katie stopped in her tracks outside the cafe, looking down the road. We stopped beside her, wary, and she looked up at me longingly. I remembered where we were then, in all the commotion it hadn't even occurred to me.

Down the road, behind the cafe—was the blue house. Our parents' house. The house I was ambushed in all those months ago. I was still nervous, and admittedly scared to even go near it. But this was an opportunity I didn't want to miss, and I knew she didn't want to either.

"We're taking a detour," I said, and the others looked at us quizzically, but agreed. They were as eager as we were to explore, but not for the same reason Katie and I were.

The house was just as I had left it, the back-sliding door

was shattered. We cautiously entered, spreading out to cover more ground. I knew exactly where Katie would go first, and I followed her past the broken door upstairs into the bedroom. Although things were scattered and broken wood lay haphazardly askew, she picked her way through her old bedroom, standing before the mirror on the wall. She lazily drew a heart in the dust on the mirror, her hand tracing the photographs pinned to the wall beside it. Photos of our childhood, of her and me, of our parents and us. She plucked a photograph of the four of us at a theme park from the wall, folding it to put into her pocket.

"Out of everything I have endured, my deepest regret was not even having a photograph to remember my family by," she whispered solemnly.

My heart broke at her words, and I walked up to the wall to pluck another photo, this one of us camping several years ago, folding it to place in my pocket. "Now, no matter where we are, we will always be together."

Her reaction wasn't what I expected when I turned to face her, she broke out sobbing, clutching me close.

"What's wrong?" I asked, my heart aching at the pitiful sounds that came from her. I had never heard her cry like this before, even the news of Mom and Dad hadn't elicited such a response.

A movement at the door, we both turned as Keira walked in with Jax, "Everything okay?" They asked, looking around the room perplexed.

Katie quickly recovered, "This was my room."

They both looked surprised as they glanced around the room, it probably didn't seem like much to them, from the champagne pink wallpaper to the golden curtains and rose red blankets, even the unicorn plushy on the bed, but it all screamed Katie. The closet door was half open, her vast collection of dresses spilled out, billowing in the breeze from the window. She stood by the window, glancing out over the front lawn.

"We'll meet you guys downstairs," Keira said, dragging Jax from the room.

When she was certain they were out of earshot she asked, "What happened here?"

"I was attacked."

"That is why you left Cave Junction?" I felt the pain in her voice.

I felt it too, having to find the courage to verbalize it, I nodded reluctantly, "This was the last tangible evidence I had of us, of our family."

An odd expression flitted across her face, so fast I couldn't quite place it. "Did you kill them all?"

Her question startled me; I paused before shaking my head.

"I didn't kill any of them."

She looked confused, yet somehow, relieved. "They let you escape?"

I paused; I had already settled on not telling the others about the Aerendor that I kept finding myself in the presence of. But what about my sister? Did she count?

I sighed. If I couldn't trust her—who could I trust?

"They were going to kill me, they caught me in the alleyway." I joined her at the window, looking out over the fog covered neighborhood. "But one of them, he came in at the last moment and spared me."

She glanced at me, and I was prepared for the disgust, for the admonition. To be told the Aerendor were demons incapable of mercy. But when I looked into her eyes, all I saw was…understanding. The hairs on the back of my neck rose. I couldn't explain why, but that look on her face. The softened gaze, the warmness behind her eyes. I couldn't help but be brought back to that moment when I had first seen her that day on the road. I had thought she was a prisoner, that I was saving her. But was she truly better off with me? She was immaculate: her hair, her clothes, her skin. A horrible, creeping thought sat at the forefront of my mind like a lead weight and refused to budge. What if—she *wasn't* their prisoner?

No. That's ridiculous. I repeated to myself, over and over. But I could say it as many times to myself as I wanted. Without Katie confirming it, the thought still lingered.

"We should get going. Juan said he saw some movement by the main road," Jax called from the hallway. His radio hissed static before he turned it off.

Katie nodded, "He's right, we shouldn't linger."

And yet she cast me a long, lingering glance, before disappearing wordlessly down the hallway.

Juan came jogging down the road, meeting Keira on the front lawn. They looked up at the window, beckoning me. My mind was reeling, I was more worried than I'd been before. What did this all mean? I tried to convince myself it was nothing to be concerned about, I didn't even ask her—she could have had the same interaction I did—maybe one was good, maybe he had shown her mercy. My mind wouldn't allow me that respite, I couldn't get the image of being chased ruthlessly through the woods by the guard that was escorting her, being *hunted*. Raekhan was no doubt still out there, he wouldn't surrender, not until he had caught us, and when he did—if he were even capable of mercy, it wouldn't be shown to me.

At the Den, Sariah and Marie took our stock and divvied it up, preparing for dinner. Jax and I reported to Ash and Deric at the fort, telling them what we had seen in the town. They were understandably worried—but not concerned enough to stop our runs into town. For now, though, Ash was determined to reinforce the only path up the side of the cliff towards the Den. She didn't want to leave anything to chance, and I couldn't blame her. Juan and Jax disappeared to begin digging pits and hanging nets. Everyone else had split off into organizing the camp so it was easier to move in and out.

Siham continued to weave baskets, mats, nets, and

even a wooden rug to lay at the entrance to deter mud accumulation. Erin and Lynn had dedicated themselves to extending the herb garden, building a raised bed and adding the roots my sister had gathered yesterday to it. Sophie joined Juan on a small patrol around the camp, making sure none of the traps had been disturbed.

Katie and I each gathered a large basket of soiled clothing. With a bottle of soap in hand, we made our way down to the river to clean them. The clouds had almost dissipated now, the fog hanging stubbornly on the horizon. We laid our baskets on the bank of the river, getting to work scrubbing the clothes as clean as we could. We worked in silence mostly, until Katie began to hum a most familiar tune. I couldn't help but join in. I decided, whatever had happened—she would tell me in her own time. I didn't need to worry about things that were no longer relevant, what mattered now was we were together again, and we were safe.

She suddenly sighed, placing the shirt she had been cleaning back in the basket before turning to me, "Fancy a swim?"

I looked up at her incredulously, scoffing, "Really, Katie?"

She grabbed my arm, dragging me up, "Come on, Wren!"

"Okay, okay!" I said, mimicking her as she stripped to her underwear.

She walked in waist deep before diving under, the light catching on her golden hair as she submerged. She came up a few seconds later, beckoning me with her hand. I smiled up at her, wading in to tread beside her. She splashed some water towards me, and I laughed, splashing some back, bringing back memories of us doing the exact same thing as children in this very river.

The problems of the world around us seemed to disappear, it was just two sisters enjoying each other's company. We were relaxed, we were happy, and more than anything—we were free. She dunked herself under the water, waiting for me to follow. She didn't have a care in the world, she was relaxed, a smile playing on her cherry red lips. The crystal-clear waters spread out her wheat golden hair, catching the sun's rays. She looked like a water nymph, her porcelain skin and freckles, her athletic toned physique, how the water seemed to love her as much as she loved it.

Katie sat there, submerged up to her neck, watching me. I swam by her, curious to whatever it was that plagued her mind. I knew her well enough to know when thoughts weighed heavily upon her. Her arms hugged her body, her eyes were lost and far off, her mouth slightly agape.

"What is it?" I asked, confused.

She paused, her eyes roving over me from head to toe, focusing on every aspect of my being as if she couldn't believe it was me. "You know I love you, right, Wren?"

I smiled at her, "Of course, Katie." Her words were genuine, but her tone was off, wiping the smile from my face. "Are you okay?"

She moved on, "And I never want to hurt you." A shadow passed over her eyes and she stared into the forest. Whatever was on her mind plagued her. Her eyes glistened with unshed tears, and she forced a smile onto her face if only in an attempt not to break down in front of me.

"I'm not proud of what I've had to do, Wren. To survive." She looked me in the eyes, "But if given the chance I would do it all again."

Embracing her, I planted a kiss on her cheek, "I love you, Katie. Make no mistake, I don't care what you've had to do, we've all made mistakes, we've all done things we aren't proud of—even things we regret, purely in the name of survival." Lynn's face flashed before my eyes, from that day in the trailer park, the betrayal written across them. "Let's just enjoy the time we have together now."

She agreed, and with tears in her eyes we embraced one last time before continuing our leisurely water antics. I wish that moment could have lasted forever, the two of us playing in the river; but eventually the sun disappeared again behind the clouds, and we had to rush to finish cleaning the rest of the clothes and return to the Den to hang them on the racks to dry.

For dinner that night Sariah had proudly made us a vegetable mash soup. It was a welcome comfort to the bitter cold bite that the rains had swept in just before sunset. Water trickled down the side of the cave wall near the entrance like it always did, but this time a raised garden box sat at the base, the plants thriving in the downpour.

Most of us sat huddled by the fire near the back of the cave. Deric had managed to limp down from the lookout on his own, with Lynn taking his spot. I offered him my bed tonight, so the hard floor of the cave didn't cause him too much discomfort. Siham had weaved wooden mats to place under everyone's sleeping bags, so they weren't directly on the cold, hard ground. It seemed to have done wonders—most of the girls had nodded off almost immediately after dinner. I couldn't help the weight that I suddenly found myself carrying. I was so used to giving in to the darkness when it beckoned. But tonight, I couldn't quite figure out why a part of me tried to fight it.

Eventually I gave in, letting the rain lull me to sleep.

I didn't know how long I had been asleep, or what had even caused me to wake. I glanced around the Den for the culprit, but everyone was fast asleep. Except instead of one sleeping bag being empty, there were two. My heart lurched when I realized it was the one directly beside me, the one Katie had chosen.

Pulling a jacket over my shirt, I grabbed a flashlight. I kept telling myself to calm down, that maybe she went to relieve herself—we had built a trench just on the outskirts of the camp, a makeshift latrine for us to still feel somewhat dignified about living in a cave. Jax was on guard, staring aimlessly into the night.

"Hey." I called to him, careful to keep my voice down less I bothered the others.

He didn't move, and I cautiously reached out my hand to touch him. He was fast asleep. A part of me wanted to wake him and admonish him for recklessly falling asleep on watch. Even a minute could be the difference between life or death. But I was awake now, and presumably, so was Katie. I'd simply take over. Dangerous, but I would let him sleep. At least, for the few moments it took me to walk down to the latrine and back. Even if my sister wasn't there, I needed to use it.

I picked my way through the underbrush along the path we had marked. I tugged gently on the ropes and strings to the traps along either side of the path, checking their tautness. I was overcautious, perhaps, but better safe than sorry.

In a small grove nearby, we had dug the latrine into the soft dirt, it was essentially a makeshift natural fence of stacked wood to hide our shame.

"Katie?" I called out to her, but there was no response. Cautiously, I peeked my head over the stacked wood and peered down with my flashlight. The light revealed an empty ditch.

My sister was nowhere to be seen.

I hated that I panicked. My anxiety would always be my downfall, and I tried to quell the shaking in my hands as I continued down the path. I knew further along it opened into a small meadow of ferns among the redwoods, and here a crystal-clear pond was fed by a small stream that ran through it.

Maybe she had sought solace in the tranquility it had to offer when she couldn't get back to sleep. I know I had done the same many times before.

I neared the meadow, and a most familiar voice met my ears. I slowed, however. Because it was not just her voice I heard, but that of a man. Careful not to make any noise, I turned my flashlight off. Everyone else at the Den was accounted for, so who could it be? She easily could have stumbled upon a traveler making their way past Cave Junction, and part of me begged for that to be the case. The redwoods seemed to part for me, and the gurgle of the stream was a welcome distraction.

I searched the darkness of the meadow, my eyes adjusting slowly. The voices rose. They were hurried, yet hushed. Gentle whispers on the bitter breeze that seemed to cut into my very flesh like daggers. Figures stood cloaked in the shadows that hugged the meadow, they huddled close together. I got as close as I dared, desperate to see their faces. They continued their chat, the woman laughed delicately, and I recognized it, the lilt in that laugh—it was definitely Katie.

Easing myself closer, I was within a few feet, enough to be able to distinguish what they said. I could only just make out the distinguishable features between them, my sister's unbound hair, jeans, and jacket combo. And the strange man. He was tall and muscular, his clothing black and tight-fitting, but it was difficult to see his face behind his hood.

He reached out his hand to cup my sister's face, and I froze to the spot.

"Soon, my love," he whispered to her.

It was hard to control my breathing. He called Katie his *love*. He knew her, and she knew him.

"We have to do it now, it will be easier that way," Katie pleaded. My heart lurched thinking of whatever it was she referred to.

It took everything in my being not to jump out from behind the cover of the trees and confront them. If she had someone she cared deeply about, why not introduce him to us, or at the very least, why not mention him at all to me?

"Does she know?" His voice was smooth, and dark— a rich blend, and yet I found it oddly familiar.

Katie sighed deeply, "No, it's easier if she doesn't."

"At the river…" He tried to argue.

"She didn't notice," Katie said immediately.

I leaned forward as far as I dared, trying to peek under the stranger's hood. His hand lowered, to grip my sister's waist, bringing her in close for an intimate embrace.

"Then we shall go," he said.

The air around us crackled, and a current of electricity bounced beneath my skin. My heart lurched in my chest when the realization hit me like a truck, knocking the air from my lungs. I could barely breathe, hardly move.

I knew who—what—so lovingly embraced my sister, and why she didn't mention having a lover. Because her lover was an Aerendor.

A soft blue light glowed around them, encompassing them like a halo. The moon took the opportunity to peek her head out from behind the clouds, casting a ray across their faces.

I couldn't stop the gargled cry that sprang forth from between my lips. The long black hair, the pensive lavender gaze—I didn't know when it happened, but I found myself running at them, my hand gripping my sister's. I fought desperately to pull her back, away from the monster she was so enthralled by.

He turned to me, his eyes wide. He casually beheld the prey he had been hunting, and Raekhan growled.

"Katie!" I screamed, trying to pull her free. Her beautiful turquoise eyes looked down on me with sorrow. One of her hands still entwined with Raekhan's and she pulled away from me. But I wouldn't relent, my grip tightening on her arm.

But it was too late, the blue light had gripped me as well, enveloping me. The electricity strengthened, coursing through my veins like a poison. The amulet at my neck glowed in response, burning the hollow of my neck where it sat against my skin. I lifted into the air alongside Katie and Raekhan and was pulled into the blinding light. The world spun beneath us, and I grasped onto her for as long as I could, with all the strength I could. She shouted above the roar of silence.

Her lips moved, and although I couldn't hear what she said, I knew she was calling out my name. My grip was loosening, and I couldn't hold on as I felt us thrust out into the darkness. The blue light dissipated around me.

I found myself face first among a dewy field of flowers and tall grass; their pastel colors kissed by the bright moonlight shining down through an unburdened, cloudless sky. I tentatively stood, aware of every ache and pain in my body. My skin still burned from whatever power had raged through me, but the amulet at my neck had muted, whatever warmth and power it carried before disappearing, leaving an innate piece of jewelry around my neck.

I found myself alone. And for the first time, truly—I was afraid. I cried out into the darkness and found myself only having the moonlight for company. No one answered my call.

"Katie!" I cried out. Over and over, I called for her, walking as if in a daze among the flowers that I did not recognize. I made towards the trees that curled and splayed toward the sky like nothing I had ever seen before. And as I stared up into the starry sky, wondering what had become of my sister, my heart sank when I beheld two moons staring back at me. Wherever I was, I was no longer home, I was no longer on Earth.

And now I could confidently say: I was the last of my kind.

ABOUT THE
Author

Currently residing in Los Angeles, Toni was raised in Australia and Japan. She spends her free time worshipping her two cats, who she can't disprove aren't vengeful deities. Hobbies include avoiding reality such as: reading, writing, playing video games, and watching the same five television shows as background noise. Featured in several anthologies, you can keep up with her works at *www.tonimobley.com*.